SADIE'S VOW

Book 1, Home At Last

Jenny Wheeler

Published by Happy Families Ltd
Copyright © 2022 Jenny Wheeler

ISBN 978-1-99-116205-2 (Paperback)
ISBN 978-1-99-116204-5 (EPub)
ISBN 978-1-99-116203-8 (Kindle)

OF GOLD & BLOOD SERIES

Poisoned Legacy #1
Brother Betrayed #2
Double Jeopardy #3
Tangled Destiny–A Christmas Novella and Prequel #4
Unbridled Vengeance #5
Hope Redeemed–A Spanish Novella #6
Book Bundle Of Gold & Blood Series One, Books 1–3.
Book Bundle Of Gold & Blood, Series Two Books 1 & 4–Elanora's Story.
Tainted Fortune #7
Captive Heart–A Hawaiian Christmas Novella #8
Ancient Deception #9
Book Bundle Of Gold & Blood, Three Holiday Novellas (Books 4, 6 & 8)
Dangerous Desires #10

Home At Last Trilogy
Sadie's Vow #1

"It is the cussedest place for women –a town of men and taverns and boarding houses and saloons." Said of San Francisco, 1869, Samuel Bowles.

"A recurring theme in many accounts was that California women in general, and San Francisco women in particular, were more attractive and fascinating than women elsewhere." 1868, Louis Laurent Simonin.

Excerpts from *More San Francisco Memories, 1852 –1899, The ripening years,* compiled by Malcolm E. Barker.

Prologue
New York, August, 1872

On the steamy summer's night when her sister Phoebe caught the eye of the Cobra, Sadie McGillicuddy lost any hope of fulfilling her vow at her mother's deathbed.

But with her typical ornery attitude, she wasn't ready to admit it yet.

"You've got to protect her, Daa," she murmured in her stepfather's ear. Shamrock Bar owner Brian McGillicuddy was leaning, nonchalant as you like, at the bar's end. Sadie had stopped by, tray laden with tankards destined for the table in the far corner, to tickle his ear.

"She's only nineteen."

McGillicuddy regarded her with shrewd gray eyes shining out of a ruddy, bulletproof face.

"What are ye worrying about, lass? She's more of a lure than you are, and that can't be bad for business."

Her stepfather cast his eyes approvingly to the corner, skimming over the heaving mass of drinkers elbowing their way up to the bar for refills.

Beads of sweat shone on his wide forehead, topped by a tumble of exuberant sandy curls. It was one of the hottest nights of the summer, and her mother had been dead for exactly one year.

How can he look so pleased with himself? Has he forgotten it's her anniversary?

She glanced down at the khaki pantaloons she wore below a long-sleeved white shirt buttoned to the collar and acknowledged that she was hardly distinguishable as a woman. And that's the way she liked it.

She gazed into her stepfather's satisfied face and told herself he had a business to run. A family of young 'uns, her three younger sisters, to feed. He didn't have time to waste mooning over the past, and neither did she.

As if to remind her of the fact, McGillicuddy said, "Ye'd better get moving with that there load. We don't want to keep the Cobra waiting." Her head swiveled involuntarily to the patrons awaiting her delivery.

King Cobra was the San Francisco boss of the Bloods syndicate, and he'd been in New York a couple of months setting up a new chapter in the Bowery. He'd formed an alliance with Brian McGillicuddy, and the last thing they needed was for him to take offense at waiting too long for his drinks.

"On my way," she said. "But I mean what I said. She's too young to be hanging out with the likes of them."

If Sadie had a talent for being invisible, her half-sister Phoebe lit up a room. Her radiance illuminated the dark little corner where she perched at a table with Cobra, Patrick Blackheart, the San Francisco chapter's second-in-command, and two flighty dolly mops, one a fake blonde, the other a scowling redhead, who regularly worked the Shamrock's floor.

Phoebe had hair the color of warm toffee. It curled over eyes that lit up like sapphires whenever anyone said anything halfway funny.

Just sitting next to her at the table makes your heart sing.

As Sadie wove her way through the mainly male crowd, ducking and diving around broad shoulders to get the mugs to the table, the condensation from the icy brew on the pewter tray numbed her fingers, but her spirits sparked warmer at the sight of her half-sister.

She was the very picture of their mother, although by the time Sadie had made her promise on her mother Grace's deathbed, the daily drudgery of raising a large family on a tight budget had long since snuffed out her mater's sparkle.

That was probably why her stepfather was so indulgent with Phoebe, she thought, as she did the final pivot around Cobra's hunched form to reach the tabletop and her thirsty customers.

Someone—Cobra, probably, from the way Phoebe was eyeing him—had said something that amused her, and her flawless face shone with joy, the pearly white teeth showing through fine red lips curved in contagious merriment.

As if sensing Sadie's approach, Blackheart turned and then moved aside to allow space for her to reach between him and Cobra to deliver the refreshments. She gave him a grateful smile, which he acknowledged with a brief flick of one black brow. He was a strongly built, olive-skinned man, with a glowering masculinity that made her uncomfortable for reasons she didn't want to examine too closely.

Cobra only had eyes for her sister. He was shorter than Patrick, considerably older, the beginnings of a paunch showing at his waistline. She guessed Patrick was close to her age—late twenties or early thirties. Cobra was forty at least. As he raised his beer mug, the springy hairs on the back of his hand were graying like those on his head.

"Thank you, Sadie," said Blackheart. "For doing Phoebe's job."

His mouth quirked.

Phoebe gave her slender shoulders a feminine shrug as if to say "More fool her," and continued as if Blackheart hadn't spoken and

Sadie wasn't standing right there hearing it all.

Yes. Phoebe and her mother looked alike, but that's where any resemblance stopped. Her mother had always been a demure Catholic girl, obedient to her husbands –one after the other - and her priests, undemanding of their attention.

For a moment, everything around Sadie faded away. The roar of men's voices, echoing off the heavy wooden beams. The energy-sapping heat, and the smell of sawdust and hops and sweat.

Sadie was back at her mother's sanctified bedside, Grace's pale, lined face soft with its own holy peace, her breath wheezing in uncertain gusts.

"Promise me. Promise me, my darling Sadie. Look after Phoebe. Don't let her come to harm. She's too desirable for her own good."

Sadie squeezed the dry skin on the hand she held lightly between her own and leaned over her mother's wasted, laboring form. "I promise, Mother. If I die doing it, I promise. And now, you get some blessed rest."

Her mother's eyes fixed on her, beseeching. Her lips flickered at the corners in the briefest of smiles.

"Swear it on the Bible." Her eyes jigged to the worn Holy Book resting right by her pillow. "Please… do it now."

She took Sadie's hand and guided it to the black leather cover. Sadie mumbled the words, barely comprehending. "I promise on the Holy Bible to keep Phoebe from harm."

Her mother's blue eyes, so like her sister's, gleamed in gratitude.

Then the dark lashes, still long and curly, gently descended onto her papery cheeks and her chest gradually stopped rising and falling.

A firm grip on her forearm brought Sadie back with a jolt. Her daydream had been so real it took her a few seconds to realize it was not her mother gripping her arm.

"Sadie. Are you still there?"

Patrick Blackheart's black eyes questioned her. The man called Cobra stared, his eyes so like those of the serpent whose name he'd taken.

"Oh, sorry. Of course." She gathered her wits into a semblance of coherence, loading her tray with the empty beer jars that littered the table.

"Can I get you anything else?" Looking at Cobra.

But he was already looking back at Phoebe, his tongue dipping in and out of his mouth like a snake's. It wasn't forked, she noted in a crazy moment, but it might as well have been.

She whisked into a quick turn and headed back to the bar.

Oh Mother, how can I win this one?

She exhaled her despair into the muggy, smoky air.

However am I going to keep my sacred vow?"

One

Day 1 April 1872

Count Adolphus Westerhoven wriggled to get comfortable on the hard leather railway seat and told himself it was only another three or four hours till he'd be disembarking at the Oakland Wharf depot.

After ten months away in his Austrian homeland, overseeing his penniless father's funeral and re-settling his unbending elderly mother with her sister, he was desperate to get back to California and re-start his life.

When he'd left, he'd just been Dolphie, outrider, protector and companion to his aunt, Countess Elizabeth Westerhoven, and that's how he still saw himself. The title meant nothing without wealth or land to back it up.

But he'd changed while he'd been away. He wasn't the same carefree fellow who'd spent years as his widowed aunt Elizabeth's fixer and right-hand man. He'd always be grateful for the way she and his distant blood relation, her husband Charles, had taken him so unreservedly into their lives when he'd been a rebellious youngster.

But he sensed a new season was unfolding for him, one where he wanted a fresh direction in his life, though he was as undecided and restless as he'd ever been about what exactly it might be. Before he'd left for Europe at the news of his father's fatal illness, he'd spent a few perilous weeks in Nevada's Virginia City as a security agent and investigator for Elizabeth and others in her extended family, including her niece, Sarah Wyndham, and her good friend, Washington Senator Hector de Vile.

He'd decided he'd had enough of being shot at, of tailing villains and meting out rough justice. His skills as a light-footed sleuth, a deadly marksman, and a meticulous observer might have equipped him well in the role, but he wanted to move on from reckless pursuits to a more settled life.

He put down the book he'd been attempting to read for the last half hour and yawned. Jules Verne's *Twenty Thousand Leagues Under the Sea* was just the sort of classic adventure he craved, but this evening he had too much on his mind to concentrate.

His insides tingled with rising excitement at the prospect of stepping back onto California soil in a few hours' time. How often, in the airless and starchy, joyless house in a village near to Salzburg, he'd dreamed of this day.

He'd sent no warning of his planned arrival ahead, sure of an enthusiastic reception at Elizabeth's Nob Hill house no matter the time of day. He stretched out his legs and put his heels up on the bunk bed opposite.

His hand crept toward Verne's volume when the door to his carriage burst open and a stranger barged in, man or woman he couldn't at first glance tell, except for the fall of honey-blond hair.

Dolphie rose in one fluid movement and faced the intruder, one hand reaching for the stiletto in his boot.

The newcomer slammed the door closed and leaned back against it, as if expecting someone else to charge in at any second.

"I'm so sorry." The voice was low and breathless but surely it was feminine, although she wore trousers and a white buttoned-to-the-neck shirt. She maintained a flat palm against the door.

"I need somewhere safe. Can I rest here a while?"

Dolphie flexed his fingers to release tense, pent-up energy.

He gestured to the bed. "Sit down, why don't you?" The woman held her ground, defending the door. After a studied pause, he raised his right brow in skeptical inquiry.

"Are you expecting guests?"

A pale pink flush climbed up her cheeks, leaving them glowing against her strawberry gold hair. The brief moments he'd spent in her company had satisfied him that, despite the strange garb, she was indeed a woman. The baggy neutral clothes didn't entirely hide her pleasantly rounded curves.

Piercing marine-blue eyes drilled into him, and then she let her hand fall away from the door and flashed him a brilliant smile.

"Hilarious," she said, and he caught a hint of Irish lilt in the phrase. "But I'm warning you, if Blackheart appears, it won't be a comedy."

"Blackheart?" said Dolphie. "Who the heavens is he, and is he as bad as he sounds?"

She laughed and shook her head. "It depends."

He took in her calm self-possession, in such contrast to the fluster when she'd first bounced in. The pantaloons were slimmer than the ones worn by a few eccentric fashion plates in San Francisco's demimonde Mission district.

They were much more practical than the fashion version, and also more masculine. Her only concession to her femininity was a jaunty red, white, and blue scarf tied at her neck.

"Depends on what?"

She gazed at him in calculated silence, as if she couldn't believe this conversation.

Then her shoulders relaxed, and she moved toward the bed.

"On whether you give him what he wants. Bloods don't like to be denied."

"Let me get this right. You have annoyed some mobster from the Bloods gang, who may pound on my railway carriage door any second now."

She trilled with a light laugh. "That's about the sum of it."

She was tall for a woman, willowy in form, and her face had an elegant symmetry; with high cheekbones, a finely molded nose, and delicate lips that quivered with quicksilver responsiveness.

"Get into bed and pull the sheets over you," he said with sudden urgency.

She looked at him as if he was mad.

"Do it. I'll pretend you're my wife."

She shrugged and followed his instructions as he stepped to the door to lock it from the inside.

He'd just turned the key in the lock when a loud hammering sent it shuddering in its slot.

"Who is it?" asked Dolphie.

"Ticket collector," roared a male voice from the other side. "Open up now."

Dolphie glanced across to the bed. The woman—it occurred to him he didn't even know her name—put her hands over her ears as if to deny the latest development and mouthed, "It's him."

She dove under the sheets and lay still.

Dolphie palmed the stiletto in one hand, flicked open the lock with the other, and in a move that owed a lot to his prowess as a fencing champion, slipped out into the corridor in one gliding movement and slammed the door hard behind him.

••••••••

He stood primed in a fencer's stance, his stiletto held horizontally in front of his body.

A towering fellow with a heavy black beard stepped back, his hands instantly held up in front of him.

"Whoa," he said. "Easy."

"Ticket collector, you said?"

Dolphie regarded the man mountain with a steady glare.

"In a manner of speaking," the muscular man responded.

"In what universe is that?" said Dolphie, thinking of Jules Verne.

The man maintained his protective position with his hands, but relaxed his general stance.

"Okay. Okay. I'm looking for my business partner, Sadie McGillicuddy. We had a misunderstanding and I'm wanting to check she's all right. It can be a dangerous world for a woman on her own."

"Sadie, you say? Never heard of her," Dolphie said. He stared at the man he assumed was Blackheart for half a minute, and then turned to go back into his Pullman car.

"Oy. Oy!" the big man protested, more loudly the second time. "She headed this way, and I've checked every other carriage between here and the one we were travelling in."

Dolphie stopped mid turn. "You were travelling together?"

"Yes, mister. Why is that so unusual? Sadie's father and me. We're in business together."

"Oh? What kind of business is that?"

"Why? What difference does it make?"

"Well, none, probably. I'm just curious."

"Keep your curiosity to yourself, brother. It's best to remain ignorant. That way, no one can blame you when things go wrong."

"Is that so?" said Dolphie, putting his hand to the carriage door handle. "I haven't met this Sadie person, so goodnight."

"No, wait…"

Dolphie opened the door, but as he went to step through,

Blackheart gave him a mighty shove, pushing him headlong into his carriage.

He spun around and raised the stiletto, but in one slashing movement Blackheart grabbed his wrist and squeezed hard. The finely wrought blade clattered to the floor.

"Cut the crap," Blackheart growled. "You're up against a professional here."

Dolphie fell backwards in a strangely orchestrated dancing step.

"Stand aside," Blackheart hollered. "You said you hadn't seen her, so why the fuss?"

He advanced to the bunk and ripped aside the rumpled sheet. The bed was empty. He stared in disbelief and then turned in a circle, scanning the room. There was nowhere else to hide. He dropped the sheet, his face a scowling, angry beetroot.

"You'd better not be playing smart with me," he hissed through clenched teeth. "The Bloods aren't to be messed with, I'm warning you."

And I'm definitely too old for this racket, Dolphie thought, as Blackheart stormed out.

He locked the door again and flopped back down on his hard bench seat.

What just happened here?

●●●●●●●●

Dolphie idly picked up the tattered copy of Jules Verne, but he had no interest in reading. Sadie had vanished. The only sounds in the Pullman car were the metallic, rhythmic clack of iron wheels on rails and the hiss of steam.

He scanned the view through the carriage windows and waited. They were in a stormy rush down the Sierra Nevada mountains, and long miles of water flumes ran near the track. Below Gold Hill a group of men flushed a high-pressure hose against a rock face, washing gold from the dirt and gravel which bore it.

A wailing whistle sounded as the Central Pacific roared through a road crossing.

"All clear, Sadie," he said in a soft voice. "You can come out now."

For a long minute, nothing changed. Just the rush of wind against the window as they plunged forward.

And then he heard a mousey scuffle overhead. Dolphie looked up in disbelief, as a panel in the carriage ceiling slid sideways and a long, lean form unfolded through a tiny slot and collapsed onto the bed beneath.

"That was tight in more ways than one," said Sadie McGillicuddy with a relieved exhalation of air.

They stared at each other, both momentarily at a loss for words.

Sadie had a smudge of dust on the end of her classic nose, which only enhanced her understated beauty. The hairs on his arms tingled, responding to a magnetic force he'd been unaware of until this instant. Dolphie had never met such a perplexing woman.

She didn't seem to give a fudge for any of the usual female conventions. A river of silence flowed between them, laden with unspoken thoughts, and it seemed to Dolphie neither of them wanted to break the spell.

Finally, he glanced at the door.

"Your pal won't be coming back," he said. "And you've got an awful lot of explaining to do."

Two

"My pal?" She half rose, her voice thick with indignation.

"According to him, Sadie," Dolphie said, studying her intently. Did it surprise her he knew her name?

"You heard him, I'm sure. He said you were colleagues who'd had a little misunderstanding, and he was checking on your *safety*. Touching, really. I can't imagine why you were frightened of him."

At his light sarcasm, her face flushed deep pink again. A satisfied warmth flooded his central core. She gave every show of being in control, but she was more transparent than she thought.

"I know him, but I'm no colleague." She poured cold scorn onto the word, glancing away to the windows, appearing reluctant to discuss it further. When she spoke next, she was still addressing the window.

"He's a business associate of my father's, that's all." She turned back to face him head-on. "And he's mixed up in my sister's disappearance."

Dolphie's heart jolted at the words.

"Explain *'disappearance.'* And *'mixed up*'?"

She stared at him, holding on to her silence. Maybe she was debating how much to tell him. He already guessed from his exchange with Blackheart that she wasn't telling him the full story.

Her forehead concentrated into parallel lines of frustration.

"My sister Phoebe. She's a few years younger than me, and she's missing from home. Whether she's run away or the Bloods have abducted her, I don't know. That's what I'm going to San Francisco to find out."

Dolphie's stomach felt as if it was falling to his feet.

"You think the Bloods have taken your sister against her will?" The disbelief in his voice echoed around the carriage. "Then why don't you call the police?"

Her eyes challenged him with answering incredulity. "You live in a different world, mister. The cops aren't interested in where Brian McGillicuddy's daughter is. They're far more interested in hitting the Shamrock Bar's owner up for their 'take.'"

She stood to leave. "I'd better get going. Thanks for your help. I appreciate it."

Subject closed. Her Irish lilt was no longer expansive, but clipped, final.

He stood to match her and was pleased to note that although she was tall for a woman, he was a head taller.

"The name is Dolphie," he said. "Adolphus, if you must." Her mouth gaped.

"Not mister. And sit down." She put her hands on her hips in silent protest.

"It's Count Adolphus Westerhoven, if you want the whole rigmarole."

She stared at him for silent seconds, and then repeated faintly, "Count? I don't believe it."

"It doesn't matter if you believe it or not, it's a fact. A useless title, with no money or land attached, unfortunately. Newly minted. My father died five months ago, and I'm returning to San Francisco after seeing to family matters back in Salzburg."

She sank slowly back down onto the edge of the bed.

"I'm… I'm sorry about your father. My mother died eighteen months ago, and I still miss her every day."

She gazed at him, her marine eyes pools of sadness.

"Dolphie," she said, turning the name over on her tongue. "I prefer Dolphie to Adolphus. You don't want to be called Count Dolphie, do you?"

He grinned at her. "Dolphie will do just fine. And now, why don't you tell me all about this missing sister of yours? I might be able to help."

••••••••

Count?

Sadie was still reeling. She'd never met a count. As far as she knew, she'd never been near one. The closest she'd got to a man with a title was King Cobra. She swallowed a despairing laugh and flicked her eyes nervously to the man sitting opposite her.

"What's wrong?" he said. "Is something funny?"

She shook her head. If he knew what kind of world she came from… Well, if he did, she was certain he wouldn't be offering to help.

She cleared her throat. Once she got started, it all came gushing out. It was such a relief to tell someone who'd listen, she couldn't hold back.

"Phoebe—that's my sister's name. Did I say already? Phoebe is wild. And beautiful. Well, exquisite, really. A terrible combination for avoiding trouble when you're not yet twenty years old. And I'm afraid Phoebe doesn't want to avoid trouble. She runs straight for it."

She flicked the silent man a quick smile, and he lifted a wry brow, as if he understood exactly what she meant. As if it wasn't strange at all when sisters acted like that.

He was peculiar in his own way, this count. He was good-looking in a Fifth Avenue, upper-crust way. Lean and spare, like a greyhound or a thoroughbred racehorse, built to move fast.

His face was like that too, strong and noble, with black eyes that looked at her so piercingly it made her heart beat faster. Scary, but not like Blackheart. She couldn't imagine him acting as anything but as a gentleman. Although, come to think of it, what did she know about gentlemen? She'd only ever seen them at a distance, getting in and out of their coaches for the opera and such.

She realized she'd drifted off into a private little daydream, and she came back down to earth with a thump. He was sitting there, watching, patiently waiting for her to continue.

"Carry on. I'm fascinated," was all he said.

"Phoebe wants to escape our life. The Shamrock. That's the bar Brian owns, if I haven't already mentioned it. He's her father and my stepfather.

"She dreams of having money, and power, lots of beautiful dresses, and never having to serve another New York scoundrel in her life. She doesn't understand yet that everything comes at a price. She thinks she can beat the odds."

"Oh?" Dolphie said quietly. "And what are her odds?"

"Her odds? About the same as mine… No, maybe better…"

She exhaled a drawn-out breath. "We're Irish immigrants in New York. I'm sure you know what that means, Dolphie. If you're lucky, you survive to become a half-decent human being. And you have to battle every day to stay that way."

"And if you're not lucky?"

"If you're a woman? Ah, you die young of hard work and too many babies, like my Ma. Leaving behind a brood of young 'uns without feathers enough to fly the nest."

Her words fell into a deep hole of melancholy. As Dolphie

watched, his eyes soft on her face, tears welled up from deep inside her, and she abruptly turned away.

It was as if, without saying a word, he understood. He sympathized. And the one thing she couldn't stand, the thing she hated even more than being ignored, belittled, not listened to, was tenderness.

Her grief caught in the back of her throat, and the memory of those last minutes with her mother rolled over her like a king tide.

She'd had no choice. She'd had to swear that oath. How could she not, with her mother pulling her hand toward the Holy Book, insistent. She'd had to give her mother that, her last living wish.

She coughed and glanced over at the kindest man she'd ever met.

"My mother…" Her voice faltered. She tried again. "I promised her I'd keep Phoebe safe."

Her voice went squeaky.

His eyes held a question, but still he did not speak.

"On her deathbed. I vowed on the Bible I would keep her from harm."

She stood up, suddenly restless, and looked toward the window again.

"I don't have a choice. I promised on the Bible. I can't let my Ma down. I have to find Phoebe and bring her back, or I'll be damned forever."

Three

Dolphie lounged at composed rest, legs stretched out before him, revealing nothing of the turmoil roiling inside. His blood churned, rebelling against the very idea of damnation.

What craw thumper nonsense was this? What kind of world did she live in? Daughterly devotion had pressured her into making a promise it was impossible for her to keep, and now she was blaming herself?

Something deep inside him told him she didn't want his sympathy. He'd caught the suspicious, full wetness in her eyes when she spoke of her mother's deathbed.

He let the quiet bubble of communion they shared linger on, intact.

He stretched back on the unforgiving seat, raised his arms along the bench back, and asked almost casually: "This Blackheart fellow. Does he know where Phoebe is?"

Her eyes widened in surprise at the change of mood, but her face relaxed. He sensed she was glad he'd ignored her momentary loss of control and had reverted to business.

She shrugged. "Depends. If she's with the Bloods, he'll know. He's the lieutenant in San Francisco—Cobra's second in charge. But she might have just run away. Decided to seek something new for herself. I don't know."

He considered her words. "Why is he on the train anyway, if he belongs in San Francisco?"

Her cheeks flushed bright pink, the query sending her right back on defense. She chewed her lip, buying time while she considered her answer.

"He and Cobra have been in New York for a while now, setting up a new chapter there. That's where my Daa comes in. He's going into partnership with them. Patrick said he'd help me find Phoebe when Brian wasn't interested. Brian says she'll find her own way home when she's good and ready.

"Patrick has got the idea she's gone to San Francisco. But whether she's run away to find Cobra, or whether they've taken her there against her will, I don't know. And if Patrick knows, he's not telling me. He's liable to get into big Bloods trouble if he gabs too much, so he's not likely to do that."

Dolphie regarded her steadily.

"Is that what your disagreement was about? Did he threaten you?"

The blush in her cheeks deepened to an embarrassed red.

She rubbed her eyes, warding off the question.

"What difference does it make?" she snapped. "He can't help. We'd both be for it if he did."

Yep. Something definitely going on there she doesn't want to talk about.

He let his arms drop to his sides, placed them on his thighs and hunched forward in a confessional pose.

"Thing is, I've got friends in San Francisco who can probably help, Sadie. They've got experience at this sort of thing. But they'd have to trust you."

The unspoken hung in the air between them

You'd have to tell them the truth. No secrets.

He leaned back again, signaling another change of tack.

"Where are you planning to stay?"

She stared at him, eyes glazed with apprehension.

"You've made no reservation? No hotel?"

She shrugged.

"Was Blackheart looking after the reservations?"

She rocked her head. "No. Nooo," she cried. "I didn't know he was going to be on the train until after I got on. Besides, he has his own home to go to."

The sea-washed eyes turned a marine blue in distress.

Her hands twisted in her lap, her fingers tightly entwined. The determined, athletic woman who'd entered his compartment with a defiant spirit less than an hour ago was dissolving before his eyes.

This was not how he'd envisioned arriving home, accompanied by some lost female. He'd already resolved he was giving up the Mr. Fix-It role he'd filled for Elizabeth for years now. He wanted something different, a change in his life.

He glanced across at Sadie. The blush in her cheeks had faded to ash. She was gazing out the carriage window, her singular beauty overtaken by desolation and fatigue.

He couldn't leave her on a railway platform at the mercy of a mobster looking for easy advantage. He'd take her home to Elizabeth's. His ever compassionate "Countess" aunt would put her up for a few days until she got herself oriented in the new city. But that's where any involvement on his part would start and end.

Sadie had rallied herself and was sitting up straighter, looking directly at him.

"I need to get my bag from my compartment," she said. "I left it there before. It's got everything I need."

'Tell me what carriage and I'll get the ticket collector to retrieve it for you."

She attempted to object, but he cut her off.

"That's part of his job."

He stood, relieved to stretch his body after the confinement of the carriage.

"I've got someone who'll put you up for a few days, until you find your feet," he said. "Then you're on your own."

Four

Where did I think I was going to stay?

Sadie shuddered at her own ineptitude and lack of foresight.

She'd been so obsessed with finding Phoebe, and with convincing her stepfather they needed to go after her, that she'd overlooked the question of where she'd sleep when she got to San Francisco.

After she'd extracted from Blackheart that he'd heard rumors Phoebe was heading for San Francisco, she'd determined to get on the next train there.

She'd assumed she could rely on native cunning and find a cheap boarding house. If that failed, she'd throw herself on the mercies of the Irish nuns.

She knew from her life in the Bowery that several Catholic orders in America brought in nuns directly from Ireland. The Daughters of Charity, The Sisters of the Presentation of the Blessed Virgin Mary and the Sisters of Mercy were all staffed by Irish nuns, and they all operated in San Francisco because of the big Irish population there. Surely one of them would take pity on a woman alone and give her a bed for the night?

And Blackheart? Her heart cringed again. She was attracted to him, she couldn't deny it. He was a handsome fellow, with his muscular frame and black eyes sparking with intelligence. Not a drunken lout, like most of the bullies and brawlers in the Bloods. He was shrewd in his judgments and she thought he held himself to higher standards. You never saw him pawing a woman in the bar. He even went to mass some Sundays.

And she'd got the impression he respected her. He didn't lust after Phoebe like practically every other one of the Shamrock's patrons.

She'd had no inkling he had followed her onto the San Francisco train with some misguided idea of protecting her, or hoping to seduce her on the long journey.

What a mess I've made of it, and I'm not even there yet. Do I have a clue what I'm taking on here?

As the train came out of a long tunnel and began a winding descent through rugged rocks dotted with Christmas pines, she and the unusual man who—unbeknownst to him—had rescued her from Patrick Blackheart's uninvited amorous advances fell into a companionable silence. And she was grateful for it, because she had a lot of thinking to do. Deliberations, she admitted to herself, she should have done before she stepped on the train.

Just how was she going to find Phoebe once she got to San Francisco? If her sister *was* hanging out with the Bloods, they were hardly going to advertise where they lived, were they?

She imagined that, just like in New York, every cop within a ten-mile radius would linger on the street outside if they knew where their base was. Now she'd burned her bridges with Patrick, she couldn't pump him for any further information.

And if Phoebe wasn't with the Bloods? Would she have to trawl every flea pit and deadfall in the vain hope of finding her?

She glanced across at Count Dolphie. He'd buried himself in a book, occasionally breaking his concentration to look absentmindedly out the window

What an unusual fish he was. She didn't come across his kind in the Shamrock. Just the sight of him gave her a strange, fluttery sensation in the pit of her stomach. A bit like what she felt when she looked at Patrick, but more intense. She wasn't sure she liked it; it was so unsettling.

"We'll put you up for a few days until you find your feet. Then you'll be on your own."

The words rang in her ears, like a warning.

It's just as well, she told herself. *You can't let yourself get distracted by anything except your quest to find Phoebe. Especially not some stupid man.*

But in the meantime, he'd be very useful.

Five

"What's that building?"

Sadie had broken Dolphie's reverie with the excited voice of a child, as the dome of the Sacramento capitol building rose like a pale planet in a forest of semi-tropical green.

"That's the California capitol building. We're passing through Sacramento. We'll be in San Francisco before long."

After an hour of thoughtful silence, his traveling companion had come alive. She shuffled herself across the still folded-down bed to sit closer to the window, watching the unfolding scene with rapt attention. Behind them to the east were the silvery Sierra Nevada mountains. On the horizon, in view of San Francisco Bay, the rising blue dome of Mount Diablo.

They crossed flat wheat lands, neat rows of orange groves, and for the first time Dolphie imagined—was he imagining, it or was it real?—that he could smell orange blossom in the air. Further away, the curving gray ribbon of the Sacramento River, full of fine salmon, wended its way down to the sea.

Dolphie had made this trip several times before, but he became aware this was a first time for Sadie. A first for everything, and she was seeing it from the luxury of a private sleeper. At one point he'd wandered back and got the railway ticket man to retrieve her carpet bag from the second-class berth she'd formerly occupied.

"What have you enjoyed most about the trip so far?" he asked.

Six days on a train were ending, and they'd met less than eight hours ago.

Sadie took her time to consider, her brow furrowing with concentration.

"The antelopes? The prairie dogs?"

He recalled the prairie dogs, fat rollicking creatures like exaggerated rats, who sat up as straight as ten pins and watched the train advance, before flinging up their heels and diving into their holes. And the antelopes, graceful animals with white feather behinds, who dashed off at the sound of the oncoming train and then wheeled around and stared at it from a safe distance.

"That was Nebraska," said Dolphie.

"Sherman?"

"Wisconsin. The highest point on the tracks. That's where we got out to change trains…"

She nodded, her eyes shining at the memory. She felt in her trouser pocket and proudly held up a pebble.

"Ah, you followed the custom and took a souvenir of the journey?" He smiled.

"Soon, you'll see the Pacific Ocean, and we'll be all but there."

They plunged into a tunnel a thousand feet long and came out in sunshine. There were pansies and golden California poppies and wild blue lupins, and the smell of orange blossom was replaced by salt spray and eucalyptus. And then the sparkling San Francisco Bay, dotted with gems of islands, lay before them.

Sadie relaxed back into her spot with a happy sigh. "I'll never regret coming, even if I don't find Phoebe."

Within minutes they were in Oakland, with hedges of fuchsias and walls of scarlet geraniums, and in no time they were onto the three-mile pier that took the Central Pacific out into the sea to meet the ferry. From the mountains they were now amid fishing boats and saucy tugs and man-of-war oceangoing vessels on cables carrying flags bearing the czar's imperial standard, the French tricolor and the rising sun of Japan.

Sadie had returned her eyes to the window, quiet and intense, taking everything in.

As they disembarked, and Dolphie awaited his trunks from the baggage car porter, he thought he glimpsed a black bear of a man with broad shoulders, loitering amongst the crowding passengers collecting up their rugs and picnic baskets and all the detritus of an overland journey.

He frowned to himself. Maybe we haven't seen the last of the Bloods, he thought. Only time would tell.

Six

Gay fiddle music and bright lights spilled through the windows of Elizabeth's turreted Nob Hill mansion as Dolphie and Sadie drew up under the oak trees at the gate in a hired hack.

The Countess had a party in progress, and it obviously wasn't for him, because he hadn't advised anyone he was arriving.

A strange little jolt pinged in his chest. Life was going on at full tilt without him, and he briefly felt left out.

He'd been away nearly a year, and he realized at that moment he'd been expecting to come back to things just as they were. Elizabeth, the "Countess" relaxing under the stars in her back garden, enjoying the night-scented jessamine. Mrs. Roderiquez, the cook, serving her mint juleps there.

And his room, unchanged, at the top of the stairs under the rafters with its Stars and Stripes Old Glory quilt ready to receive him.

He paid the driver and followed along as he wheeled the first of his two trunks up the paved path to Elizabeth's front door. That was new, too.

When he'd left, the path had been a countrified shell and pebble walk that sometimes stuck to the bottom of visitors' shoes, something Elizabeth had complained about because fragments got tramped into the house.

He rapped loudly to make himself heard above the sounds of revelry, but when Mrs. Roderiquez opened up, her jaw dropped in astonishment and then she squealed in delight.

"Mr. Dolphie!!!!" Her happy cries brought Elizabeth swooping in a minute later. "Count Westerhoven, if you please," she corrected with fake formality, and then swept him up into her arms, laughing her welcome in his ear.

That's better, he thought. This feels more like a homecoming.

It was a few minutes before he could disentangle himself, direct the hack man to bring in the second trunk, and step back to introduce Sadie, who'd held back in the shadows.

"Elizabeth, I have a guest with me. Sadie McGillicuddy. I met Sadie on the Central Pacific, and I wondered if she could stay with us for a few days, until she gets herself sorted?"

Elizabeth turned to the young woman, her face welcoming and expectant. She was wearing a rather formal-looking royal blue gown with gold military braid down the front and at the cuffs, but her smile was gentle.

"Sadie, you're most welcome," she said. "It won't take Mrs. R. a minute to make up the bed in the spare room. Your first visit to California, is it?"

Sadie stepped into the light of the hallway, shoulders back, the same confident, forthright young woman who'd stormed into his compartment.

"I am honored to be here, Mrs. Westerhoven. Thank you so much for your hospitality. And yes, my first time in California." She gave Elizabeth a gracious smile that lit up her eyes.

Elizabeth took Sadie's hand and gave it a welcoming squeeze before turning back to Dolphie.

"As you see, you've found us partying. I've some new friends to introduce you to, Dolphie. Come right in. If you're hungry, there's plenty of food still out on the buffet. Please help yourselves after I've done with the introductions."

Dolphie took Sadie's carpet bag from her and stood aside to allow her to follow Elizabeth inside. He dropped the bag quietly in the hall and trailed them into the drawing room, where some faces were familiar.

He recognized the deceptively unassuming, and now very wealthy businesswoman Sarah Wyndham, and her darkly handsome Hawaiian sugar merchant boyfriend Kaleo Manolo. Mercurial Alex de Vile, son of California's Senator to Washington Hector de Vile and an accomplished photographer. He'd got to know them all well during their Virginia City escapade before he left for Europe. He noted Hector's absence with a pang.

He'd read of his death in tragic circumstances in the London newspapers on his way home, and he hadn't yet passed on his condolences to Elizabeth and Alex. He'd have to leave that till later. Now was not the time.

Elizabeth paused in front of one stranger, a dark-headed, fit-looking man who was probably a decade older than Dolphie, but exuded a youthful vitality.

"Jack Cabot, meet my dearest nephew, Dolphie Westerhoven, and his friend Sadie."

Jack stepped up with a bright grin. "At last I meet the legendary Adolphus. I feel as if I've been waiting too long!" He turned to Sadie and made a brief mock bow. "And Sadie. Pleased to meet you."

Elizabeth hesitated, her hands clasped in front of her, ever the charming hostess. "We've had some developments that are too complicated to go into right now, Dolphie, some happy and some sad. But this is one of the very happiest."

She drew to her side a thin, pale-faced girl, who shrunk against Elizabeth's assured form, her delicate countenance pinched with worry, obviously overwhelmed by the attention.

"This is Cordelia Cabot Carruthers, Jack's niece, not long arrived from New York." She gestured to the middle-aged woman with tired eyes and a prim set to her mouth who stood at the girl's shoulder. "And her guardian, Susannah Carruthers. Cordelia, Miss Carruthers, meet Count Dolphie and Sadie."

Susannah Carruthers's eyes flitted from his creased suit to Sadie's trousers and her mouth pursed the tiniest fraction in judgment.

This pair don't meet my approval, was the unvoiced message, and from her infinitesimal stiffening at his side, Dolphie knew Sadie felt the censure too.

The woman, dressed in a modestly styled, olive-green gown designed to be as unobtrusive as Elizabeth's attire was to make a statement, gave them a silent nod, and turned back into the room.

So much for that, thought Dolphie. He glanced up and caught a naughty sparkle in Jack's eye. They exchanged conspiratorial grins, and he liked the man immediately.

"We've had a long journey and as you can see, we're rather travel worn," Dolphie said with a hint of apology. "Perhaps it would be better if we retired and let you get on with the festivities."

"Don't even think of it," said Elizabeth robustly. "We're going to feed you first, and then, if you wish, Mrs. R. will organize baths for you."

She turned to Sadie. "Sadie, is that all right with you? Can you stand to stay awake for another couple of hours?"

Sadie dipped her head in assent and smiled again. "I'm so excited to be here, Mrs. Westerhoven, I don't think I could sleep right now even if it was in the most comfortable of beds."

"That settles it," said Elizabeth with satisfaction. "I can promise the bed will be comfortable when you reach it, but let's organize food first."

Seven

Later—much later—when the housemaid had shown Sadie to her second-floor room, Alex, Sarah and Kaleo had departed to their own homes, and Elizabeth and Susannah—having seen Cordelia to bed—were relaxing over hot chocolate in the drawing room, Jack and Dolphie got down to man talk over a brandy nightcap in the library.

"I've got so much to catch up on, Jack, I don't know where to start," said Dolphie. "Hector's death, all that drama at the Imperial Club the night he died in the fire, I'd be grateful if you could catch me up on that some other time. I don't want to ask Elizabeth, it might be too painful for her.

"Right now, though, I'm curious about how this young niece of yours came to be back here. And the woman who's her jailer," he said with a grin. "I gather at some point she was sent to relatives back East?"

He scanned his new acquaintance's aquiline profile, seeking some clue as to Jack's attitude. "She's just arrived to join you, is that right? Sheltering under your wings, so to speak? Is it too sensitive to ask what happened to her parents?"

Jack's face darkened. "She wasn't exactly 'sent to relatives.' Her wastrel father sold her to a couple she—and we—didn't know, like merchandise."

He spat the words out like poison in his mouth.

"No!" Dolphie yelped, the words charged with latent anger, and Jack nodded, his face set in weary resignation.

"My sister died suddenly, and her husband was—still is—an arch rogue. He's a gambling man, never much of a husband or father, and when Tasmin—Tammy died, he adopted Cordelia out to a wealthy New York couple who had no children. For a fee."

He reached over and opened a cigar box. "Want a Cuban?" When Dolphie nodded, he proffered the box and a light.

"As a result, I'm pretty hot on the whole topic of child abuse. I consider selling kids for money is just plain trafficking. It's reprehensible. I begged her father, Dandy Durkan, to let me take over as her guardian, because I adored Cordelia, and I'd spent a lot of time with her."

He took a sip of his drink and drew on his cigar before continuing"

"Tammy was too interested in partying so she wasn't much better than Dandy. He sold her from right under my nose. I confess, it devastated me."

"How long ago was that?"

"Coming up seven years ago. When she was four."

"And how do you now come to have her back?"

"Her stepmother died nearly a year ago and her stepfather wasn't up to taking good care of her. The woman you saw—Susannah—is Cordelia's aunt—her stepfather's sister. She's here as a minder, to check me out and give the final approval for me to take her over."

"And how's that going? She seems—well, not the easiest of people, from what I picked up. I got a distinct whiff of disapproval for turning up unannounced with Sadie like I did. A 'not done at all, James' sort of attitude." He mimicked a snobby English voice.

James grinned. "She is rather proper. Used to the New York scene with all their social rules. Here in California, we don't go in for that sort of stuff, so she doesn't fit comfortably here."

"Is she planning to stay on with Cordelia?" asked Dolphie.

"Heaven forbid!" said Jack with a laugh. "I, for one, couldn't stand it. And I'm sure she wouldn't want to either. She's got her own life back in New York. I gather she's staying until she's settled Cordelia into a suitable environment."

Dolphie tapped his cigar ash into an ashtray on the side table.

"She can hardly object to Elizabeth," he said. "You couldn't find a better mentor for a young girl, though I suppose someone very proper might consider she's a little unorthodox."

Jack grinned and nodded.

"I admit I don't know her at all well, but I get the impression in Susannah's book unorthodox is bad and conventional is good. We will need to learn how to give and take on both sides. I've no intention of letting go now we've got Cordelia back."

"We? Was Elizabeth involved in this one, too?"

"Dear Elizabeth. It's all thanks to her Cordelia is here. She wrote to a minister relative of hers in New York asking him to make inquiries about Cordelia and it all went from there."

He softened his voice to a confidential whisper.

"Elizabeth is from one of the old missionary families very close to the Hawaiian royal family. That's how she first got to know Hector. From strong Methodist stock. Should be Susannah's first choice as a surrogate grandmother, but we'll see.

"Her minister cousin discovered Cordelia was in poor shape. She's spent a lot of time alone, with her adoptive mother dead and her adopted father incapacitated by grief. He was burying himself in his work and Cordelia was so lonely and unhappy it was affecting her health. You can see what a thin little waif she is. We aim to fix that!"

"There's that 'we' again," said Dolphie. "Can I be frank? Is there something going on between you and Elizabeth?"

Jack laughed. "No, no. Not now. Years ago, maybe, but not now. She was on the verge of marrying Hector when he died and it's hit her hard, though she puts up a good front."

He lifted his empty glass to eye level and tilted it toward Dolphie.

"Do you want another of these? Or a coffee? Or even hot chocolate? Mrs. R. will still be bustling around the kitchen if we need anything."

"Hot chocolate would be just the thing," said Dolphie, as Jack rang for a servant.

"You were saying about Elizabeth and Hector…"

"Yes," Jack said. "She's still picking up the pieces. Hopefully. Cordelia is a distraction for her.

"As you know, with her work for abandoned and abused women over the years, she has a real soft heart for the underdog. So, she's jumped right into helping Cordelia grow into a strong young woman. She's a wonderful ally to have. Managing Susannah would be so much harder without her."

He gazed into his glass reflectively. "I was a mess for a few years there, after we lost Cordelia. I didn't handle it at all well. Elizabeth can take the credit for dragging me back from the brink and shaming me into being the man I'm meant to be."

His eyes fixed on Dolphie and he winced self-consciously. "I'm afraid I blamed Elizabeth when Cordelia disappeared. I proposed we marry and raise Cordelia together, but she wouldn't go along with it. She had more sense than I did. I see that now."

He paused as Mrs. R. bustled in with their hot drinks.

"I feel like I've had a second chance and I won't mess up this time. Whatever it takes, I'm seeing Cordelia through to becoming a happy and healthy young woman. Anyway, enough about me. What about this young woman Sadie who you met on the train? How on earth did that happen?"

Dolphie told the story of Sadie barging into his Pullman compartment.

"How she got past the guards, I don't know," he said. "You know what they're usually like at patrolling to make sure only first-class ticket holders get in. She was in second class with some mobster she knew from her father's bar in New York."

"Charming. For goodness' sakes, don't let Miss Carruthers hear that part of the story."

Dolphie laughed.

"She's got another 'abused and/or abandoned woman' story to tell. She's looking for her younger sister, Phoebe, who's gone missing from the family home. She believes she's come to San Francisco chasing after some man she's infatuated with."

Jack laughed. "Another 'to be censored' story. Miss Carruthers will have a fit! She's most particular about Cordelia not being given improper ideas."

His handsome face was a picture of unrepentant delight.

"Does Sadie have any idea where her sister might be?"

"She thinks she's chasing after one of the top guys in the Bloods gang. Heard of them?"

Jack looked astonished. "This story gets more bizarre by the minute. As a matter of fact, I have," said Jack. "I used to spend time in the Barbary Coast and saw a lot of those types. They are one of the new gangs coming up—a mix of Irish and Italian. They've taken over entire blocks from the Chinese syndicates and the Sydney Ducks."

"And what kind of reputation do they have?" asked Dolphie.

"Pretty much standard mobster stuff. Peddling liquor and girls. They run gambling joints and exercise that Sicilian code of silence stuff. Keep a tight rein on their own ranks. Nobody defies the boss and lives to tell the tale."

Dolphie thought of Patrick Blackheart. Was he paid to keep an eye on Sadie? Would he tell his Cobra overlord everything he knew about Sadie's interest in her sister?

"Do you trust her?" asked Jack.

Dolphie shrugged. "As far as I can throw her," he commented with a laugh.

Jack guffawed. "And she's a strong, sturdy woman, so not too far. What's with the clothes?"

"The men's attire, you mean? She says it's purely for comfort and practicality. I think it's to discourage male attention myself. If you look past the clothes, she's a beautiful woman, and she's working for her father in a bar. It signals to the drinkers she's not available in the plainest possible language."

Jack sipped contentedly. "I admire her courage. It's twenty years since the suffragists like Amelia Jenks Bloomer tried to get women into pants and it never really took off, did it? But good on her for plowing her own field."

There was a gentle tap on the library door and Elizabeth slipped into the room, pausing to assess their mood.

"I'm off to bed. Susannah's already gone. I don't want to interrupt your getting-to-know-you session." She flashed them a smile. "But I've some domestic news before I hit the pillow."

Her eyes crinkled at the corners in frustration. Not good news then, thought Dolphie.

"Susannah has announced she doesn't consider Sadie a suitable person for Cordelia to be associating with in this house. She's moving both of them to a hotel tomorrow."

There was a stunned silence in the warm, accommodating room, and then Jack spoke.

"For all the tea in China! What's wrong with the woman? Does she think the child's made of eggshells?"

"She considers it sets a very poor example for Cordelia to see a woman in bloomers. She might get ideas of becoming a mad suffragist."

Dolphie cut in. "I brought this on the house by inviting her to stay, Elizabeth," he said. "Maybe it's best if I find rooms for Sadie and myself somewhere else."

"Not necessary, Dolphie," said Elizabeth.

He shook his head and screwed up his mouth in vexation. "I don't want to abandon her. She knows nothing of this city, and she's taking on a mammoth task. I'll go with her and help her find her way, at least for a day or two."

"I won't hear of it," Elizabeth said. "I don't know the full story, but let's sleep on it and find a solution before Susannah departs tomorrow. Jack, I'm relying on you to come up with something typically irresistible to keep her here."

Eight

Brothel queen Sophia Morrigan fluttered her long black lashes at Patrick Blackheart and enjoyed the warm surge that rose from within when his sexy black eyes gleamed in response.

He was a handsome devil, this Bloods man who'd arrived from New York last night, and she wasn't inclined to waste any opportunity to exercise her courtesan skills. Goodness knew she was well out of practice.

She'd been vaguely aware of him about town, but her new "understanding" with the Bloods meant they were now working more closely together than they ever had in the past.

After the disastrous "affair" with Senator Hector de Vile—attempted affair, if she was being ice-cold honest, it never even came to a kiss—and then Grigor's untimely death, she hadn't been in the mood for dalliance.

There was also the petty matter of being charged with two counts of murder for their deaths. She'd got off those by paying a lot of dollars out in bribes, but the notoriety that came with the title "Queen of Death" she'd already earned now carried more weight, and it certainly put a dampener on romance.

She glanced up and saw Blackheart was still watching her with those sharp, calculating eyes. He was a virile fellow, and he seemed to have brains, too, which was always a welcome addition. At least one man had noticed she was female. She flicked him a flirtatious smile and turned her attention back to King Cobra, head boss of the Bloods and her new business partner in the chain of brothels and gaming dens she ran across the state.

Cobra was desirable in his own way too—money and power always made a man sexy, and he had a brooding allure, but he was too old. She was only thirty-four, and he must be close to fifty. She'd got fair warning he was an old-school mobster from the bruises and worse he'd dealt out to her brothel nancies. That settled it for her. Their relationship was going to be nothing but business. Blackheart? He might be quite a different story.

The three of them—Cobra, Blackheart and herself—had enjoyed French onion soup followed by sole in wine at Jack's Restaurant on Sacramento Street, and they were now meeting just around the corner and a block away at to her brightest and best house of pleasure, a Palladian-style masonry pile on Montgomery Street called The Other White House.

From the outside, it looked more like a rich man's private club than a brothel, and that's how she wanted it. White columns rose behind a clipped laurel hedge, with black wrought-iron lamps giving it an air of exclusivity.

"You take care of Teo for me, there's a good man," Cobra was saying, searching his lieutenant's expression for any sign of insubordination. Blackheart didn't hesitate.

"Done," he said. He tapped his fingers on the table, as if reflecting.

"What?" said Cobra sharply, always sensitive to dereliction.

"I'm wondering who will take over watch duties on Phoebe if Teo is out of action. He's the one on that job, isn't he?"

Cobra's frown creased in irritation.

"Phoebe's here now. What makes you think she needs round-the-clock attention? Thanks to Sophia, we've got her safely tucked up out of harm's way at the Golden Girl."

He reached out and tapped Sophia familiarly on the forearm, a cool smile accompanying the gesture. She had to fight the urge to avoid his touch. There was something creepy about Cobra, she decided.

"You have got her under your care, haven't you? She's not to be used in the house—she's my special project. I don't want anyone else getting their hands on her except me. You understand?"

"Of course, Cobra. Your special project," Sophia Morrigan soothed.

"So, what's the problem, Blackheart?"

Blackheart hesitated again. Sophia was pretty certain this was a calculated pitch. His deputy was running rings around Cobra... and this new girl was his weak point.

"Brian McGillicuddy's on our tail. That weird daughter of his, the oldest one, Sadie. She's got a bee in her bonnet about Phoebe 'going missing.' Her father apparently hasn't told her what's going on. She's come out here to track her sister down and take her back home."

Cobra roared with laughter. "What a fool. She doesn't know her old man and I have done a deal?"

"Apparently not. He knows she'd create trouble if she was aware. And she's souped up with some deathbed promise she made to her mother to keep her sister out of harm's way."

"Mother of Mary, Phoebe's in the safest place she could be. What's she on about?" Cobra sounded indignant. "You can't get any safer than a Bloods boss's concubine. No one else is going to dare touch her."

"Mmm. Maybe Sadie doesn't see it that way. She being in with the nuns and attending Mass every Sunday and everything. She's a proper Irish Mick, even if she works for her Daa in the Shamrock. I think we need to be careful. Get her on our side," said Blackheart.

"What can a doll who knows nothing about nothing do?" Cobra sneered. "You said it yourself. She's a bar moll from the Bowery. She's got no chance. She's already found some pretty heavy-hitting friends. You heard of The Countess?"

Cobra scowled, and Sophia sat up straighter.

That witch who would have married Hector de Vile if he hadn't died? What was she doing involved in anything to do with Sophia's business?

She felt hot prickles stinging up her arms.

Blackheart continued, appearing to not pick up on her sudden interest.

"I followed her off the train last night. She picked up this fella and they went to that flamer's big house. Stayed there overnight, so far as I could tell."

Cobra snorted. "So what?"

Sophia was alert to a sudden sense of danger. She thumped the table, as if she'd just had a great idea.

"More liquor, my friends? What's to your liking?"

She waved her arm to summon the house manager she kept on duty when she was entertaining. "More refreshments for our guests, Guido."

When their glasses were full, she clinked hers first with Cobra's, and then Blackheart's.

"I know this woman, the Countess, Cobra, and I can tell you, she's a nuisance. Patrick is right. You can never be too careful. She's given me the devil of some problems. She's got some opium fiend friend with a chip on his shoulder about abandoned children who used to hang out in the Barbary Coast.

"It might be just the sort of thing they'd get into—getting the idea Phoebe's being ill-treated and coming to rescue her. I think you'd be a smart man to take notice."

Cobra's pupils contracted into tiny black points of darkness.

This man does not like to be told anything. He's too stupid to see what he's got here.

"Okay. Okay. I hear what you're saying."

He wheeled on Patrick Blackheart.

"Deal to Teo and then send them a reminder, then. You know the score. Give them the usual 'Keep your nose out of it' message."

For a half second, Blackheart's lips tightened. He knew he was working for a dolt, too—Sophia could see it.

Then he got to his feet, pushing up from the table.

"Will do, Boss." He nodded to Sophia, his hooded eyes masking fervent desire. "Be seeing you, Angel. I've got work to do."

He gave Sophia a playful bow and left.

Nine

"What do you mean, Cobra wants to see Teo?"

Phoebe pressed her plump lips into a rebellious pout. Perched on a high stool at the intimate bar, she crisscrossed her legs like a ruffled pea hen adjusting its roosting position.

They can't take Teo away.

Teo Martinez, her Bloods bodyguard, had been the one constant in her life since leaving home. He'd told her stories of Marisol and his children, of his life in San Francisco before he'd found a place with the Bloods. They'd become friends on the week-long journey out here.

Now she'd been in San Francisco two days and she had seen nothing of the Bay's talked-about sights, nothing but the luxurious interior of the Golden Girl parlor house, with its red and purple satin bed linens and cushion covers, the musical ceiling chimes and warm and encompassing sandalwood fragrance.

She couldn't argue that it wasn't superior accommodation, but she'd seen nothing of the celebrated mid-afternoon promenade of fashion when the townswomen gave passersby an impromptu fashion parade.

She hadn't yet eaten at any of the much-vaunted restaurants, or gamboled in any of the dozens of Pacific Street dance halls she'd heard so much about back home at the Shamrock.

Nor had she clapped eyes on King Cobra, her reason for coming here. Why wasn't he dying to see her, she wondered? He'd been eager to break out of the starting gate back in New York.

And now Patrick Blackheart was here demanding that her personal minder, Teo Martinez, had to leave her? She didn't want to admit it to herself, but Theodoro was her anchor, the only familiar touchstone she had in this strange place. Behind her air of arrogant assurance, she felt vulnerable and exposed.

If Martinez disappeared, what was to stop someone from recruiting her into the other side of the business? She wasn't so naïve as to not understand that for all its embellishment with potted ferns and string quartets, the Golden Girl was a high-class brothel.

"I need Teo here, with me," she said, her voice sounding a lot more assured than her wobbly insides felt. "Cobra said he was to be my minder. Has the boss changed his mind?"

She cast an evasive sidelong glance at the brooding presence on a stool next to her. Teo Martinez was a muscular giant, well over six feet tall, with a bullish neck and heavy black eyebrows that met in the middle.

He spoke mainly in grunts, but he'd been a reassuring presence on the train ride out West, effortlessly protecting her from the unwelcome attentions of other male passengers.

And she'd had no fear of unwanted advances from him. He was a happily married man, and besides, they both knew that as Cobra's marked woman, any breach of propriety on his part would result in instant execution. The Bloods did not suffer that kind of betrayal.

Now though, as she surreptitiously scrutinized the man who'd been her constant companion for the last eight days, she detected a sour whiff of fear. Teo was worried, and her heart raced with a matching dread. The other side of Teo sat her new friend—the only other person she knew in the city—a girl called Isla who used to work for the Golden Girl's owner but was not one of the parlor's "pretty waiters." Not yet anyway.

"Isla, will you stay with me?" she asked, her voice trembling despite her determination to appear strong. It suddenly struck her that if Teo was in trouble with King Cobra, maybe she was too. Had someone been feeding him lies about them?

"You're good, Phoebe," Patrick Blackheart said, as if detecting her uncertainty. "Cobra's busy with the Bloods. He's still crazy for you, don't worry. He just wants you to rest a few days, help you get over that train ride and to look your best, you know? Before he comes to visit."

He winked at her.

He's still crazy for you.

A great lump formed in her throat, and she swallowed hard. Closing down on the sense of relief she felt sounded a lot like hiccupping.

She clutched her throat and aped a cough to cover her anxiety.

For the first time in her mad escapade, she wondered what she was getting herself into. And if she'd ever be free again.

•••••••

"What's the story with Cobra?" asked Isla, after the men had gone and the effeminate young man who tended the bar poured them more non-alcoholic fruit punch. Not entirely to Phoebe's taste, but Isla said she didn't drink alcohol.

"He's my intended," Phoebe said. "I've come from New York at his request."

Isla's eyes shot wide open. She was unusual, this new friend of hers, with snow-white straight hair cut to chin level and an elegant face which could be that of a guy or girl.

She said she was sixteen, but she looked thirteen. Phoebe felt ancient beside her at nineteen. And yet Isla was far more at home in the Golden Girl parlor than she was.

"All the way from New York? Aren't there girls he likes in San Francisco?"

Isla raised her finely sculpted brows in unabashed surprise.

Phoebe blushed and shrugged.

"I guess, but he wants me."

"You're betrothed to the big boss of the Bloods, King Cobra? Does that mean you're marrying him?"

Phoebe's throat filled with another wave of raw fear.

"I… I suppose so… He didn't exactly say."

Isla frowned. "So, what? You're going to be his concubine instead?"

Phoebe's ears roared with indignation. This girl was a straight shooter, that was for sure.

"Concubine? No! He said I'd be his number-one woman. That I'd share in his wealth and power. I can have as many dresses I want. Dresses and jewels. He said I would be with him, no matter what. That sounds like a wife, doesn't it?"

Isla's unlined forehead wrinkled into parallel lines of doubt.

"I suppose so," she said. "It depends on the husband. And the wife."

"Listen," said Phoebe, with an urge to ensure this girl understood.

"Girls like us, we only get one shot at getting it right, or we end up on the ash heap. I saw it with my own Maa. This is my shot. While I've got my youth and looks. Men go crazy for it. But I'm not stupid enough to think it will last. I haven't been with anyone… you know what I mean?"

She felt the color rising in her cheeks and was relieved when Isla grinned knowingly.

"Sure. I understand. You're making him beg for it."

"You're right there, kid, but I've only got so many rolls of the dice before he wins the game. My next few moves… well, that's why I'm upset about Teo. I hope it's not a sign."

A puzzled cloud crossed Isla's luminous pale face.

"A sign? What kind of sign?"

"Of bad luck. You know. Like the Devil's Bedposts. The four-poster…"

Isla's eyes screwed up in confusion.

"The four of clubs. The card, dummy."

"Ohhhhh. You're worried something's going to happen to Teo and it will rebound on you."

"That's right."

Phoebe squirmed on her stool. She stood and stretched like a cat, as if shaking off bad luck.

"Tell me, is there a beauty parlor around here? I need to get prepared for Cobra's first visit. I can't afford to waste any of my chances."

<h1 style="text-align:center">Ten</h1>

When Susannah entered the breakfast room early the next morning, the first person she saw—and the last person she wanted to have to deal with first thing in the morning—was Jack.

She closed her scratchy eyes for a few seconds, vainly hoping that when she opened them again, he would no longer be standing at the sideboard, loading his plate with thin sage sausages and potato pancakes.

She rested her hand on the doorpost for half a minute, but when she opened her eyes he was turning with his full plate to seek a place at the dining table. Her insides contracted as their eyes met.

He was such an annoyingly debonair man, far too attractive for someone who was a good decade older than she was. Whenever she looked at him, she felt as if their ages were reversed. She was all washed out and weary, while his "leaves were still fresh and green" in the words of Jeremiah.

He looked like he'd be bearing fruit well into old age. And he couldn't even thank righteous living for his vitality, she grumbled to herself.

From what she'd heard, he'd been living a perfectly dreadful life in a Barbary Coast hellhole until recently. Why he had now set himself up as some sort of savior for his niece Cordelia, she could hardly imagine.

"Good morning, Susannah." Even to her dulled ears, his cheerful ebullience sounded forced. She felt like answering honestly and acidly, "What's good about it?"

She was going to have to go to the inconvenience of relocating to a downtown hotel with Cordelia today, and doing it in such a way as to not upset her gracious hostess or admit to Cordelia there was anything amiss.

The girl wouldn't be happy about the move. Susannah sensed she was already feeling very much at home at Elizabeth Westerhoven's manor, which was lavish in its furnishings while also wrapping itself around you like a comfortable mohair rug.

And although Jack did not live here—even he would see that would be most improper—he spent a great deal of time here. It needled her that Jack and his niece shared a deep bond which the years of separation had not broken.

Cordelia remembered him from her early childhood and plainly adored him. She would be most unhappy about moving house, but what choice did Susannah have?

Instead of indulging her urge to snap, she rallied up as much emotional warmth as she could and replied without rancor. "Good morning, Jack." She settled in a chair opposite him and waited for the servant to pour her a hot coffee.

He glanced across at her. "Not eating this morning?"

She shook her head. "I'll be fine with coffee. I find I have little appetite first thing in the day."

They allowed a drawn-out, awkward silence to fall, both preoccupied with their own thoughts. Then, with cringe-worthy bad timing, they both spoke at once.

"I had something…" from Susannah.

"Elizabeth tells me…" from Jack.

They both hesitated, and Susannah caught a hint of a lopsided grin curling from one side of Jack's mouth.

He's always one to make a joke of life. Just because he seems to come through everything unscathed.

Familiar prickles of irritation ran up the back of her neck.

It was all right for the handsome boy-man who did what he liked and could emerge from his opium haze, all forgiven, trust fund intact. If a woman of his class so much as put her toe out of line, she'd be cast out of society forever. Look what happened to his poor sister, Tasmin. Cut off without a cent when she eloped with the card shyster.

"After you," said Jack.

"I'm sure Elizabeth has told you I plan to find alternative accommodation for myself and Cordelia today," she said. "I don't think it's fair to lean on Elizabeth's kindness when she has new guests to see to."

Jack's eyes measured her with a calculating gleam.

"Come on, Susannah. We've known one another long enough to be honest, haven't we? You find the environment 'unsuitable.' Isn't that closer to the truth?"

The mettle she'd called on so many times over the years rose in force within her.

"If you're determined to call a spade a spade, then yes, Jack. That's exactly right. I don't want Cordelia getting wild ideas about what is and isn't socially acceptable. You're not exactly an exemplary model in that regard."

That hint of a lopsided smile showed on his lips. There it was again. Heat poured into her face as she regarded him with blatant resentment. All the stress and tension that had been gathering inside her bubbled over.

"You've really got no idea what it's like for a girl like Cordelia, on the cusp of womanhood, with so many confusing rules to understand and obey if she's to make a decent way in life, have you, Jack? One foot wrong, and she risks social exclusion.

"She's already got the severe disadvantage of reprehensible parents. Goodness knows where she'd be if it weren't for my brother and his wife…"

Jack took a sharp indrawn breath, and the congenial expression that was one of his most attractive—if annoying—features vanished. His face darkened with irritation.

"Excuse me," he said sharply. "Do you mind?"

"Oh? Now we're the model of propriety, are we?" she mocked.

"You don't like it when someone finally drops the pretense and tells it like it is? Poor Jack…"

Where is this coming from? Stop talking right now….

But she couldn't. It was as if all the years of fighting for a place in the sun, for something she could call a satisfying life even if it didn't match the conventional expectations of marriage and family, burst from her.

The years of hiding away in her studio, painting under a pseudonym because her brother would consider it brought shame on the family name for her to want to paint—be a serious artist, not dab at watercolors between afternoon teas. She'd done that in secret defiance, but it had never been enough.

His head jerked up, and his gorgeous cutting cheekbones shone with little red spots. Was it anger? Hurt?

"I didn't realize…" His voice was quiet and puzzled in tone. "I accept our family hasn't done nearly enough to support Cordelia." He stopped, as if without his usual confident bonhomie he didn't know quite where to navigate himself.

"I want to learn, Susannah. I want to understand what I have to do to make it up."

He ran his hand through his hair, distracted, disconsolate, and she was undone.

His humility, his willingness to accept her rudeness without reproach, punched the wind right out of her sails.

What a complicated chameleon of a man Jack Cabot was. She'd never met another like him. The artist in her, the spontaneous creativity she'd had to keep locked down her whole life, saw him anew, and she wanted to paint him. Like this, Right now. Thoughtful, deep. Remorseful.

"Jack, I…Forgive me. I'm forgetting myself."

"No, Susannah. No. You're quite right. I have no clue how to raise a young woman who can be true to herself and also fulfill social expectations. And I'll need help from women who know how to negotiate the rapids, if I'm to do it."

They locked eyes in a shocked silence, which was broken by a tentative tap on the open door. They looked up in unison and gaped.

Standing in the frame was Sadie, limpid blue eyes framed by red-blonde curls that had clearly seen the help of a maid's hand, in a pretty peach silk frock with a wide velvet cummerbund waist.

Jack clicked back into the role of a gallant in the blink of an eye. He rose and gestured the new arrival in. "Sadie. Good morning. Come in, come in. Make yourself at home. You remember Susannah Carruthers?"

Sadie dipped her head in lithe grace.

"Yes, of course. I hope I'm not interrupting your conversation."

Jack shot Susannah a wry smile. "We'll have plenty of opportunity to continue another time, I hope."

Sadie crossed to the table and slipped into a seat beside Susannah. She glanced at the older woman, a tentative set to her mouth.

"Good morning, Miss Carruthers. I'm sorry we had little chance to talk last night. And I feel I must apologize for barging in on the party as I did. I know the Count is family here, but I'm extra baggage."

She shot Susannah a wan smile. "I really wouldn't have accepted the invitation if I'd had anywhere else to go. But I'll sort that out today…"

Susannah felt herself warming to the young woman. Tall, well mannered, polite, and looking so lovely in the dress. "You're here on your first visit?"

"Yes. I would never have come, except I'm searching for my young sister." She glanced at Jack, her eyes uncertain. "I gather you've recently been reunited with your niece, Mr. Cabot. I'm hoping for the same good fortune in finding my sister, Phoebe."

Susannah's eyes widened, and she shot Jack a foxy, covert message. "Tell us all about it, please do. Knowing Cordelia's story as we do, I'm sure we both have a small notion of what you're going through."

And so she did.

Eleven

Sadie gazed around Elizabeth Westerhoven's breakfast table and surreptitiously pinched her thigh through the fine cambric lawn skirt she was wearing… a gift from her hostess.

The Countess, as Sadie had learned Elizabeth was called as a kind of family joke—her husband Charles, Dolphie's relation, had links to the ancient ancestral title that Dolphie now held—had insisted on giving her several frocks she'd had made for her niece Sarah Wyndham.

Sarah had meantime apparently inherited a goodly sum from her uncle Bully Pike, and could now afford to buy finer dresses for herself.

It was just one aspect of the fairy-tale world her chance encounter on the train had dropped her into. Mrs Westerhoven was insisting she stay on as a guest "while you investigate your sister's whereabouts."

And after yesterday's heart-to-heart talk with Susannah Carruthers over breakfast, she'd somehow broken through the older woman's frosty reserve and discovered an unexpectedly independent-spirited woman underneath.

She got the impression in different circumstances—sipping fruit punch at a women's only club in Manhattan, for example—Susannah might even be fun to be around.

Susannah had been surprisingly supportive of her wish to find Phoebe and take her back home.

She didn't need to know all the gory details.

As Sadie felt Susannah melting with sympathy at her story of her lost sister, a cascade of the ice-cold shivers she'd experienced ever since Florian's death threatened to overwhelm her.

It was back. That creepy 'someone's walking on my grave' feeling she'd had ever since her brother bled out on a New York sidewalk, the victim of a brawl with the Bloods rivals, Satan's Horsemen.

If Florian hadn't been killed, if Cobra hadn't promised her grief-ravaged father the Bloods protection and vengeance, then none of this would have happened.

The Bloods wouldn't have hung around the Shamrock for weeks on end. Phoebe wouldn't have become besotted with Cobra. But if Susannah knew all that, she'd never let her into the charmed circle. And then probably none of the rest of them would either.

A burning hatred flushed through her, banishing the familiar freeze of the graveyard shivers, a gushing hot acid she wanted to tip right over Cobra and his henchmen.

She glanced up from her toast, suddenly aware Susannah was saying something, and she had no idea what it was.

No. It wouldn't be wise to let her know any of this.

Sadie picked up her toast, nodded and smiled, and did her best to pick up the conversation where she'd left off.

And Susannah didn't mention another word about finding somewhere else to live. Sadie had heard a lot more than she let on as she hovered outside the breakfast room, waiting for a suitable pause in the conversation to enter.

Her eyes flickered to the abundant trays of bacon and eggs, potato pancakes and crusty toast in a heavy brown bread she'd never eaten before, that she gathered came from Germany and was Dolphie's favorite.

Elizabeth preferred French croissants, so there were some of those too, steaming fresh and crumbly when you pulled them apart with your fingers in the most ladylike way, of course, with your fingertips resting lightly on the crispy exterior. She'd watched Cordelia break one open and copied her.

With a jolt, she became aware someone had addressed her. Her eyes flicked to full alert, and she glanced up from her plate to detect who was speaking.

Elizabeth. She sat at the head of the table like a proud mother hen surrounded by her chicks. Perfectly poised today in a dark purple gown edged in cream lace, her black hair piled on the top of her head and falling to her shoulders.

She held a platter in her hand and was proffering it to Sadie. "Another croissant, dear? We're very proud of our French bakeries. They've been with us since Gold Rush days. You must taste some of our fair city's delights while you're with us." She smiled warmly.

Sadie's heart plucked with a sudden, unexpected melancholy.

This is what it feels like to have a home where people care for one another.

She swallowed hard and cleared her throat.

"I've had a wonderful meal, thank you." She hesitated, still not sure of the correct way to address her hostess, who'd insisted she call her Elizabeth. She couldn't, though. The familiarity just wouldn't come out of her mouth.

Elizabeth's eyes narrowed in amusement.

She's guessed I'm ill at ease.

"If you don't feel comfortable calling me Elizabeth, then I suppose Countess will have to do," the regal Mrs. Westerhoven said. Her deep-set eyes held Sadie's own with a mischievous twinkle. "It's what the Count calls me most of the time, anyway." She threw Dolphie a teasing glance.

Sadie gave Elizabeth a grateful smile, and was about to add something—she immediately forgot what—because Mrs. Roderiquez bustled into the room with an urgent air, holding something in her hand. A woman's bag?

"M'lady," she said, waving the bag in the air. "Someone left this on the doorstep." She faltered, suddenly aware she had the undivided attention of everyone at the table.

Elizabeth's brows lifted in surprise.

"What is it, Mrs. Roderiquez?"

The housekeeper came to a stop and held up the bag with distrust.

"It's a bag. A woman's bag, Mrs. Westerhoven. It's not your bag, is it?"

Elizabeth shook her head. "Not mine, no."

"I didn't think so. I'm pretty sure I've never seen it before."

She glanced from Elizabeth to Dolphie and then back to her mistress.

She was plainly uncomfortable about saying more, and uncertain of how to continue.

Her mouth opened and closed like a goldfish. She licked her lips.

"What is it, Mrs. R?"

Elizabeth's brow furrowed in concern.

"Thing is, marm, I don't rightly know, but something seems wrong. The cat…" She glanced around for Elizabeth's beautiful long-haired Persian blue. "The cat is acting right strange around it. And it smells awful."

She lifted the bag to her nose and wrinkled it as she sniffed, as if to confirm the statement.

She advanced to Elizabeth's chair, holding the bag out in front of her like it might contain lighted dynamite.

Sadie shot to her feet, her eyes desperately seeking Dolphie's as she registered the hard floor under her.

"No… no. Don't." She gazed at Dolphie's astonished face, a beseeching plea in her eyes. On her lips. "I think I recognize that bag. And please, Countess, don't touch it. Please."

She turned to Dolphie, aware that her hands had somehow lifted themselves to her chest and she was wringing them in dread.

"Dolphie. I'm sorry, but I'm going to need your help."

Twelve

She didn't want to believe it. Didn't want to even look at it. But she couldn't deny it.

The sight of that bag, even without Mrs. R's obvious upset, had struck terror, like a knife in her soul. And it had taken her right back to a night at the Shamrock Bar a month ago. The night she'd first grasped that King Cobra had his fangs into her sister and would not let go.

They'd closed up for the night, and she was doing the rounds, making sure all the benches were cleared and the place locked down, when she'd heard giggles coming from the bar kitchen. She'd peered around the door to see Phoebe seated on a stool at the long table, with Cobra standing behind her massaging her shoulders.

Her sister groaned with pleasure, but her attention wasn't on the big man who stood behind her, pressing himself against her back as he moved flexible fingers across her shoulders and to the base of her long neck.

Phoebe fingered a generous fall of glamorous golden fabric decorated with hundreds of tiny mirrors. Shards of reflected light fell across the old oak, giving the worn wood a golden glow. Sadie's sister caressed the cloth, her face rapt and gaze inward, as if she was holding something precious.

Sadie drew up, halted by a feeling she was witnessing a sacred moment, one that held tremendous significance for her younger sister, and she could not bring herself to break the spell. Goodness knew they had little enough to celebrate. She stood trapped in the moment like a reluctant spy, but finding it impossible to sneak away.

As she gaped, she noticed Phoebe's neck hung with five tiers of a matching choker, the fragments of mirror glass sparkling like golden diamonds. And from her shoulder hung a bag with a closure flap in the same golden mirrored fabric. The same purse now deposited on Elizabeth Westerhoven's front steps.

From when she'd been a small girl, the displays of crafted goods in the local markets had enchanted Phoebe. At first it was the puppet dolls, but as she grew older, most of all, she'd cherished the dazzling array of rainbow saris, sparkling with mirror work. The merchants called it sheesha, the tiny mirrors which were embroidered into the cloth, thousands of them into each garment, so that when its wearer moved, they glittered on a cloud of gold.

Phoebe had always said she wanted to be a princess, and the sheesha cloth had been the closest thing she'd seen to realizing that fantasy in their hard-scrabble world. If she'd confided this to Cobra, if she'd inveigled him into buying her a full matching outfit, the dress, the bolero, the bag, the necklace, there was a lot more going on here than Sadie or her father realized.

She'd stolen away that night, and she'd secretly looked at the sheesha dress when Phoebe had not been around. Just to satisfy herself it wasn't a mirage.

Now, here was the bag. In Elizabeth Westerhoven's breakfast room. And that could not be a good thing.

She stood and gazed around the table, wishing she were somewhere else. Wishing she didn't have to say what she was about to say.

"I recognize that bag."

Everyone stared, their jaws dropping in astonishment.

Susannah moved her chair closer to Cordelia's, as if proximity could protect her from the unpleasant and the scandalous.

Sadie cast a wild glance up the table to Elizabeth, as if seeking absolution.

"It's my sister Phoebe's bag. One of her special belongings. She loved that bag."

She hesitated, swallowed, and her face softened as she glanced from Cordelia to Susannah.

"I think it's best if Dolphie takes possession of it."

She turned to Dolphie. "And after that, Dolphie, we might need to talk to the sheriff."

Thirteen

Dolphie grabbed up a couple of serviettes as he took the bag from Roderiquez. As she handed it over, he caught a whiff of it. He recognized the smell from backstreet slaughterhouses and understood any minute now a brown rusty liquid was likely to leak out. Above all, he wished to save Cordelia from what he anticipated she'd see. He signaled to Jack with his eyes as he stood, and Jack jumped up and threw his arm around the back of Cordelia's chair.

"If you ladies have finished breakfast, how about I accompany you on a sight-seeing tour today? It's a perfect day for it, and you've seen nothing of the Woodward Gardens yet, have you? If we go now, we can enjoy our stroll before it gets too hot."

Great idea," said Susannah. "We'll change into walking shoes, get our parasols, and meet you at the front door in a few minutes. How's that?"

They exchanged an understanding look. Cordelia glanced from one to the other. "Why did Sadie say they might need to talk to the sheriff?" she asked, demolishing in one breath the idea she hadn't picked up something unusual was afoot.

Jack scrambled for a reply. "Ahh. Maybe she suspects there might be stolen goods in it? Something like that."

"You mean the thieves are trying to return them?" she asked.

"Perhaps. I guess we'll find out later."

Jack smiled inside. Her first thought was something positive. How nice to be young and naïve. While he loitered in the hall waiting for his morning companions to return, Dolphie disappeared into the library with Elizabeth and Sadie.

He poked his head around the library door. The three were gathered around Elizabeth's desk, the bag lying on a bed of serviettes which were already stained a dirty brown.

"Are you sure you want to be here?" Dolphie asked, searching first Elizabeth's and then Sadie's faces. They looked as if they were holding their breath, strung out by the suspense of not knowing.

"Yes," they said in unison. Elizabeth added: "Come on, Dolphie. Whatever horrible thing awaits, we have to know about it."

Dolphie moved his focus to the doorway, where Jack lingered.

"They're right," said Jack. "That parcel was left on Elizabeth's doorstep for a reason. It's not a random event."

There was the sound of footsteps in the hall.

"I'll catch up with you later," he said, and pulled the door closed with a determined click.

Dolphie hesitated. The little dip in Sadie's white throat was pulsing like a tiny bird's heart, and her normally dewy skin had a sickly sheen.

"Please, Dolphie," she said. "Just get it over with."

He nodded and opened the fabric flap of the bag. Inside sat an item, chicken, or rat, or something else, wrapped in paper soggy with red wetness.

Suppressing a shudder, he edged his hand in and drew out the dripping bundle. Carefully he peeled back the paper, one layer, then two, until the contents were plain. A wave of nausea threatened to overwhelm him, and he sat down with a thump, as if kicked by a horse in the chest...

Elizabeth glimpsed the mess and folded forward, clutching her stomach, clearly suppressing an impulse to vomit.

A human hand, a left hand, hacked off at the wrist, fingers and thumb intact, lay displayed on the polished desk. A tattooed hand. Dolphie leaned in to examine the blue inking. D-E-V-I-L. One letter on each digit, starting at the index finger.

Sadie gave a soft cry and crumbled to the floor, before he could jump up and catch her.

••••••••

Later, when gallons of strong black coffee laced with brandy had revived them, they reassembled around the cleaned-up desk, the mangled mitt sequestered in the cellar on a bed of ice.

"Teo. His name is…" Sadie's voice faltered… "*was* Theodoro Martinez." Her face was ashen, the sickly film of sweat now turned to rivulets stained dry on her cheeks.

"He was Phoebe's minder when Cobra was in New York. If something's happened to him, I hate to think what might be also happening to Phoebe…"

She glanced at Elizabeth. "And Jack's right. There's nothing random about the delivery. It's a message to me to stop looking for her."

Fourteen

D-E-V-I-L

There wasn't any mistake. The hatchet man who'd been entrusted with her sister's safety in New York had been murdered right here in San Francisco.

A deep ache in Sadie's guts confirmed what Patrick Blackheart had hinted at but never actually told her. Phoebe was being held by the Bloods. Willingly or not, she did not know. Her sister was infatuated with their boss man, she couldn't deny that.

But was she stupid enough to run away to him? King Cobra had returned to the West Coast a full week before Phoebe went missing, but it was quite possible that Teo had accompanied her on the train a week later. As she lay on her back in Elizabeth's charming guest room with its flowered curtains, she tried to ignore a bone-shaking headache and piece together what Teo's horrific death meant for Phoebe's safety.

His own mob had murdered him, no doubt about that. No one else knew about her presence in San Francisco, or her stay in this house. The Bloods' rivals, Satan's Horsemen, the hoods who had killed Florian, were perfectly capable of killing Teo, but they didn't know about Phoebe or the gold bag.

The only other person likely to know about the dress, the bag, the entire outfit, and what it meant to Phoebe, was the man who bought it, Cobra, or one of his abettors. Otherwise, there would be no reason to deliver a mutilated hand to this house. But why had a loyal soldier fallen from grace?

She shivered and wished once again that her father had not welcomed the Bloods into the Shamrock after their mother's death. Her brother might still be alive, and Phoebe would never have developed this crazy infatuation.

Had Teo forced himself on Phoebe and this was payback? Surely, he wouldn't be that stupid? He'd been one of the King's most trusted lieutenants, so what had he done to deserve this brutal, humiliating death?

She heard a light tap on the door and probed her temples with her finger to ease the thumping tension in her head.

A tentative female voice called through the sturdy wooden panels.

"Miss Sadie. A family gathering in the drawing room. Mr. Dolphie wondered if you feel well enough to join them? Starting in fifteen minutes."

It was Elsie's voice. The young servant Elizabeth had assigned her, the girl who'd done such an excellent job on her hair yesterday.

She ran her hand over the top of her head, massaging her skull as she rose from the soft mattress, so unlike the coarse horsehair pallet at home.

She ached all over. She couldn't sleep. She'd have no rest until she knew Phoebe was safe, so she may as well get on with it.

"Coming, Elsie," she said. "Why don't you come in and see if you can work your quick magic on this hair again before I go down?"

••••••••

By the time she made her way downstairs ten minutes later, she'd splashed her face in cold water, Elsie had done her hair, and her head still felt like the Central Pacific was thundering between her ears.

But she'd come to one silent conclusion. Her presence in this kind, welcoming house presented a hazard to everyone here. She had to find somewhere else to stay, like it or not, and she marched into the drawing room with her mind firmly made up. The prospect terrified her, but she saw no other option.

As soon as she appeared in the doorway, Elizabeth sprang forward and drew her in with a consoling hug. "Sadie. We're all so sorry. Now that the sheriff's done his job, we're working out what we need to do next."

Police Captain Teddie Blackmore had collected the hand earlier in the afternoon, and taken statements from her, Dolphie and Elizabeth before departing. But a gangland murder of a man he wasn't sorry to see die? The lawman had no inclination to pursue the matter. Nor had he been interested in her request for help in finding Phoebe.

"Runaway girls, miss? There are hundreds of them in this city, and the vast majority of them don't want to be found."

Sadie drew back from Elizabeth and surveyed the room. Jack and Susannah were back from their sightseeing activities, but Cordelia was nowhere to be seen. Probably enjoying milk and cookies in the kitchen, playing with the cat and watching the staff prepare dinner.

Dolphie occupied a corner armchair. He stood as she entered and gestured to a chair close to his. "Sit there, Sadie. Did you get any rest?"

She licked her parched lips and shook her head. "Not really. I keep going over it all in my head."

She glanced around her, still standing, her hands steepled in front of her in silent prayer.

"I'm so sorry I've brought this obscenity upon you all. No one should have to see something like that."

"You, along with everyone else here, Sadie. It's not your fault," said Dolphie. He'd remained standing and pointed to the chair again.

"That's what we're here to talk about."

She sat down with a sigh, but still she wasn't finished.

"These people… these gangsters… they never used to be a part of our lives. Not when my Maa was alive. She wouldn't have let them set foot anywhere near us. But that all changed when my brother Florian was killed last spring. He was just unlucky. Killed by one of the Blood's rivals, the Satan's Horsemen, in a street brawl.

"My Daa was flattened by the loss. So when the Bloods suggested they partner up, offer protection and revenge, Daa fell for it. Now we're all paying the cost."

Dolphie nodded. "That helps explain the connection a little better. But it doesn't explain what's going on now, and whether it affects Phoebe. Or should I say how it affects Phoebe? The fact they delivered it here does indicate they're holding Phoebe."

Sadie ducked her head in agreement. "That's right. That bag, that horrible bag… it was part of a very smart ensemble—sari, bolero, bag and necklace, all in the same gold mirror fabric. Cobra bought it for Phoebe. She had a fantasy about it being her wedding dress."

She shuddered, as icy fingers crawled right up her spine. "I'm not sure what they're trying to communicate by using that bag."

"If she was in on it, she'd know the effect it would have on you," Dolphie suggested, his voice low.

Denial choked her. "Phoebe wouldn't have been involved. She liked Teo. Trusted him."

Dolphie's voice was even quieter, more concerned.

"You don't know what's been happening this last week, Sadie. Things might have changed. These mobsters are pretty volatile when challenged."

It was true, she knew, but she didn't want to think of it.

"So, what can we do?" she said.

"The police aren't interested in mob quarrels, so there'll be no help there. Jack's got some feelers out with some of his old friends on the Barbary Coast. Meantime, I think you and I need to move to a city hotel. It will draw the focus away from this house."

His eyes lifted to where Jack and Susannah sat together on a coach, with Elizabeth to their right in a chair.

"That's right, Jack? You're happy with that?"

Jack locked eyes with Susannah and turned to Dolphie.

"I am, and so is Susannah." He paused, and Susannah spoke.

"I am sorry, Sadie, but it's for the best. We can't have Cordelia getting any hint of what's happening. It's all just too distressing."

"I fully understand," Sadie said staunchly. "In fact, I don't see why Dolphie has to leave as well. I don't want anyone becoming a target because of my dreadful family. No one."

Elizabeth lifted her hands from her lap in protest.

"Something awful has happened here, Sadie, but your family is not to blame. Please. I know from my charitable work. These situations can become dangerous. We need to take precautions, but we still want to help you find Phoebe."

Sadie's eyes filled with tears. They were so kind. So determined to help. For a long minute, she sat, her throat so choked up she couldn't form words. Dolphie apparently took her silence as agreement.

He rose from his chair. "Jack and I have a few things we're pursuing, but we'll be back for dinner. I'll make arrangements for us while we're out. After dinner, we'll move downtown. Why not pack your things up for the move and get some rest before we eat?"

A broiling storm inside her weary body left her feeling skewered to the seat. She barely had the energy to raise her head, look into his eyes, and nod.

She held herself in check until she stumbled back into the nicest room she'd ever slept in, locked the door and threw herself down on the counterpane that matched the floral curtains.

She clutched at her ribs as she rocked from side to side with frozen sobs she wanted no one to hear but could not contain. There was no way on earth she was going to allow the staunch-hearted Count to risk his life on her behalf. Before dinner came, she'd be long gone. Where to? She had no clue.

Fifteen

As was their usual custom, Elizabeth's extended family gathered in the dining room ten minutes before they were due to eat, ranging themselves around the table, sipping cool lemonade or light gin or a glass of sauterne or cider while they caught up on the day's news.

Their hostess gazed around her diverse guests with happy anticipation. Susannah had noticeably relaxed from the formal and reserved stance she'd adopted when she'd first arrived, Elizabeth was glad to see, and Cordelia's health seemed to be responding to Jack's prescription of good food, fun and California sun.

Her adoptive father—Susannah's brother Thomas—had warned them, the New York physician said, that with her fragile health, she was in danger of developing tuberculosis if she didn't already have it. But Jack refused to accept that grim diagnosis.

The extraordinary events surrounding the morning delivery put an undeniable dampener on their usual lively spirits, but they were all doing their best to pump some cheer into their chatter.

"We saw some beautiful white swans at the gardens today, Aunt Elizabeth." Cordelia's voice sang with a happy energy that had been absent when she'd arrived two weeks ago, and her face was showing more robust color too, Elizabeth noted with satisfaction.

Earlier in the afternoon, Susannah told Cordelia the 'parcel' had contained mysterious old bones the policeman was looking into. She'd looked puzzled but accepted the explanation without further comment.

"I'd love to take some stale bread and go and feed the swans one day," she added now.

"We can do that," said Elizabeth. "Even better, I'm sure Cook can find some stale cake for them."

Cordelia laughed. "Stale cake? I'm surprised there's any left to go stale with Uncle Jack around." She shot her uncle a fond look and Jack winked back at her.

She's looking so much healthier than when she arrived, Elizabeth mused to herself. *But speaking of appetites, Mrs. R will be wanting to start serving our first course soon, and Sadie's not downstairs yet.*

Maybe she's asleep. She looked exhausted earlier.

She rose and went to the kitchen, where Elsie was sitting with spoon raised, about to start on a bowl of chicken soup.

"Elsie, could you pop upstairs and remind Miss Sadie we're about to start dinner?"

A confused look crossed the maid's face. "She wasn't there when I looked in earlier to see if she needed a hand, Mrs Westerhoven. And none of her things were there. I thought she must have gone to stay somewhere else."

An emptiness opened up in Elizabeth's spirit and replaced her earlier inner sense of happy anticipation.

She hurried back into the dining room and caught Dolphie's eye. He'd been ribbing Jack, but he held up his hand to signal he'd be back in a minute and crossed to where Elizabeth stood near the door into the hall.

"I think our New York guest has taken off," she said. "She's not come down for dinner, and Elsie says all her clothes are gone. Do you want to go up and check on that?"

He was back within minutes, holding up a slip of white notepaper.

He leaned close to Elizabeth's ear, so she was the only one who heard.

"Tucked into the edge of the dressing room mirror," he said. "She says thank you and sorry, but she can't put anyone else at risk. She'd rather go it alone than have someone else die."

Elizabeth rose to address the table, ever aware of Susannah's insistence on protecting Cordelia.

"Sadie's resting in her room with a headache. We'll send her meal up."

•••••••••

Dolphie's meal passed in a daze. While he'd been out with Jack earlier in the day, he'd passed by the Occidental Hotel and booked two rooms—one for him, one for Sadie. Now it seemed that was a wasted effort. Sadie McGillicuddy was rejecting his help.

He recalled the talking-to he'd given himself after that first meeting on the train. He'd been suspicious of Sadie's motives, and skeptical about some of the things she'd said. She'd certainly withheld details she didn't want to reveal—the true nature of her relationship with Patrick Blackheart, for example.

He let a wry smile slip to his lips as he remembered what he'd told her. Wasn't it something along the lines of "I'll help you out for a couple of days, and then you're on your own?"

And she'd taken him at his word. At the first sign of trouble, she'd let him off the hook and gone her own way to save him and the others from danger.

He accepted the gravy boat passed to him by Jack on his right with a polite nod and doused his roast beef before passing it on to

Elizabeth. Cook had done her usual fine meal and he wasn't tasting any of it.

"You're lost in your own little world, tonight," said Jack. "What's up? And what's this about a headache?"

He raised one brow in skeptical inquiry.

"Sadie?" Dolphie glanced around him, checking for eavesdroppers.

Jack laughed. "And why are you looking so furtive?"

"I'm not looking furtive," Dolphie said, his face cracking a grin. "I'm just checking if anyone's listening."

Jack looked perplexed. "They usually are. Why is that a problem now?"

Dolphie couldn't help himself. He surveyed the scene again. Susannah and Elizabeth were deep in conversation about the San Francisco art scene. Elizabeth had over the years been a big supporter of young developing artists. Cordelia was feeding the cat forbidden tidbits, taking careful note not to get caught as she did.

Dolphie ducked his head close to Jack's ear. "Sadie's run off just like her sister. She doesn't want to put any of us in danger, so she's cutting loose. In so many words..." he added with a "figure that one out" helpless gesture with his hands.

"As if she will get very far without us."

Jack stared at him, and then like him, looked around the table.

"They are a pair, I'll give you that. Two crazy women on the run."

"We can't leave her to it," said Dolphie. "She'll get herself killed and dumped just like that other fellow. They might well decide to deliver us her hand too. If she's not careful, we'll never hear of her again."

Jack topped up Dolphie's wineglass as well as his own.

"I think she's well aware of the odds of success," said Jack. "Perhaps better than we are."

"Fair comment," said Dolphie. "But I can't leave her to try and do this on her own. It's just not right."

"Spoken like the newly titled nobleman who just three days ago was adamant he was finished with security details. Who was looking for another occupation other than defender and preserver of vulnerable women… or men," he added as an afterthought.

"Make fun of me if you like, Jack, but don't you agree?"

"Most wholeheartedly," said Jack with a mischievous twinkle. "But I suspect there may be a little more to your dedication than simple chivalry. This woman has got under your skin."

Dolphie shook his head, smiling indulgently. "It's pure chivalry, Jack. You've only known me three days, so forgive me, but you've got it all wrong. I just don't want to see a well-meaning woman who doesn't know a fig about the way this city operates get herself killed."

"Just as well you're talking to a man who knows how this town's underworld works."

He smiled as a servant leaned in to remove his empty plate, while another placed the evening's dessert—it looked like blackberry crumble and cream—before Elizabeth for her to serve.

Jack continued in a low tone: "While you were negotiating your rooms at the hotel today, I had a nice little chat with Isla."

He tapped the table with his fingers absentmindedly.

"She's a young girl Elizabeth and I got to know while you were away. Another of Elizabeth's 'rescues.' An orphanage girl Sophia Morrigan was grooming for great things in her empire of shame. An intelligent wisp of a thing.

"From talking to her I've got a pretty good idea where Sadie's sister Phoebe is staying. You interested in coming with me to visit?"

"No second invitation required," Dolphie said.

They clasped palms in quiet understanding and picked up their spoons to tuck into dessert.

Sixteen

She had a plan, even if she didn't know one square in San Francisco from another. She had a plan.

She scuttled through the back passages of Elizabeth's warm-hearted house and slipped out the servants' door at the back, hugging her carpetbag to her chest. It was twice the size it had been on the train, bulging with the frocks Elizabeth had insisted she should have "until you can get something you prefer."

Sadie regarded them as being "on loan." She was not stealing them. But she'd realized within a day of arriving in San Francisco that her wardrobe of two sets of khaki trousers and white shirts she'd worn as her uniform around the Shamrock made her stick out like a sore thumb here, and she didn't have the money or time to spend shopping for girlie frocks.

She told herself she'd return the dresses to Elizabeth as soon as she could, but most urgently now she needed somewhere safe to stay. As soon as she was settled, she'd write to Elizabeth, let her know she was doing fine, and explain.

She hugged her bag close, the Pocket Derringer Florian had bought her tucked on top of the dresses, making a reassuring hard lump against her body. She'd never had to use it, but she knew how to, and she took comfort in the thought as she tiptoed through sweet-smelling shrubs and folded into Pine Street, slipping out of sight of the house as fast as she could.

Step one accomplished. No one had seen her leaving, nor had anyone called out to ask her what she was doing. Now for step two. She would walk in the general direction of town until she saw an empty hack passing by. She'd hail it, and ask the driver to take her to the nearest mission run by Catholic nuns.

The Daughters of Charity, The Sisters of the Presentation of the Blessed Virgin Mary and the Sisters of Mercy. She went over their names like a faith chant in her head. They were all staffed by Irish nuns, and they all operated in San Francisco because of the big Irish population there. Surely one of them could provide a bed for a lone woman of excellent character.

She would explain her dilemma and offer to pay for a room for a few days while she worked out what to do next. She was confident that the Sisters would welcome a little extra income for an empty cell. She was counting on them.

She was scuttling along Pine Street with her head ducked low when she heard the familiar grind of iron wheels on macadam. She turned and saw a battered old hack trundling toward her, pulled by an aging mare.

She waved her hand to hail her fare, and the driver alighted at the kerb to take her instructions.

He raised his brows in surprise at her request but didn't demur from taking her to the nearest mission, which he said was down the hill and close to Chinatown. It shouldn't be an expensive fare either. That was a blessing.

He'd opened the door for her and she was about to get in, when a much bigger coach pulled by two horses hauled up alongside. The hack driver gazed across lazily, more from curiosity than concern, but what he saw made him freeze.

His face turned a chalky white as he stood, mute and staring. Then he raised his hands in the air and yelled something she didn't understand.

What was the problem? She peered through the cab window to the vehicle alongside. Then she understood. They were both—she and the driver—staring down the steel length of a double-barreled shotgun.

Seventeen

Elizabeth Westerhoven's maid Elsie knew she shouldn't be loitering in Pine Street after dinner, but she'd had a brief reprieve from her evening duties and she couldn't resist the temptation to step out and hope to spot Fred Osborne, the night watchman, on his rounds.

She knew he often passed by on his rounds in the early evening, because they'd "happened" to cross paths a few times in recent months. Fred was young, genial, with an open farm boy's face, a ready smile and kind gray eyes. Not at all like the wizened old chaps who were more commonly found doing the rounds at night.

She stood in the shelter of an overhanging tree and tapped her toe lightly to calm herself. Pine Street was one of the quietest and safest streets in the city, lined as it was with the palatial homes of the wealthy, many of them fitted with their own security and the occasional guard dog. She was far more likely to get into trouble with the Countess for neglecting her duties than from a passing robber.

And really, being out for a few minutes would do no harm. That amiable lady she'd been attending wasn't there anymore. She'd definitely scarpered. Taken all the Countess's dresses with her too. So there wasn't anything for her to be doing right now, except waiting for a quick chat with Fred.

Her face warmed at the thought of it. She looked up and suddenly was aware of a woman approaching down the street from the direction of Elizabeth's house. And not just any woman. It was Miss Sadie.

Elsie backed into the overhanging bush until the greenery hid her from view, holding her breath in case dust from the tree made her sneeze. The footsteps approached at a fast clip and passed by. Elizabeth's house guest was deadly set on going somewhere in a hurry.

Then she heard the noise of a cab, trundling down from further up the road. She edged out of the greenery to see what was going on. Ahhh. Sadie had hailed the cab. That made sense. She was talking to the driver; her stuffed bag clutched to her chest. Elsie felt a little pinch as she caught sight of it. If the Countess hadn't given this woman those dresses, a couple of them might have been hers.

Her nose tickled, and she pinched her nostrils as she suppressed a sneeze. She caught the faint murmuring of Sadie's distinctive voice, and the cabman's gruff replies. Sounded like a sweet little bird, she did.

Elsie stayed where she was, watching. Another cab was approaching, not such an unusual thing in Pine Street. The residents came and went as they pleased, with coaches and drivers to take them wherever they wished.

And then she spotted him, coming from the other direction. Fred, with his big night watchman's lamp swinging on a chain and his baton in hand. The city didn't provide their night watchmen with guns, and Fred couldn't afford to buy his own.

Elsie's heart sank. She couldn't step out when all these other folks were about! The Countess might hear about it. She shrank back, her frustration rising. She'd risked getting into trouble to steal a few moments with Fred, and it looked like she was going to miss out on seeing him after all.

Such is the lot of a ladies' maid.

She stayed in hiding and listened. She caught the faintest thud of footsteps. Probably Fred's getting closer. No click of the door closing on Sadie's hack. And then two—then three—she lost count, lots of things—so many she couldn't keep track, happened all at once.

A man's voice—probably the hackman's—shouting something she couldn't understand. A sharp shot, followed by a man's loud curse. And then Fred, calling in his steady, deep voice.

"Stop! Stop in the name of the law."

And then another shot, and Fred, screaming in pain. And Sadie crying out: "No… Noooo…"

Elsie peeked through the branches.

A man as big as a boxer, a shotgun dangling from his one arm, had grabbed Sadie. He was holding her by her arm and cursing as she pulled away, desperate to escape. Elsie could see it was a hopeless business.

The man was much larger than she was, and the shotgun was swinging dangerously. His fingers were still on the trigger. A black felt hat, pulled down low over his face, made it impossible to see him.

Fred was lying in the street, clutching his knee, his mouth jammed shut. She guessed he was fighting to stay quiet to avoid another bullet. Then the big guy hauled Sadie after him, her feet bop-bopping on the sidewalk as he dragged her into the second cab. Sadie was making strange cat-like cries as he bundled her in behind him and they moved off.

For a few more long seconds, Elsie remained pinned in the undergrowth, too frightened to emerge. What if there was another armed man still out there? But as the sound of the coach died away, the hack driver, who'd cowered behind one of his wagon's wheels, stepped out and ran for Fred.

She followed his lead and rushed to the night watchman, who was clutching his blood-soaked trousers and whimpering.

"Oh Fred," she cried. "Are you all right?"

"Elsie? Go and get someone," Fred muttered through clenched teeth.

"Get help now."

Eighteen

"All taken care of."

Patrick Blackheart twisted the whiskey glass he held in his fingers, flicking his eyes away from Cobra's beetled brows, losing himself momentarily in the shining amber liquid.

If only everything in life was clear as Lake Tahoe moonshine.

He ricocheted his gaze back to the boss man, seated at his shoulder in Cobra's private bar in their Montgomery Street hideout. The general store frontage downstairs gave no hint of the lushly furnished second-floor office and residence.

Cobra's glaring eyes were wide open, the yellow flecks in the pale hazel iris giving an eerie sense of gazing straight into a reptile's soul.

Not for the first time, Blackheart asked himself the question; was there a human in there? Talking to King Cobra was like attempting to communicate with a dragon—or a snake.

"I delivered the hand earlier today."

Cobra's mouth twisted in a satisfied smirk.

"That will teach him for having sticky fingers."

Blackheart waited for Cobra's next gloating dig. Everyone knew it was suicide to siphon off Bloods' funds. But he'd convinced Cobra that Teo had been stupid enough to do it.

"He thought he deserved special treatment because he was taking care of my girl?" he jeered.

He tipped back his glass, sluiced the last drops down his throat, and held the empty tumbler out for a refill. Patrick obliged.

"Speaking of women…" he said, wheeling his body to face Cobra full-on. "What do you want me to do with the sister? We'll be picking her up anytime now, is my guess."

"The man-woman?" Cobra said dismissively. "What is it with that chick-a-biddy? What's wrong with her?"

Blackheart shrugged. "Doesn't like men, I guess."

"Doesn't like men?" Cobra roared with laughter. "Nothing like her sister then, is she?"

Blackheart tamped down the urge to put a fist right in his smug, dumb gob.

He dipped his head in agreement. "Naah. Nothing like her. But that doesn't answer the question. What are you going to do with her? You can't make her cold meat when you're in partnership with her old man."

Cobra gazed at his lieutenant with wickedly amused eyes.

"Why not? He doesn't need to know."

Blackheart shrugged. "If Phoebe ever discovered it, she'd scratch your eyes out. Or worse." He paused with a wicked grin of his own. "Cut off your balls."

Cobra's cheeks flushed bright red. The joke was wearing thin.

"I'd like her to try."

"I wouldn't underestimate them. Those girls are tight as a drum, even if they are very different sorts."

There was a commotion of shouting and feet thumping on the stairs leading to the residential level and both men jumped to their feet, drawing guns as they did.

A knock came on the outside door.

Slinky the house manager's raspy voice, like a tin roof creaking in the wind. "Who is it?"

"Regge Luigi!" Luigi rules. Cobra's password.

Slinky Bill pulled the door open and, after more scuffling of feet, stood back to let the visitor—or visitors, it sounded like more than one—in. Blackheart gazed in quiet dismay.

Fat Thumbs George limped into the room, one meaty hand holding a woman by the shoulder, the other jamming a revolver against her temple. He was dragging a bloody leg behind him, like a wounded chicken. The knee of his trousers was ragged, and the blood flow freshly scarlet.

"Blasted harlot shot me," he roared.

He gave her a mighty thrust in the back and Sadie fell forward into Blackheart's arms, blood oozing from a gash above her right eye.

Fat Thumbs shot two bullets into the panelled ceiling, as if his pent-up frustration at being bettered by a woman required expression.

He twirled the revolver on his index finger and glared at the boss.

"Damn bitch. I hope you'll let me show her what's what before we cook her goose."

Nineteen

Jack loitered in the street outside Daphne Partington's house in the Mission District and waited patiently. It was 8:30 p.m.—not late by Isla's standards—and he was certain that if the irrepressible girl-woman was out on her frequent nightly investigations, Daph would have insisted that her security man, Sylvester "Sylvie" Rushton, would be right there at her shoulder as protection.

Since Isla had gone to live with his socialite fashion designer friend six months ago, she'd grabbed at her chance to learn new skills and beef up on an education that had been sadly lacking at the orphanage where her stepfather had dumped her and her sister.

He smiled to himself as he reflected how much both his and Isla's lives had changed in the last year. She'd played a significant part in bringing him back in charge of himself.

The young woman had infused him with new hope and purpose, as she'd told her story. One so similar to that of his niece Cordelia, only with a much rougher ending. Cordelia's stepfather had sold her to rich New York merchants, people happy to pay for the privilege of adding a well-born child into their household.

Although the Carruthers were strict disciplinarians who put appearances ahead of love, they'd given Cordelia a good start in every other way. She'd been safe, well-fed, and educated.

Isla wasn't so fortunate. When she'd reached ten, the age of consent, the orphanage sold her into indentured service with Sophia Morrigan, a woman who peddled a lot of the children she sourced straight into prostitution.

Isla had avoided that fate, thanks to her physical immaturity and remarkable survival skills. Morrigan had recognized her potential and was training her as "personal valet," possibly grooming her for brothel management, when Jack had first seen her last year.

Something about the girl's gut-wrenching determination to survive had inspired him to dig himself out of the hole of opium-fueled despair he'd fallen into after he lost Cordelia.

He'd galvanized himself to renew his efforts to uncover the fiends who engaged in the despicable trade of children for profit, and he and Elizabeth were giving Isla all the support they could in her search for a sister she'd been separated from in the orphanage.

A flash of light showed at the end of Daphne's street, and Jack's senses went on high alert. The hack had barely rolled to a stop before Sylvie swung down from the cabin. His crooked white teeth gleamed in the lamplight.

"Bit late to be out for you, isn't it, Gov? Now you've got responsibilities at home?"

His full, dark lips stretched in a wide, teasing smile.

"I'm sure Missie will be happy to see you, even though it was only what—three days ago she saw you last?"

Jack gave Sylvie a playful swipe, half handshake, half bear hug. He watched as Isla tripped with the lightness of thistledown down from Daphne's cab to stand beside them.

She was a Nordic waif, her hair white-blonde, her slim elfin face lit by azure eyes that missed nothing. Her face had filled out a little with Daphne's milk coffee and croissant breakfasts and wholesome beef dinners, but she was still a slip of a girl, presenting as much younger than her sixteen years.

She reached up and gave him a familiar peck on his cheek, like a younger sister greeting her older brother, though he was old enough to be her father and then some.

"Jack," she said. A single light, breathless word with a Celtic lilt that conveyed a world of emotion. "Nothing wrong, is there?"

He gathered his arm protectively around her shoulder, light in his touch.

"Nothing you need to worry about, sweet one," he said. "But things it's best you know."

He turned to Sylvie.

"Can we sit and talk in Daph's coach for a while? I'll bring it in later, if you like, and you can go to bed."

Sylvie laughed. "I'm happy to wait. I don't trust you silver-spoon boys with the horses. You wouldn't know how to store tack if your life depended on it. Give me a whistle when you're done."

Jack gave him a playful push on the arm and gestured to Isla to climb back into the cab ahead of him. "Have it your own way, Masta," he laughed. "I did offer."

•••••••••

Jack pulled a silver flask out of a shoulder bag and poured them each a small tumbler of the non-alcoholic mint julep Elizabeth's cook always had at the ready. Isla savored the fresh mint on her tongue and smiled. "Always the perfect host, Jack," she said.

"Except when I'm not," he quipped.

She caught his muted smile in the dim light.

"Something's happened, hasn't it? Not to Cordelia, I hope?" Her voice sounded squeaky, bouncing off the cab wall.

Under the turquoise silk Daphne had insisted she wear out

tonight, her heart was beating faster. Her hand reached into the reticule on her lap and she stroked the rabbit's foot tucked inside. Daphne. She was like a weathervane pointing true north, proving that lost girls could come home to a safe family.

She'd had a pretend rabbit's foot when Jack had brought her to Daphne, one she pictured in her mind when she lay awake and wished on the moon, with her eyes screwed up tight. Wishing harder than anything, she'd wished in a way some folk might call praying that she'd find Lillias before it was too late.

And then Daphne had given her a real rabbit's foot that she carried with her everywhere. When she was feeling low and losing hope, she'd stroke the soft fur to remind herself to never, ever give up.

"Nothing's happened to Cordelia," Jack soothed. "We'll get to that. What's upset you? I can tell something has."

Amazing how Jack picked up on her moods. Before she met him, she didn't remember anyone ever noticing or caring how she felt. She licked her dry lips.

"Something bad's happened to one of Cobra's men. They've offed him. And because Sophia and Cobra are together a lot lately, it might affect things at the Golden Girl. I thought it was good for you to be warned."

Jack knew that although Isla no longer worked for Sophia, she still had a lot of close friendships with Sophia's girls, and slipped effortlessly between the two worlds.

"There might be ramifications coming," she added in a worried voice.

Despite Isla's disquieting report, Jack smiled.

"Ramifications? Big word. Very good."

One thing Elizabeth and Daphne were doing was making sure Isla caught up with her lessons.

"Bad stuff." She grinned. "Bad stuff could be coming. Just could be. Nothing definite."

"We've already had a warning about something like this," Jack said. "So it doesn't surprise me."

Isla's eyes sparked with curiosity.

"It's only just happened, so how would you know?"

In the pale light cast by the coach lamps, Jack's face darkened further.

"His body probably is down a manhole somewhere. Or already washed out to sea. However, they left one of his hands on Elizabeth's doorstep."

Isla's hand flew to her mouth.

"On Elizabeth's doorstep? Why?"

"I suppose for the usual reason the Bloods do this kind of thing. To frighten Elizabeth. Make her—and all of us—feel intimidated. Leave a warning."

"A warning about what?"

Jack sighed. "Elizabeth's got her nephew staying there. A chap called Dolphie. She's been close to him for years—you didn't meet him when you stayed there because he was visiting his family in Europe."

Isla nodded. "I remember Elizabeth talking about him."

"Dolphie has a friend called Sadie, who's here from New York, searching for her lost sister, who's tied up with the Bloods somehow."

Even in the dim light, Jack saw color draining out of Isla's already pale face.

"Sadie? Her sister isn't called Phoebe, is she?"

Twenty

The doctor had been and gone and Elizabeth's coachman Bert was delivering Fred to the Catholic sisters' hospital. Fred would make a full recovery, they'd been told. Though he'd bled profusely, the doctor said the shotgun pellets hadn't damaged his kneecap.

Elizabeth and Dolphie sat with Elsie as she answered Police Captain Teddie Blackmore's questions. Teddie was far more interested in a night watchman being shot at than he'd ever been in a crim's severed hand.

"The mayor won't stand for it." he said. "He says if we don't do our best to protect the men who protect us, we're in a sorry state."

He also was rather less concerned about Sadie's abduction.

"I don't know where you picked her up from, Westerhoven, but she seems to attract trouble. First that hand…" He broke off his sentence and rolled his shoulders uncomfortably. "Gives me the shivers, just remembering it,"

Elizabeth and Dolphie had little to contribute as Teddie Blackmore went through his interrogation, trying in particular to extract any further details of the shooter's appearance, or that of any other accomplice.

"I was hiding in the hedge. I couldn't see much, I just heard noises. Except for when I popped my head up and saw him dragging Miss Sadie away. He had a black hat pulled down over his face. I didn't see enough to recognize him again, sorry."

"What about the way he moved?" said Teddie. "Did he look like a man who rode horses, say? Or more like a man who walks everywhere."

"Walks," said Elsie without hesitation, and then paused. "Though I don't know why I'm so sure. I only saw him for less than a minute, and he was limping as he was dragging Ms Sadie away. That's because, like Fred told us, she got him one in the leg. He'd have probably killed Fred if she hadn't."

Mrs. Roderiquez came in with a tray laden with hot coffee and warm rock cakes smelling of nutmeg, mixed spice and dried fruit

"These were to be for breakfast, but Cook figures you need them now," she said to Elizabeth.

Teddie allowed himself to be persuaded to stop work to eat, and two cups of coffee and two rock cakes later, he resumed his questioning.

"And Elsie. Tell me about Miss Sadie. Was she fighting this man who grabbed her, or did she go willingly?"

Elizabeth felt the hairs on the back of her neck bristle, but said nothing.

"Oh. she was struggling, sir. She was dragging her feet along the ground, trying to slow him down. She fired at him. Fred will tell you that. But it was useless for her to stop him, and I suppose he scared her. If she fought too hard, he might have shot her, too." She swallowed.

"I was terrified he was going to shoot me if I put my head up, I know that."

"And could you tell if she knew him? Did she call him by any name, for example?"

Elsie looked momentarily confused. "Call him? I don't think so. The cabbie yelled something I couldn't understand."

"Did he now?" Teddie said. "I'll have to talk to him as well, then."

Elizabeth rose to her feet. "Elsie is looking exhausted, Police Captain. I really think if you have further questions, they should wait till the morning. She needs her sleep. I think she's told you everything she knows, twice over."

Else shot her a grateful look, and Teddie Blackmore rose, taking his dismissal in his stride.

"I expect you're right, Countess," he said. "If I think of anything else, I'll come by tomorrow."

●●●●●●●●

"What was that all about?" Elizabeth sounded aggrieved as she lowered herself to the capacious sofa with a tired sigh. "Does he really think Sadie is involved in a plot to kidnap herself?"

Dolphie shrugged. He lifted the cup of steaming chocolate to his nostrils and inhaled the scent of European winters and velvety sweet spice. "He has to ask the questions, I suppose."

He studied the frothy little bubbles that sat in whirls on the top. When he dipped his tongue in, he caught a hint of pink marshmallows.

"She is rather more familiar with the identity of mobster associates than one would expect from a young woman of good standing. And where did she get that gun, for goodness' sake?"

Elizabeth gulped back her chocolate and choked out a mocking chuckle.

"What's that supposed to mean?"

He responded with a shy grin.

"First, there's that Blackheart character she hinted assaulted her on the train. Assaulted? No, she didn't exactly accuse him of assault. But she was supposedly trying to escape him when she floundered into my carriage."

His eyes flicked to Elizabeth, all humor gone. "I think it's more likely he moved in on her, and she didn't know how to deal with it."

He put his cup down with a clatter and reared back, running his hand across the top of his head.

"I think if they were not exactly good friends back in New York, they more than tolerated each other. And I think he got on that train to keep an eye on her, whether she knew it or not, wanted it or not."

Elizabeth gazed at him shrewdly. "You've been doing a lot of thinking about this young stray," she said with one eyebrow lifted. "Got a personal interest here, by any chance?"

His heart picked up pace and he could feel his face warming.

"She's aroused my curiosity," he said, with a tilt of one side of his mouth. "Let's leave it at that, for the present, shall we?"

Elizabeth smiled. "As you wish. You know I'd be delighted to see you wed."

Dolphie feigned alarm.

"Don't get ahead of things, Elizabeth. I've no clue what we might be getting into here. We know he knew where she was, because someone must have followed us when we left the train. They knew where to deliver that hand. But that doesn't mean she's in cahoots with them."

He sat forward and grasped his cup again.

"I completely believe her story about her missing sister. That isn't a con. And now with this latest incident, we've got two young women apparently detained against their wishes. Whatever Blackmore's view, I don't think for a moment that Sadie went willingly. I'm sure of it."

Elizabeth gave him one of her warmest, most engulfing smiles.

"I'm sure you're right on that one. The question is, what are we going to do about it?"

They both jumped at a loud rattle at the front door. Dolphie stood. Elizabeth had insisted all the staff retire after they made their last chocolate, and they certainly were not expecting any visitors at this time of night.

He returned minutes later followed by Jack, looking as fresh and unruffled as when he'd left them four hours ago, immediately after dinner.

He paused in the doorway and grinned at Elizabeth, some old ember of their dampened romance flickering momentarily in his eyes.

Dolphie pointed to an armchair. "Sit down, you old rogue, and tell us what's making you look so cocky."

He caught Elizabeth's attention. "You were just asking what we're going to do about it? I think the answer has just walked in."

"Going to do about what?" asked Jack, piqued at a hint of fresh developments he was in the dark over.

"Your news first, old champ. Then we'll tell you ours."

Twenty-one

One moment Sadie was in fear for her life from the shotgun-wielding, pistol- packing madman Fat Thumbs, a man plainly convinced that he was entitled to shoot a night watchman, but that retaliation was strictly verboten. She suspected his outpouring of rage was magnified because a woman had brought him down.

She was glad she'd winged him, because she wasn't at all sure what he'd have done to her if he'd had full use of his arms and legs.

But if she'd been frightened when he'd dragged her up shabby dim stairs to she knew not what, fright turned to stark terror when he propelled her across the room toward Cobra. She was expecting a bullet in her chest or her back before she hit the floor.

When Blackheart's arms enfolded around her, breaking her fall and protecting her from the raging accomplice and his waving gun arm, it seemed like her first lucky break of the day. The masculine, woodsy smell of Patrick's skin enveloped her. She'd found safe harbor.

She hung limply off his shoulders, her buckling knees collapsing under her.

Then, with a quick awareness that appearing close to Blackheart might be bad for both of them, she let go of him and sank to her knees as he too released her, a dark, blank look on his face as he turned toward Cobra.

His sudden release left her bereft and exposed. She'd glimpsed warm, strongly muscular safety. And then, just as suddenly he'd abandoned her, leaving her alone and vulnerable again. She felt Cobra's calculating appraisal on her without looking up.

"Get up," he barked at her.

Then he whirled on Fat Thumbs.

"And you can vamoose!"

He waved a meaty arm in the direction of the door and immediately switched his attention back to Blackheart.

"By the ever-living, jumping Moses. Now what? Shooting at a night watchman? How dumb can they be?"

Sadie scrambled to her feet, nursing the bruised knee her clodpate attacker had delivered when transferring her from the coach to the street. She swiped down the side of her face and saw her sleeve come away red. Blood. He'd left his mark then.

She shuffled to one side, leaning on the back of a rickety wooden chair, and surreptitiously surveyed her surroundings. The bag containing all her earthly possessions hung heavy across her chest, but the Derringer was lost on the street.

Cobra leaned with his backside against a scarred, dark wood desktop scattered with loose papers and dirty plates and glasses. The air was thick with the smell of tobacco smoke and stale food. A scruffy day bed stood along one wall half covered with a threadbare blanket.

She mustered her fraying tenacity, gathering her panicked thoughts up into a new resolution to win through.

She was in some sort of headquarters, where she guessed Cobra spent a good deal of his day. In the weighty silence, Blackheart looked to Cobra, seeking further instructions.

The highbinder who brought her here—Fat Thumbs, was it—

stood his ground until Cobra rounded on him with flashing eyes.

"I told you to git. Do it! Before I do it for you."

Fat Thumbs limped for the door, muttering under his breath as he left.

Before Cobra could speak again, she took the plunge.

"Where is my sister?" Her voice sounded powerful and determined, despite her insides feeling like jelly. "I want to know where she is, and that she is safe and well."

She stared at him defiantly.

"And I want to know what makes you think you can treat me like this, dragging me in like a dog off the street? I thought you and my father were in partnership. Is this the way you treat a partner?"

A flash of surprise shot across Cobra's beefy tanned face. He licked the pulpy red lips which were already glistening wet, and an unpleasant smirk lifted one corner of his fat mouth.

"Listen to her. Does she think she's Lady Muck? Methinks she's been seeing too much of her friend the Countess?"

Sadie ignored his mocking tone and pressed on.

"Have you got Phoebe here, too?"

She studied Cobra's darkening face, hardly daring to look at Blackheart.

"That blockhead you employ shot a night watchman. There are witnesses to my abduction, you know. Both the night watchman and the hackman saw everything. Probably the cops already know his name. And you can bet my friend the 'Countess,' as you call her, will be with the police in her parlor even as we speak.

"You'll have Police Captain Teddie Blackmore on your back every time you stop to blow your nose if you hold on to me."

Cobra's fists clenched at his sides, and his face pinched up in frank dislike.

"You've got a big mouth for a woman," he said, his voice

venomous. "But keeping you would be a lot more trouble than it's worth."

He turned to Patrick Blackheart.

"Throw her out, will you? I don't care where. In the middle of Chinatown, all the better. Let's see how she survives alone in the Barbary Coast."

Sadie leaned on the chair more heavily and steeled herself for her last assault.

"I'm not going anywhere until I've seen my sister, and satisfied myself she is safe."

She set her jaw tight and prepared herself for a blow, but none came.

"Take her to Sophia's joint, will you, Patrick?" Cobra said, turning away. "And then chuck her in the gutter."

Twenty-two

"She's mad about him. Sadie. You're in for a big let-down if you think otherwise. I can tell you."

Sadie sat opposite Blackheart, her knee injured in her struggle with Fat Thumbs resting, hot and swollen, on the hack seat opposite her and beside him. It was unthinkable for her to walk it, so they were on the short ride to 'Sophia's'—whoever she was. Sadie hadn't yet mustered the bravery to ask. She was still light-headed after the violent attacks she'd experienced over the last few hours.

First, she'd thought she was going to die. Then, when Patrick appeared, she'd felt things would be all right. And now, unbelievably, she was on her way to see her sister who it seemed was alive, unharmed, and in Bloods' custody. Whatever that entailed. She'd find out as soon as she laid eyes on her.

"Is she here of her own free will, Patrick?"

"You can ask her that yourself, Sadie. But yes, she is. More than that. She's just as determined as you are in a different way. You won't tear her away from here. I'm betting on it."

For the first time since she'd set out on this mad quest to save her sister from perdition, Sadie's heart faltered in her chest. She'd only ever considered Phoebe had run away or been abducted. She hadn't considered she might have deliberately come here of her own free will.

She shook her head. "I won't believe it till I hear it from her own mouth," she said staunchly.

His gaze roved her face, gentle, assessing, and the strange warmth he generated in her glowed again, warming her from the inside out. She dragged her eyes away. She had to keep alert. Memorize where she'd been, and where she was going.

The scene outside the hack abruptly demanded her attention.

It was late—it must be coming up to midnight, and the sidewalks swarmed with San Francisco's party people, the night-lifers who crowded the club and bar scene and then collapsed into bed at dawn to sleep it off till the next evening.

The sidewalk thronged with revellers, Spanish señoritas in brilliantly-colored full skirts, their beaus on high-peaked saddles wearing tight-fitting glittering jackets, riding alongside them.

Elegant California belles on the arms of togged-up gentlemen. Skin tones of every hue, from the whitest Englishman to dark Southerners and the rising chatter of a multitude of tongues. Italian, German, French, Spanish and many others she didn't recognize… The New York she knew never looked like this. She pulled herself back.

"Will Phoebe still be awake? Shouldn't she be in bed?"

Blackheart laughed.

"Wake up, Sadie. She's not a baby anymore."

The hack was slowing, and the driver drew up outside a fine antique-looking plastered white building with a columned street frontage and striking golden door. Clipped ovals of trees—Sadie guessed they were mini cypresses, half her height—lined a short walk from the street to that welcoming door.

"What is this place?" she asked, directing her attention back to Patrick.

"It's The Other White House," Patrick said, flicking her an ironic smile. "But we're going to one part of the establishment, called the Golden Girl."

"And who owns it?"

"I think that's best not discussed; not by me, anyway."

He helped her out, but once she'd planted her feet on the ground, she refused his arm and limped her way up to the golden door. A young Negro with the body of a Michelangelo's David and a face of shining beauty to match sat on a stool in the entry.

Patrick leaned in to him and gave him instructions Sadie could not hear.

The custodian considered her with frank appreciation, his black eyes sparkling.

"I'm Bennie, your host for the night. Welcome to The Golden Girl." His eyes widened coquettishly. Did he wink? Before Sadie could decide if he had or not, he turned and gestured for them to follow.

They veered left and up a circular staircase lit by a gorgeous stained-glass window in green, purple and clear leaded frames and came out into a central hub with several doorways leading into different rooms.

She drank in the extensive range of entertainment on offer, from "drawing room" conversations in a comfortable lounge room dotted with sofas and armchairs, to a cabaret-style dance floor with stringed quartet next door and the staircase climbing higher, to who knew what?

She didn't want to imagine. She could see it would be easy to ignore the "business" side of the operation. To sip cocktails and relax with pretty girls for company. To dance with one of those girls to the music of the double bass and violin.

For a fleeting moment, she registered relief that rude bawds did not confront her. This was sexual commerce in a sophisticated guise.

Bennie led them into a small and very private bar, some distance from the rest of the house activity. Sadie got the impression it was a discreet space for personal guests of the house, like some sort of segregated *Arabian Nights* harem.

As Bennie departed and she and Patrick moved into the room, she saw there were two young women seated at the bar. Phoebe and a white-haired pixie who looked a lot younger than her sister.

She felt a jolt of disapproval. What was a young girl like her doing in this kind of establishment? She quickly suppressed the thought.

Not your fight. Focus on getting Phoebe out of here.

Phoebe glanced up, smiled as she recognized Patrick, and then froze when she saw Sadie limping behind him.

She jumped down from her stool in alarm.

"Sadie! What's wrong? How did you hurt yourself? It's not Daa… or one of the young ones, is it?"

Sadie limped into an enveloping hug, her heart galvanized at the sight of her sister. Phoebe's face screwed up with worry over the questions she'd asked, but her skin was as pearly as ever. One quick glance told Sadie her sister was at the peak of good health.

"No, no, dear Sis, nothing like that. I was just worried about you. That's all. Whatever possessed you to run off like that without telling us where you were going?"

Phoebe's frown of concern melted into one of confusion.

"Tell no one? Daa knows where I am. I left with his blessing."

Sadie's face mirrored the bewilderment Phoebe had shown seconds before.

"But I don't understand. I asked him if he knew where you were and he shrugged it off. Said not to worry, you'd be fine… I thought you'd run away."

"I am fine," Phoebe cried, her voice edged with annoyance.

"Why wouldn't I be?" Her eyes flicked to Patrick, who had held back to allow them space to meet. "She takes the cake, doesn't she, Patrick? If you want to get a drink and come back later…."

He nodded with a grin.

"Good idea. I can see you might be some time… Come and get me when you're ready."

Twenty-three

Phoebe hadn't realized how lonely she'd been feeling until she Sadie walked into the place. Her heart flooded with excitement at the sight of her sister, looking the prettiest she'd ever seen her, all dressed up in a pink and white gown she'd never seen before and could never have imagined Sadie wearing.

"Gorgeous dress," Phoebe exclaimed. "Where did you get it?"

Sadie sighed. "It's a long story."

"What happened to your face? It's bleeding. And what's wrong with your leg? Why are you limping?"

"An even longer one."

They stared at each other, seemingly at an impasse, and then simultaneously both burst out giggling.

"I'm so glad you're here, Sadie. I've missed you." Phoebe reached over and gave Sadie a careful hug. "I only just realized it the moment you walked in here, but I have."

She patted the seat on the other side of her.

"Sit down and tell me everything." She gestured to the seat on her right. Sadie's heart jumped, as she remembered they weren't alone. In the excitement of greeting Phoebe, she'd totally forgotten she was with a friend.

Phoebe gestured to the woman seated next to her. "This is Isla, a new friend I've made here in California. Isla, my sister Sadie."

Isla dipped her head. "Nice to meet you, Sadie. I'll push along if you two want to talk."

"Oh, you're welcome to stay," Phoebe said quickly. "I might need your support," she added with a sly grin.

She patted the seat beside her left again. "Come on, Sadie. Sit down on the other side of me and tell me all the news. I haven't got anything else to do, and we've got all night. So, tell me. Starting with the dress."

"I'm feeling more of a fool every minute," said Sadie. "I can't believe Daa knew where you were and didn't tell me."

She hesitated. "Mind you, I had it firmly fixed in my head something bad had happened. You'd run away and got into trouble. Or been abducted."

"Abducted? Sadie! You're crazy."

Sadie told her of meeting Dolphie, and of going to stay with the Countess. But for reasons she didn't want to examine too closely, she mentioned nothing about Teo and the severed hand, nor about Patrick's unwanted advances. She stopped herself.

Are they really unwanted?

She brushed the thought aside.

"Elizabeth lent me some dresses because she didn't want me wearing trousers around the house. It was awkward," she added, not wanting to mention Cordelia either. "They've been very kind, but I need to find independent accommodation. I can't keep sponging off their kindness."

"Isla knows somewhere you could stay, I'm sure. Wouldn't you, Isla?" She turned to her young friend. "Do they have any spare rooms at that place you told me about? Where you used to stay before you went to where you are now?"

"Oh? You don't live here too?" Sadie had just assumed.

There you go. Jumping to the wrong conclusion again.

Isla shook her head. "I used to, but the Countess helped me, too." She hesitated, as if she'd already said enough. "I live somewhere else now."

"I'd be interested in seeing what it's like," said Sadie. "Maybe you can show me later."

She turned to Phoebe decisively. "But now, Phoebe, I've told you all my news. Oh, the children and Daa are all fine by the way, nothing to report there—so now it's your turn."

Phoebe felt her stomach tighten and then flutter with nervousness. This would not be easy, because Sadie had always disapproved of Cobra and the Bloods. That was probably why her father hadn't told her anything about their "arrangement."

"I'm here to be Cobra's first woman. With Daa's blessing," she said in a rush. "It's what Cobra wants, and what I want too."

Sadie's mouth dropped open, as if she couldn't believe what her ears had just heard.

"Oh, come on, Sadie. It can't be that big of a surprise. You know what he was like at the Shamrock. He's head over heels."

"First woman?" whispered Sadie, as if the words were stuck in her throat, reluctant to emerge into the light. "Since when is it okay for a girl from a good Catholic family to be a gangster's moll? Maa is rolling over in her grave."

"Oh, stop being so dramatic," Phoebe said, her blood rising to the boil.

"I've got no intention of being a kitchen slave like our mother was. She was a wife, and she was still a slave to food and family. I want something better for myself, and Cobra can give me that."

"Something better? I know Maa had it hard, but Daa loved her. She always said she was blessed."

Phoebe made a disbelieving shushing sound. "Don't give me that, Sadie. She died of overwork and underappreciation. That's not happening to me."

"Oh, so what IS going to happen to you?" Sadie's voice had a clipped, disbelieving edge.

Phoebe answered with earnest assurance. "I'm going to have money. As many clothes and rings and necklaces as I want. No one is going to push me around or make me into a kitchen skivvy. Other people will work for me, while I enjoy myself."

"Oh? And when the dew is off the rose? When another bright young thing catches Cobra's eye and you've got two kids hanging off your skirts? What then? Tossed out in the gutter, that's what."

Phoebe felt as if a big hollow had opened up inside her. "That won't happen. He says he'll love me forever."

Sadie scoffed. "And I wonder how many poor fools have believed that one and lived to regret it." Her glare transfixed Phoebe. She couldn't escape it. Sadie's passion just drew her in.

"Tell me, if he 'loves you so much'"—she gave an ironic emphasis to the phrase—"then why doesn't he marry you? In the Catholic church. With all the trimmings?"

Phoebe could see; it was as plain as the nose on Sadie's face. Sadie didn't believe Cobra would marry her.

And in that instant, she understood what she had to do. Marriage was the only option. Because Sadie was right. She had no protection if he dumped her when she was past her prime, however hard she worked at keeping her man enthralled.

Even a church wedding wouldn't protect her from that humiliation. But at least she'd have the satisfaction of knowing he couldn't marry anyone else.

"My mind is made up, Sadie." She dramatically spread out her hand she'd been keeping hidden to display the sparkly green ring.

Sadie looked down at her hand. "It's an emerald, I think. Teo brought it with him from Cobra when he came to escort me out here."

At the mention of Teo, Sadie gave a vague eye roll. Phoebe wondered if she'd forgotten who he was already.

"I didn't just hightail it from New York by myself, like you, you know," said Phoebe with satisfaction, ignoring the change in her sister's demeanor.

"Cobra sent Teo with a ring—like a pledge—for my security. Teo and Cobra—they're both good men, she said defensively. "And Cobra adores me."

She paused, waiting for the familiar tide of warm confirmation that rose within whenever she reflected on how much Cobra loved her. He told her so all the time.

"So, you can forget about any silly ideas of talking me out of it. What do you have to offer instead? Thankless drudgery as a slavey for Brian at the Shamrock until you're old and wrinkled? Is that what you want?"

Sadie's green-blue eyes widened in surprise. She hadn't expected Phoebe to go on the attack, she could see that, but it was time her older sister understood. She wasn't a kid anymore.

"I know you're the oldest, Sadie. It should be you marrying first. But you don't seem to get it. If you don't find someone like Cobra to look after you, that's what you've got in store. And I already know I want more."

Twenty-four

"I've just come from Isla," said Jack, draining the chocolate pot of its last dregs as he spoke.

"Bit late for her to be up. Isn't it?" Elizabeth said.

Jack laughed. "You know Isla. A law unto herself. It's what's enabled her to survive like she has."

Dolphie's face twisted into a question.

"I don't know this Isla. I've only heard a bit about her from Elizabeth."

"You'll like her," said Jack. "She's remarkably on the ball for a young woman. She's had to stay on top of things. She even outwitted Sophia, and that takes some doing."

"Sure. Fill me in on those details later. What's Isla got to do with this Sadie business?"

"Isla is looking for a sister of hers who 'disappeared' from an orphanage—probably sold into indentured service like her, so she hangs around some of the bawdy houses sniffing for any word of her."

Jack took a sip of lukewarm chocolate and glanced up, his eyes feverish with tamped-down excitement.

"And guess who she found there yesterday?"

Elizabeth gazed at him, transfixed.

"Where?" said Elizabeth.

"Not Phoebe?" said Dolphie.

Jack laughed. "At Morrigan's latest place. The replacement for the Imperial Men's Club. The Other White House. And far from being beaten and abused, she's untouchable—a little princess protected by the top man. She's a very willing 'captive,' with her eyes set on securing the boss's favors for life."

He put his cup down with a clatter. "It appears the only piece of intelligence Sadie had right was that Cobra has got eyes only for Phoebe, and his infatuation, passion, call it what you will, is returned in full ardor.

"Phoebe is whole-heartedly 'sold' on the match. She sees it as a way of escaping a life as her father's slave."

Dolphie sat up, his eyes not leaving Jack's face. "Wow! I wonder how Sadie got the story so wrong, then?"

"No idea. But now, tell me what's been happening here? Why are you both up so late, for starters? Any sign of Sadie? I'm surprised I found you still dressed and awake."

"Sadie, we can say with certainty, is now a guest of the Bloods, like her sister. Maybe they'll meet up and clear things up between them."

"Oh? How on earth do you know that for sure?"

"Because they grabbed her on the street outside here and shot the night watchman—who, it appears, is some sort of 'sweetheart' of Elizabeth's girl Elsie—while doing it."

"My gosh, things are heating up," Jack said. "Why do you think they went to all that drama over leaving the hand, if they planned to kidnap her anyway?"

A peaceful silence stretched between them as they considered the question. It was late, and they were all tired.

Elizabeth finally answered. "It's hard to say. Perhaps the death of that poor man had nothing to do with Phoebe. It was over something else, completely unrelated, but it provided a convenient opportunity to intimidate. That's what a lot of these gangs thrive on, isn't it? Intimidation?"

She sounded despairing.

"And now they've got Sadie as well as Phoebe. It's just not right."

Dolphie stood, suddenly resolute.

"There's only one way we can know if they're both happy with the arrangements or not, and that's by asking them."

He spoke to Jack. "And that's what we've got to do, isn't it, Jack? Ask them if they want to be there. And if they don't, then help them escape."

Twenty-five

"She thinks she's my mother. It's not fair."

Phoebe didn't intend to sound like she was moaning, but she understood that's how she'd appear to Isla.

"She only wants the best for you," said Isla, thinking how nice it would be to have someone—anyone—who cared enough about you enough to want to protect you.

"I suppose…"

It was the day after Sadie's unexpected arrival. Isla had taken her to a bare-bones boarding house—no frills, but clean and safe—on Kearney Street, and she'd rented a basic room with a made-up single bed, a chair and a bedside table, for the next week.

Patrick had been furious when he'd returned to discover she'd already left without telling him, but Phoebe had soothed his anger. After all, she pointed out, Cobra wasn't concerned. He just wanted her to mind her own business. And Patrick could reassure him she, Phoebe, wasn't going anywhere.

Now that Sadie had heard from Phoebe's own mouth that she was happy with the arrangements she hoped with all her heart her sister would find some other cause to keep herself busy. Go back to New York and look after the younger children, for instance.

Isla said something, and Phoebe started, lost as she was in her own musings. "She's worried about you, Phoebe. I think that's kinda nice. For a sister to care that much."

Phoebe gave a soft huff. "You care for your sister like that, don't you? That's why you hang around places like this? 'Cause you think she could end up somewhere like this?"

Isla's dark brown brows contracted under the snowy fall of her fringe.

"I sure hope not, but it's always possible. There's nothing especially 'golden' about the Golden Girl for the ones who work here. You haven't seen what it's like. You talk about slavery.

"Working in a brothel is slavery of the worst kind. You've got no rights as a person. You're just an object. There's nothing glamorous about it. You don't even have to be attractive. Just meat for the slaughter."

Isla cast her a sideways glance.

"If you didn't have Cobra's protection, you could end up in the bedrooms upstairs like anyone else. What would Sadie do then?"

Phoebe felt a cold chill run up her backbone.

Me? A common whore, even in a place with fancy furnishings?

She stuck her lip out, but remained silent.

"No, I'm serious, Phoebe. It seems to me it's all a bit of a game to you. A romantic adventure. But what if the wind changed to the other side of Cobra's face? You'd be in a pretty perilous situation."

Phoebe started to object. "My Daa…" And she ran out of words. Her father was busy in New York, and anyway, what could he do? He'd been powerless to do anything when her brother Florian died. He'd turned to Cobra for protection and revenge.

Isla picked up the challenge. "What would your Daa do? What could he do?"

Phoebe shrugged, accepting Isla's argument.

"So maybe Sadie isn't so wrong after all. So, I ask again. What lengths would Sadie go to protect you?"

Phoebe's cheeks flooded with blushing guilt.

"I reckon she'd go to any lengths. Even offer to stand in my place. And that's pretty amazing, because she doesn't even like men that much. Not like me."

"Liking men and wanting to sleep with every jackeroo who can put up the money? Those are two very different things, gal."

Phoebe pushed the hair out of her eyes, secretly brushing aside a tear as she did.

"Where did you get to be so worldly wise, Isla? You're not even as old as me."

"You're better off not knowing," Isla said with a sad smile. "I just think you could show your sister gratitude for caring about you so much."

Twenty-six

Well, Mother, what do you want me to do now?

Sadie lay on her back on her narrow bed with a hard horsehair mattress which reminded her of every niggly bump and weary bone in her body—and there were plenty of them—and rested her hands behind her head. The clock at the head of the stairs, an ornately carved antique which was the only piece of fine furniture she'd seen in the house, chimed out two gongs. Two a.m.

She exhaled a long sigh of frustration.

She'd fallen onto her bed of nails in an exhausted state, expecting to drop dead asleep before her head hit the pillow. Instead, she'd been unable to settle. Her body thrummed with an unhappy awareness that Phoebe was in awful danger and had no clue of it.

She chided herself for not telling her about Teo's death. The news would devastate her, she knew that. The pair had formed a bond while Cobra thrust them into each other's company. It was something else her eagle eye had missed and Sadie recoiled from being the one to tell her.

Yet surely, this was part of the problem. Phoebe entertained fantasies of being Cobra's "kept woman" without understanding the realities of the world she was falling over herself to enter. Sadie was certain that when the reality punctured her girlish dreams, soft-hearted Phoebe would run. She'd want nothing more to do with Cobra. But by then it would probably be too late.

What if I told her about Teo?

She probably wouldn't believe you. She'd think you were making it up to get her out of there.

What else can I do?

Like a shooting star in a clear night sky, the thought came to her.

Talk to Patrick.

Patrick knew the world of the Bloods better than either her or Phoebe. And he liked her.

You're trading on your power as a woman

No, I'm not. I'm just asking for advice from a friend.

Keep telling yourself that for as long as you can believe it.

What else can I do? I'm desperate.

And what would your Maa think of that? Trading yourself for your sister?

That's not what I'm doing…

Sadie heard the grandfather clock strike three a.m. before she fell into an exhausted sleep, wanting to believe she'd find the best way out for Phoebe before it was too late. She had to.

Twenty-seven

Sadie rolled out of bed the next morning, every joint in her body creaking and sore. She didn't know whether to blame the hard horsehair or the thrashing nightmares about severed hands that had woken her several times before the gloomy dawn.

She splashed her face with cold water, put on another of Elizabeth's borrowed dresses—this one a lemon and apple-green botanical print—and did her best to dress her yellow-gold hair so strands of curls softened the sharp line of her jaw.

She surveyed herself critically. How she looked had never been important until now, but today she needed to appear as comely as she could. She was out to tame a Cobra, or if not him, his second in command, and she knew from the derisive way the boss man had raked his eyes over her in the past that her "girl-man" self wouldn't cut it.

She pinched her pale cheeks to bring more color into the dull skin, patted her hair. At least the frizzed-up hair made her blue eyes stand out. She drank two glasses of cold water from the water jug at her bedside and strode down the creaky stairs past the clock she'd heard chime every hour through the night. Shoppers and salespeople buzzed like bees in a hive, filling Kearney Street's sidewalks.

Nine o'clock and a new day. She knew many of the shop owners and their staff would have been up since dawn preparing, and it felt as if it were half gone already. She paused for a moment to orient herself, remembering the route she'd taken with Blackheart and then Isla to get here last night. The Golden Girl had only been a short distance from the Bloods' headquarters.

Once she got back here, she was certain she'd recall the route she and Patrick had taken the night before. She was taking the risk of tackling King Cobra in his den, and she guessed from the run-down frontage of the merchant shop at street level he preferred to operate incognito. He'd be furious she'd remembered clearly enough to return.

Would he be so angry that he'd "disappear" her the same way he'd made many of his rivals and enemies vanish? She was under no illusion about his ruthlessness. She supposed that's how organizations like his operated. By the law of the jungle. If he thought she was standing in the way of something important, he'd dispatch her without a second thought.

Forty minutes later she was on the street opposite the general goods store, gazing across at the obscure entrance to the Bloods' headquarters. Two Bloods guards loitered there, but it wasn't obvious they were security. The kaleidoscope that she was fast understanding was normal San Francisco life bustled on, with hustlers and buyers, streetwalkers and waifs all going about their business while the temperature slowly climbed to its daily peak and the air filled with the fragrance of hot popcorn and horse dung.

••••••••

Sadie sat in the window of Belle's coffee shop, well into her second café au lait, before she saw Patrick's familiar broad shoulders disembarking from a hack on the traffic side. He disappeared around the back on the vehicle, pulling a coin out of his pocket for the fare as he moved with the sureness of a prowling panther.

She jumped to her feet, gulped down her last of her cup and shot an apologetic grimace to Belle, who stood at her till like the guardian of a treasure hoard.

She pointed out the door, mouthed "Got to go" while dodging around an irate driver with a cartload of hay, and made it to the other side just as Blackheart's back vanished upstairs. A motley-suited henchman stepped into her path, blocking entry.

"Patrick," she called. "Patrick." Louder.

"Sorry ma'am," he said, and shouldered her out. "No unauthorized entry here."

She stepped out of his reach. Patrick Blackheart's deep baritone interrupted her next protest.

"Miss McGillicuddy," he said. The security men turned, abruptly, astonishment on their faces. "It's okay, boys. I know the lady."

And to her: "To what do we owe the pleasure?"

"I need to see Cobra," she said. "It's urgent."

She glanced around her. "And I didn't know how to find him any other way than to come back here and wait for you."

He glanced at the heavies and then back at her. Then he took her by the elbow and propelled her across the street to Belle's.

"This isn't a good idea," he hissed as they crossed the busy thoroughfare. "If there's one thing Cobra can't stand, it's pushy women."

Twenty-eight

Her empty coffee cup was sitting where she'd left it, and Sadie was back in her same seat. Belle must have had a run of customers and they hadn't had time to remove it. But this time, she wasn't alone. Sitting across from her was Patrick Blackheart, his narrowed dark eyes regarding her with a glint of humor that shone through his hard-faced exterior.

"What are you thinking? This isn't some charitable club Cobra is running. You know that, don't you?"

Sadie glanced around nervously and drummed her fingers on the edge of the table, wondering if Belle knew who Blackheart was and what he did.

"Of course I do," she hissed in an undertone.

Blackheart was exerting his usual unsettling effect on her. She seemed to expand into her dress so it was uncomfortably tight, and a nervous flutter started up in her stomach. Her eyes moved of their own accord to his red mouth, surrounded by the springy, full black beard that beckoned to be touched.

Her eyes flew from his moving mouth to the top of his head, where equally luxuriant black hair fell from a side part over his ears.

"Sorry," she said breathlessly. "I didn't catch that last bit."

"I said, what do you want with Cobra? An obvious enough question, given the circumstances. Didn't your sister satisfy you with her answers last night?"

"Um, yes. Yes, she did. She imagines she's in love, and Cobra's in love, and when they get together, life will be perfect forever more. But we both know life's not like that."

His red mouth twitched.

Why am I always looking at his mouth?

Because it's easier than looking into his eyes.

Her mouth dropped open at the implications of that unwanted revelation.

She looked at his right ear, trying to focus on what he was saying.

"*We* might know that, but if your sister doesn't, what do you expect you can do about it?"

"I've got to do something," she said. "My mother's ghost won't let me rest if I don't."

He gave her a hard look then, and his brow contracted, as if she'd confirmed she'd lost her mind. He raised his eyes to the counter, where Belle stood gazing at them in undisguised fascination. Apparently she knew who Blackheart was.

He raised two fingers, and Belle nodded.

"This might take a little longer than I'd anticipated," he said.

"I think we need more coffee."

•••••••••

While they waited for their coffee to arrive, she told him about the deathbed vow her mother had extracted from her. Increasingly, she felt it had caught her unawares, that her mother had demanded it under duress.

As much as she adored Grace, a prickling unease settled in her chest. Her mother knew her weakness for wanting to protect those she loved, and she had played on it.

Blackheart stayed silent, his eyes roving her face as she told him her story.

"Phoebe's young. She thinks she's in love…"

Sadie's voice trailed off as the coffee arrived, brought by a dark-haired maid who regarded Patrick with unabashed delight, which he ignored.

"That might be so, but Cobra is set on her. And what Cobra wants, Cobra gets."

"She doesn't know about Teo yet. I didn't have the heart to tell her last night. She's going to be very upset…"

"Won't make any difference," Blackheart said.

"How do you know that?" Sadie cried. "What if it makes her change her mind?"

Blackheart shook his head. "I told you. It won't make any difference. She's come this far and Cobra can't afford to lose face. She can't back out now. I mean, they're practically engaged."

She sprang at the opening.

"Then why aren't they engaged? If he wants her so much, why doesn't he marry her?"

Blackheart shook his head in disbelief. He lowered his voice and in an urgent whisper he said, "There's a good reason why a man like Cobra gets to the age he has without a wife."

She gazed at him with expectation in her eyes, and he exhaled sharply.

"And no, I don't know what it is. I just know there must be one. Probably he's got more than one wife back in Italy, for all I know."

Sadie felt the pink rise in her cheeks at what she saw was her own naivete.

She stared at him. "Of course he would. How stupid of me."

Blackheart looked deep into her eyes.

"And apart from that, she's part of the deal."

Sadie's heart leaped in her mouth.

"The deal? What deal?" Her mouth was so dry she could hardly get the words out.

Patrick gazed at her for a long minute, as if reckoning up something.

"For the oldest daughter, the one who takes care of pretty well everything in your family, including all his young brats, your father doesn't tell you much, does he?"

A sickening nausea threatened to overwhelm her.

"What deal?" she croaked.

"Your father's deal with the Bloods."

Twenty-nine

At last! Cobra was here at last! Phoebe twisted the emerald ring—she was sure it was a real emerald—and smiled up at him through her long, dark lashes.

His darkly powerful presence, that aura that had most attracted her from the moment she'd first laid eyes on him, shone out of him, as overwhelming as it had been that first day when she walked in on him with her father.

He was a real man. Not like one of those boys who hung around the Shamrock, getting drunk and hoping to trap her in a corner and paw her. After the first couple of times being japed into that kind of encounter, she'd got wise to them. No, that wasn't Cobra. He was pure class.

His tough jawline with its neatly trimmed flecked beard, the determined set of his mouth, even the dangerous glint in his eye which said she should not deny him… she found his relentlessness irresistible.

And that his eye had landed on her, and he'd liked what he'd seen, when he could have his pick of any woman he wanted? That made her feel hot and flustered in ways she didn't want to examine too closely. Blessed be the Holy Mother Mary. She knew she wanted to be at this man's side every minute of every day.

He brought his finger to her chin and lifted her head to gaze into her eyes. She noticed for the first time that he had a ring on his finger with an identical green stone to hers, although the mounting was in a more masculine gold setting. She gently took his hand and held hers up alongside, so the two rings sparkled together.

"It's like we're betrothed," she whispered, her heart so full she could barely speak proper words.

He must have bought his ring at the same time as mine.

He raised one black brow above an amused grin. "What crazy ideas young girls get," he said with a husky laugh, as if the idea had not occurred to him, and she felt her heart plummet again.

She must not get him angry, but she was going to stand up to him. Prettily stand up to him, of course. She'd make herself irresistible. She leaned into his right ear and breathed softly, licking the lobe for a few seconds before pulling back.

Her eyes fixed on his lips, she whispered, "Why is it so crazy? You say you'll love me forever." He lifted her face up with his finger and peppered her cheeks and then her closed eyes with butterfly kisses. For such a powerful man, he could be gentle, something else she found unspeakably seductive.

"You never know, maybe we will. Would that keep your sister happy?"

I know the walls have ears, and this is the confirmation of it.

"My sister?" she said with forced gaiety. "What has Sadie got to do with it?"

"She's already stirring up trouble, and she hasn't been in the Bay more than a couple of days. If she goes on like this for much longer, she'll be feeding the sharks."

Phoebe felt ice in her guts. "Trouble in what way?" she asked.

"Threatening us about the shooting of some night watchman? Harassing me about you."

"Harassing you about me? What's that about?"

"I have no idea. Maybe she's jealous?"

She shook her head.

"She's a true believer in the holy state of matrimony. Holy Mother of Mary and all that. The only thing that would satisfy her is marriage."

"Is that so?" said Cobra. "Well, maybe if you let me taste the wares…"

He dipped his lips to hers and kissed her lips, beginning gently but soon deepening the kiss, groaning with pleasure as he progressed.

"I promised your father I'd take things slowly, but I can't wait forever."

What a strange thing to say, Phoebe thought. What has Father got to do with any of this?

And then she lost herself in Cobra's tantalizing kiss.

Thirty

So their weak-chinned father had sold Phoebe short. Phoebe's father, Sadie corrected. He was only her stepfather, the man her mother married in a rush after her father died. Thank the creator, none of Brian's blood ran in her veins.

She'd gone on a long hack ride with Patrick Blackheart as he'd detailed the whole miserable story of her father's dealing with Cobra. She could see why Brian hadn't come clean and told her about it, because she admitted to herself if she had known, she would have ripped his head off. Figuratively speaking, of course.

And she had no doubts if she'd been in charge of the Bloods negotiation, she'd have got a better deal out of it. As Patrick explained it, Phoebe had been "given" to King Cobra as a "prize of war" in return for a revenge killing of several Satan's Horsemen members, in turn a payback for their brother Florian's death.

Like the Sabine women of ancient times, Phoebe was war booty. Sadie fought to repel angry tears, clamping her jaw tight and looking out the hack window so Patrick wouldn't see her flooded eyes.

Her father valued a dead son so much more highly than a live, beautiful virgin daughter, he'd traded her like horse meat. And he'd not even secured a future for her as a wife, but accepted her fate as a kept woman, to be passed on to someone else when Cobra tired of her.

And all for what? Florian was gone. The threat to the rest of the family was small to nonexistent, because none of them held any value for the Horsemen. On the contrary. Now her father had stoked the war by his declared allegiance to the Bloods, they would be in more danger than before. All for cheap revenge and a flood of watered-down booze.

She tasted stale bitterness in her mouth, the flavor of lies and defeat. How could her stepfather have seen this arrangement as a win? Cobra had taken exactly what he wanted at no cost. And Phoebe, all wrapped up in her romantic fantasies, had no idea she was merchandise between too tired old men with no vision above their belt lines.

She turned to Patrick Blackheart. "What do you make of it, Patrick? Is this a deal, or what? Cobra takes the virgin daughter and gives what in return? A supply of cheap liquor? If he decides he's tired of supplying the Shamrock and tupping Brian's daughter, he can throw them both over, and there isn't a blighted thing either Brian or Phoebe could do about it. As it stands, we're totally powerless."

Blackheart regarded her with baleful eyes.

"Ye are not wrong there, lass," he said, reverting to the singsong inflections of his native language. "And ye are a lot smarter than your Daa for seeing it."

They were returning up Montgomery Street, the city's principal thoroughfare, but Sadie was too deeply engaged to take much notice. Patrick had confirmed what she knew to be true. And he'd paid her a compliment. Hadn't he? She stared at him.

He'd reverted to that deep, blank mask his face often wore, a carefully cultivated veil of neutrality.

As she stared at him, Sadie knew what she had to do. There was only one way to outsmart Cobra now, and it was a painful payback to resort to. But if Phoebe was set to lie with this man—and Sadie could see now, there wouldn't be any way out of it—then by the Archangel Gabriel, she'd do it as his wife. That would give her lifelong status in both church and community, no matter how things developed between the Bloods and her family in the future.

Even if it meant Cobra was committing bigamy.

He wouldn't care about that, she was pretty sure. And she'd just pretend the idea of any first (or second) wife had never been mentioned.

"Take me to see Phoebe again," she blurted.

She glimpsed the momentary shockwave that penetrated Patrick's mask of indifference.

"What? You're not going to tell her about the deal, are you? She's a vain little thing. It would only cause more trouble."

She grinned, suddenly seeing the funny side.

"I'm not going to tell her about the deal, Patrick," she said in a level, ironic tone.

"Nor about Teo," she added as an afterthought.

He gave a deep sigh. Relief, she guessed.

"At least not yet." Her mouth twitched with mischief. "And if I do, I'll make sure you're protected."

Her heart did a little flip of satisfaction as she saw his eyes light up in response to her teasing.

"But it's time we girls got together to scheme some deals of our own."

Thirty-one

Patrick dropped her two blocks away from the Golden Girl and she walked up the busy street to the front door, confident neither Cobra nor any of his minders would have seen her alighting from the hack in Blackheart's company.

She strode in through the doors and bobbed greetings to Bennie with an outward confidence she didn't feel inside, grateful that she had already been here once and the staff recognized her as "Phoebe's sister." She sensed that already gave her status in the place and she used it the best she could.

A willowy redhead she hadn't seen the other night appeared to be acting as "day manager" on the upper floor. She paused before a desk rather like a hotel booking office and beamed her best "Miss High and Mighty" smile. The sort of smile that said, *I'm sure you are falling all over yourself to be of help to me because I am such an important person.*

She leaned toward the redhead with a confiding air, her voice low.

"I'm Phoebe McGillicuddy's sister, here to see her from New York. And our time together is so precious." She allowed a long, loaded pause before resuming.

"She is in residence, isn't she? And she indicated she'd welcome an afternoon visit…"

She'd assumed the woman was close to her own age, but as she looked into her face, saw that even the generous coating of face powder couldn't disguise the criss-crossing weary lines around her mouth and eyes that made her look a good ten years older.

The redhead frowned. Her jaw hardened, signaling there was a problem, making her look even older.

"I'm afraid Miss McGillicuddy is receiving a private visitor and is not available, Mrs…" She conspicuously examined Sadie's left hand, and seeing her bare fourth finger, theatrically corrected herself. "Miss…"

Sadie caught a parochial school cadence in the carefully modulated voice. Convent educated. How had she ended up in this fancy house? She was peering at Sadie, still fishing for her name.

"McGillicuddy. Miss Sadie McGillicuddy. Same as my sister…"

She'd taken Brian's surname when her mother married him. At this moment, she wished she still used her father's name, McGraw.

"Well, I am sorry, Miss McGillicuddy, but your sister is unavailable at this time."

"Oh. I see." She glanced around her. She was standing in the entrance to a pleasant lounge, lit with subtle glowing table lamps, and set up in comfortable seating clusters for getting-to-know-you conversations. Meetings, she assumed, between the "party girls" and clients.

"Then I think I will just wait until she is available," she said, with a hint of steel in her carefully articulated words. She'd been nun-educated too.

The woman stepped quickly from around her desk.

"I don't think…"

But she didn't get any further, because just at that moment, two visitors interrupted them. The Cobra walked in with Phoebe hanging adoringly off his arm.

Phoebe spotted her first and stopped in her tracks. "Sadie. What are you doing here?" The query wasn't welcoming. Rather, it had an exasperated ring.

What does she want now?

Cobra placed his hand protectively on the hand that clutched his arm.

"Well, well. Whatever's wrong now?" Cobra asked waspishly.

"Nothing, Mr. Romano. Nothing at all. I was just hoping to see Phoebe again, because I don't know how long I can stay… Daa needing help at home and all…"

She struck a humble note, one of appeal. She regarded Cobra with a soft expression.

If this man is going to be my brother-in-law, I need to get him on my side.

"Were you just leaving?"

She flashed him an appealing smile.

"Phoebe is very fortunate to have a benefactor like you." She allowed the merest hint of hesitation before mouthing the word "benefactor."

Cobra narrowed his hard eyes in shrewd assessment and then broke into an ironic grin.

"'Benefactor.'" He rolled the word on his tongue, as if tasting it, testing it. Evidently, it met his approval.

"Yes. Phoebe's benefactor. How clever of you, Miss McGillicuddy."

She shot him one of her most winsome, docile smiles in return.

"I'm happy to keep Phoebe company if you have things to attend to."

"As a matter of fact, I have," he said.

He turned to face Phoebe and, lifting her hand to his lips in the most elegant, cordial manner, kissed her fingers.

"I'll see you tomorrow, little bird. Until then, *Arrivederci.*"

●●●●●●●●

"What was all that about?" Phoebe asked, her voice laden with suspicion, as soon as they were back in the privacy of her own sitting room.

"Don't tell me you've changed your mind and you actually like Cobra?"

She simpered. "He grows on you, don't you think?"

Sadie hid her smile. Her sister was desperate for her approval. Under the defiant attitude, she sensed doubt and insecurity.

"I suppose…" she said noncommittally. "I know I have to change my approach, anyway, Feebs. I don't want to lose you."

Phoebe's eyes filled with tears. "I've missed you Sadie," she said. "It's getting pretty lonely here as the big boss's woman. So far, it's been nothing like I thought it would be…"

"What did you think it would be like?" asked Sadie.

"Oh—like at home, I guess. With everyone sitting around together talking and drinking. You know. Patrick and Teo and the other boys. I even miss Daa,"

She laughed self-consciously.

"I've been here mostly on my own. The only person to talk to has been Isla, and she's a bit of a queer one."

"Queer? In what way?"

"She seems to know an awful lot about the place, but she's not exactly part of it. I haven't worked out where she stands yet. For her age, she's very cynical."

"Maybe life has taught her to be," said Sadie, making a private note to get Isla to herself and interrogate her. "What did she say that makes you think that?"

Phoebe's face flushed with embarrassment. Softly, in a tentative voice, she said, "She told me off about you, actually. She said you had it right, and I had it wrong.

"That Cobra could chuck me over any time he wanted, and there wouldn't be a thing I could do about it. That if I'm not careful, I could end up working upstairs like the other girls."

Sadie's skin went cold.

"You're not thinking…"

"What?" Phoebe's eyes were incredulous as she scanned her sister's face.

"That I want to end up upstairs? Are you kidding me? Of course not. That's why I've made some very important decisions."

"Oh? And what are they?"

Phoebe's determined good humor evaporated, replaced again by the unworldly naif.

She shrugged self-consciously. "There's only one, really. One important one."

"And what's that?"

"I have got to get Cobra to marry me. I'm a fool if I accept anything less."

Her eyes flickered over Sadie's face. "I know you will hate the idea because you don't like him much…"

Sadie's throat was choking up over her racing heart. She had to take a big breath before she could get any words out.

"No, no, no, Feebs," she said urgently. "Those are my thoughts exactly. You're right. It's the only way. You have to get him to marry you. We just have to work out how."

Phoebe's mouth dropped open. Her hand flew up to cover her gaping expression.

She made a choking sound, as if she was trying to form words without success.

"Just for once, we see things exactly the same way," Sadie reassured her.

They'd both risen to their feet in excitement at their exchange, and Sadie was pitching herself up onto her tiptoes and then relaxing, as if she couldn't contain her excitement. Phoebe's eyes sparkled with mischief.

They were staring at one another like that when Isla strode in and stood between them.

"Jack and Dolphie are here to rescue you before any of Cobra's guards get back. There's no time to lose…"

The sisters looked to Isla and then back at one another, and simultaneously burst out laughing.

Isla's smooth, unruffled face crinkled into confusion. "What's wrong? Don't you want to be rescued?"

"Too late for that," said Sadie. "We're finding another way."

Thirty-two

She'd only been apart from Dolphie for one night since they met, but when he walked into the small bar area where she had met Phoebe for the first time the night before last, Sadie realized with a jolt she had forgotten what a commanding presence he carried with him.

He moved with such effortless grace, his gaze direct and crystal clear. He carried a natural understanding of what needed to be done, without having to ask.

Sadie felt a repeat of her response on the train; her heartbeat accelerated, her arms tingled from shoulder to wrist.

There was something about him that went straight to her core, no doubt about it. But if she was going to help Phoebe make the best of the mess she was in, she had to focus her entire will and purpose on that one thing.

And besides, as much as she warmed to the knowledge that he was risking danger to "rescue" her, she also felt a tingle of irritation at the assumptions he'd made without checking with her first.

She felt the color rising in her cheeks as they settled around the table and called for drinks. A light cider for her and Phoebe, whiskey for the men.

The idea that they needed rescuing for a start. They were in a mess of their father's making, for sure, but Dolphie and Jack swooping in and plucking them out of it offered no long-term resolution. Cobra would simply come after them in retribution.

They were putting together their own rescue package, one she didn't feel comfortable talking about with Jack and Dolphie. They had strolled in with a patrician air of certainty, confident they were an equal, if not better, match for anything Cobra might throw at them.

Their born-to-rule authority reminded her all over again that she was from a different world, from the opposite side of the tracks. Dolphie might have no fortune, but his family had reared him with expectations about life. That he would triumph.

Whereas people like her and Phoebe and even Brian, had learned at an early age, the world wouldn't bend for their needs and they'd better get used to playing second fiddle.

She could never explain why the only solution for Phoebe was to marry a mobster and prepare to be deserted in the future—though Sadie wasn't about to frame the deal she was going to persuade Phoebe to go after in those terms.

She was ashamed to admit the truth of her father's deal with Cobra to anyone, and besides, Phoebe didn't know about it and that was the way she wanted it to stay.

They'd moved from the private sitting room to the bar when Isla returned from the front desk with Jack and Dolphie in tow. It just wouldn't do for two men to visit Phoebe in her private quarters, especially if Cobra heard about the visit. There was no doubt in Sadie's mind he would consider them as a rival gang and treat them accordingly.

They settled awkwardly around a small occasional table to talk, meeting eye-to-eye rather than shoulder-to-shoulder at the bar. And awkward it was going to be, Sadie realized as they exchanged stilted opening greetings.

"Glad to see you're unhurt from the other night," said Dolphie. "It must have been terrifying."

"What was terrifying?" Phoebe asked. "You didn't mention anything about this, Sadie."

Sadie darted her annoyance to Dolphie.

"It was nothing, Feebs. A misunderstanding."

Jack gave a snort of derision.

"Tell that to the night watchman who's still off work, hobbling around on crutches."

"Ahh," said Phoebe with familiar satisfaction. "The night watchman. Cobra mentioned something about a night watchman. He got shot somehow, didn't he?"

"How is Cobra?" asked Jack with robust familiarity, as if he was a close buddy. Sadie was fairly confident he'd never laid eyes on the man.

Phoebe's eyes rested on Sadie, as if seeking guidance as to the response.

"He's being Cobra," she said, her voice laced with suspicion. "Why?"

Jack looked amused.

"Well, seeing as a couple of nights ago we were all feeling rather threatened by him, I thought the question needed asking."

Phoebe's brow crinkled in confusion.

"Threatened? Why?"

Sadie broke in abruptly. "Just another misunderstanding, Feebs." She glared a warning at Jack and Dolphie.

No mention of Teo and the severed hand.

They seemed slightly taken aback, but the slightest dip of their heads showed they'd got the message.

"We're handling things, Dolphie. In our own way. We don't need your help, much as we appreciate your offer."

Dolphie steepled his hands, as if absorbing the rejection in his fingertips, and then asked, "Oh? How exactly are you handling things?"

"We have our ways," she joked, hoping to deflect his attention.

Phoebe interjected, all bright innocence.

"I'm preparing to marry Cobra," she said. "That should solve any 'issues.'"

Jack stared at her, plainly appalled.

"Marry him?" he said. "Do you realize what you are getting yourself into?"

Phoebe gazed back, her eyes unfocused, in momentary shock at his vehemence.

"Yes, of course. I love him. We love one another."

Her voice was faltering and lame.

Jack let out a snort of disbelief. "He's probably got two wives and a string of children he's left behind in Sicily."

Phoebe went pale.

"No, he hasn't," Sadie lied. "We've already checked with Father Gregory."

Jack in his turn, stared at her, momentarily speechless.

"Father Gregory," Sadie ad-libbed. "The priest at Mission Dolores. He's from the same area as Cobra back in Italy. And it's not Sicily," she continued with forced certainty.

All eyes were now on her.

"Look," she said, in a more conciliatory tone. "Phoebe and I are handling things. Everything is going to be fine. We thank you both very much for your concern about us, but really, it's unwarranted. It was all just a big misunderstanding."

She stood up abruptly, unable to handle their speculative eyes, as

Isla rushed in, unusually agitated.

"Sophia is on her way." She gestured to Jack. "You don't want to be here when she gets here. You'd best go now or there'll be fireworks."

She looked around wildly and gave an apologetic laugh. "Bad choice of words, sorry. I mean, there'll be trouble."

The last time Jack and Sophia had a confrontation, two men had died in a fireworks explosion.

Jack and Dolphie stood up with a deflated air.

"I guess that's it, then," said Dolphie, casting a glance in Sadie's direction, half hoping, she thought, for a reversal of her stance.

"Thank you very much for your concern, Dolphie. I am very sorry for getting you involved in the first place."

Dolphie cast one last searching gaze her way, as if to penetrate her shield, and then followed Isla out.

And instead of feeling jubilant at having convinced him she was fine, she felt like a deflated hot-air balloon.

Checked with Father Gregory, indeed.

Oh Father forgive me, she silently prayed. *I had to do it. That's three lies of omission or commission. About Tea. About Daa. And about Father Gregory. Forgive me.*

Thirty-three

"Why are they so uptight?" Phoebe wrinkled her nose with disdain. "Anyone would think we can't take care of ourselves. Who do they think they are?"

You'd be more than uptight if you'd had Teo's severed hand on your doorstep.

Sadie shrugged. "You know what those biggest toads in the puddle are like. They think they own you. Not our sort."

Her heart knocked with guilt against the wall of her chest. She'd just been abominably rude to a gentleman who'd shown her every consideration. Maa would be turning in her grave. Not only that, Dolphie and Jack were decent men, who cared about others. Dolphie had dug her out of the trouble she'd got herself into, and she'd treated him shabbily.

She heard her mother's soft Irish lilt in her head.

Sadie, my girl. I taught you better than that.

Sadie clenched her hands under the table.

I can't do everything, Maa. You made me swear to keep Phoebe out of trouble. That's all I can manage right now.

Phoebe continued to look like she smelt something bad right under her nose. Sadie's attempt to build solidarity by being disloyal hadn't satisfied her.

"Where did you say you met that Count fella? On the train? He's acting like your life is in danger or something."

"Don't worry about him, Feebs. Let's get back to what we agreed on before they arrived."

Phoebe's face was blank.

"About Cobra marrying you," Sadie prompted.

"Ohhhh. Yes, of course." Her sister's face lit up like pink candy floss at the reminder.

"That."

"So, how are we going to make it happen?"

She swallowed hard, hedging for time, reluctant to get to the kernel of the gnarly problem. She would not suggest Phoebe seduce him. That would almost certainly have the opposite effect. For Cobra, Phoebe's chief appeal, she guessed, was the fact that she had never been with another man.

"I mean, how much sway do you have over him? Be honest now. What would you have to do to get him to agree to the idea?"

"Well, certainly not sleep with him," said Phoebe. She bit down on the words like hard toffee in her mouth.

Not so naïve, then. That's good.

Phoebe shifted on her barstool, gazing around her.

When they'd first sat down, they'd had the space to themselves.

Now three more people sat at a table across from the bar, a portly balding older man who looked like a butcher, and two much younger girls, one a curvaceous blonde, the other a brunette with tight black curls that gave her the appearance of a schoolgirl.

"I have to create a sense of urgency, don't I? Or make him jealous."

Sadie shivered, thinking of Teo.

"That might be too dangerous."

She hesitated, cautiously scanning Phoebe's enchanting face. She really was as flawless as the newly fallen snow.

"You didn't get too friendly with Teo, did you? You know what I mean? He didn't get fresh with you?"

Phoebe brows rose to her hairline, appalled at the suggestion.

"Teo? Of course not." Her face collapsed into an anxious query. "Which reminds me, where is he? He hasn't been here for days now. I miss him. I must ask Cobra where he's gone."

Sadie felt cold leak down her body.

"Now that you're safe here, I guess Cobra thinks you don't need a personal bodyguard like before. He's probably got him assigned to other duties."

She reached across and squeezed her sister's hand.

"I wouldn't ask about him. Cobra might get the wrong idea. He might be the jealous sort. Setting him off might be a bad idea for everybody."

Phoebe sighed. "You're probably right. Fine, no playing the field," she laughed. "Chance would be a fine thing. I never get to meet anyone in here."

"And you won't hold him off for too much longer now you're here. We have to act fast."

"What was that you said about Father Gregory? How do you know him? You've only been here a few days."

"Ahhh… I confess. I made that part up."

"You did? So Cobra could be married already?" Phoebe's sparkle dimmed. "I don't know why I didn't think of that. It just didn't occur to me."

"More likely, he's a widower," Sadie said with a confidence she did not feel. "Wives die young in Europe. All the time."

Phoebe's face bore a despondent cast. "I guess," she said. "If you say so."

"I'm sure Father Gregory will know all about that side of things.

I will talk to him for real this time. He might even agree to officiate."

That was something she needed to do tomorrow. Find a priest willing to officiate. For that matter, make sure Cobra had in some dim, dark day in the past actually been born into the Catholic Church. Most Italians were. That, and try to ignore the lump as big as an orange that threatened to fill her chest whenever she thought of Dolphie.

One thing was for sure. She'd sacrificed any hope of him ever wanting to have anything to do with her in the future. And that had to be a good thing, didn't it?

There isn't room in your life for a man like him, anyway.

Thirty-four

"She certainly knows how to gild the lily, doesn't she?"

Sadie slung the remark in a low undertone to Patrick Blackheart, who sat on her immediate right around the crowded saloon table. She was referring to Sophia Morrigan, the big-time owner of the Golden Girl, although she did little of the day-to-day work—she paid others for that. They all sat, crammed elbow-to-elbow around the oval oak tabletop, partying up to celebrate Cobra's latest business coup.

More than a dozen of Sophia and Corban's associates and retainers sat under an umbrella of sound, the rising jocularity imparting to their words an intimacy they wouldn't usually carry.

The more they drank, the louder the joking and singing became, and the more it felt like she and Patrick occupied their own private bubble while the party boiled on around them, with Sophia and King Cobra at her right shoulder leading the charge.

It was the night after she'd cut ties with the Pine Street gang. That's how she thought of yesterday's meeting. She had heard nothing from Dolphie, Jack, Elizabeth or Susannah since, and frankly, after the way she'd treated them, she didn't expect to.

Tonight's celebration was all about Sophia and Cobra

congratulating each other on their most recent business coup. As far as Sadie understood it, they'd acquired control of a big saloon and associated brothel and gambling hall in Sacramento, which until recently had been a Satan's Horsemen monopoly.

She did not want to know about the finer details of the deal and how they'd pulled it off, and no one offered that information, anyway. What had become clear over the course of the evening was that Phoebe's magnetism drew attention from every corner of the room, from young bucks foolhardy or ignorant enough to pay homage at her throne.

In the general melee of finding seats Phoebe had been shunted down the table, out of Cobra's sphere of influence, separated far enough away from the mob boss to obscure their relationship and to draw a steady stream of would-be admirers who did not realize they were attempting to steal the mob boss's girl from right under his nose.

Phoebe looked especially transcendent, in an emerald gown that gave the in-love glow of her flawless ceramic skin the beam of a lighthouse on dark cliffs. Sadie had never seen her looking more beautiful.

She was also suddenly aware that in the familiar halls of their home bar, the Shamrock, Phoebe enjoyed an unspoken but real mantle of protection through being the owner's daughter.

Brian held on to the quick temper and iron fists that had brought him success in the boxing ring as a younger man, and no one at home risked stirring him up by coming on too strongly to his youngest daughter, the jewel of the house. Phoebe had played up to that, without even realizing it.

From East Coast to West Coast, Phoebe rose like a star in their midst, drawing male admiration while making no appeal for it, and Sadie saw immediately Cobra didn't like it.

Several times when Phoebe had been cold-called by young bucks seeking a dance, or the honor of allowing them to buy her a drink, Cobra had stepped in and claimed ownership. Taking her for several turns around the dance floor himself to fend off the attention of others, his face a blend of pride and irritation at the attention she was attracting.

"Don't encourage any of them," she'd hissed into Phoebe's ear halfway through the night. "He's not impressed at having to defend his territory."

One particularly persistent horsey Adonis had so annoyed Cobra she'd feared he might draw on him, but Patrick had warned the feller off before they came to blows.

"Is it always like this?" she'd asked Patrick at one point.

"Like what?" he said, brows contracted in a question even as his black eyes carried that familiar hint of humor. He was always laughing at her, she thought. Was she floundering that badly?

"So loud. So crazy. The Shamrock's pretty tame by comparison."

Patrick shrugged. "It's crazier than Morrigan's last place. The Imperial. That had a bit more class."

"And what happened to that?"

"She had a fireworks party and it partly burnt down. They're still repairing it."

"Heavens! I never thought I'd say it, but New York feels tame by comparison."

"I like the Shamrock," Blackheart said. "It's got a nice family feel about it."

Sadie felt unreasonably hot and pleased at his comment. She shot him a grateful grin. "Phoebe and I are still finding our feet here. Not sure we'll ever fit in."

His eyes raked her face. "How long are you planning on staying?"

She gave a light shrug. "I guess just till I'm satisfied Phoebe is okay."

"And how will you judge that?"

Admiration at his precise clarity warred with irritation at being pinned down like a butterfly in a scientific collection. He had an unerring talent for pinpointing the key issue in any situation. Come to think of it, he'd be very good at Cobra's job.

She challenged him with her eyes. "When I've got her married to him, I guess."

He stared at her, wordless.

After a long pause, he glanced up to where Cobra sat, as if checking the man was still present, and then back to her. "You're serious."

She took a sip of her lukewarm drink. It had been sitting untouched for so long, it had absorbed the heated intensity from the goings-on around them.

"That I am. It's the only way I can see to fulfill the vow. As you've explained, there's no escaping him." Her eyes shot up to where Sophia and Cobra held court.

"And to be fair, she doesn't want rescue. The very idea annoys the heck out of her."

Dolphie's wan face swam into her mind's eye again, and she felt a stab of regret that she'd given him the wrong idea from the start.

"So, you're the one who always hits the bull's-eye. How does Phoebe get him to marry her?"

"*You are* serious."

He glanced around him again, as if fearing being overheard, but no one was paying them any attention.

"Get Phoebe to meet Consuela."

"Consuela? Who's she?"

"Cobra's sister. He's terrified of her."

She gazed into Patrick's eyes, mesmerized by the deep triumph sparkling there.

"I don't believe you. Truly?"

"All true. I'm only telling you this because you're the most remarkable woman I've ever met. And Consuela will love you."

Her heart did a full revolution in her chest. Had Dolphie been a figment of her imagination? Was she gazing at the real thing?

"And what if he won't make the introduction?"

"Then I can give you her address and you can introduce yourselves. Just don't mention my name anywhere near it."

He flashed a brilliant grin that lit up his face, and she had the feeling she was seeing him in an unguarded moment for the first time.

"It's about time Cobra got his comeuppance, and Consuela is one of the few people in this world who can give it to him."

Thirty-five

Patrick Blackheart wanted this woman more than any other in his thirty-eight years of bachelor's life. He'd bided his time, turning down plenty of easy options, women who were pretty and sexy and who threw themselves at him.

He'd been watching for the one who would be not just a bed partner, but a partner in life. And Sadie McGillicuddy was it.

He smiled to himself as he reflected on the party conversation from last night. That younger sister of hers, Phoebe, yes, she was a beauty. No argument about that. But Sadie? She was exquisite in an understated way. And she had a brain. He could go on. Immense courage and conviction and inner resilience which led her to put the needs of others before her own. Not just once or twice, but repeatedly.

For her, living selflessly was a way of life.

Together they could build not just a marriage, and a family, but a dynasty.

He just had to convince her of that fact.

He cringed inside when he remembered that excruciating scene on the train. He'd badly misjudged things there—let his desire for her demolish his normal cool-headed logic.

He'd caught the fiery spark in her eye more than once. She was attracted to him, that was obvious, but he'd misjudged how a well-bred Catholic girl would react to a direct approach. He had to take it a lot more slowly this time and lay out the logic of it for her.

Then she'd see the light. He'd never been more certain of anything.

••••••••

Two days after the Golden Girl confrontation with Sadie, Dolphie Westerhoven's Old World pride was still smarting from the knock back the New York girl had delivered.

He'd told himself he was tired of being the knight on the white charger. He'd said he wanted a change of season in his life. No more deliverance of men or maidens in distress, even on behalf of his dear aunt, the Countess.

He'd returned from his father's death and months in Europe, ready for a new life in his beloved California, a different life altogether. One that was more stable, less nomadic. He wanted to put down roots, start a family of his own.

And then what had he done? Picked up a wench on a train, taken her home, and set about trying to "rescue" her.

And not just her, but her wild-eyed, lovesick sister as well. And yet within half a day Sadie McGillicuddy had transformed herself from a woman on a mission to "save" her sister to someone who was in no need of any help at all, thank you very much.

Talk about women! It was all so darn confusing.

His face reddened at the embarrassment.

How had he got it so wrong?

One minute it appeared she'd been abducted by the Bloods mobsters. The night watchman had taken the scene as genuine enough, and had a wounded leg to prove it. And then there was the matter of the severed hand on their doorstep.

These were the people her sister wanted to marry into? He recalled sitting so close to Sadie at the bordello bar their thighs were almost touching, when she'd assured him coolly that she had no need of him at all.

Thanks a lot and begone. That's the message now.

He wondered if the story about the deathbed promise—that story that had so touched him with its pathos—was all a con. And as for the claim that she was fleeing Blackheart's assault on the train?

He was a fit, dangerous-looking fellow, no doubt about that. But Dolphie had always been skeptical about whether she'd given him the full facts of what went on between them.

He ran his hand down his face, his fingers gently massaging his overheated skin from temple to throat.

A hard-headed man would accept he'd had a narrow escape from an opportunistic con woman and walk right away. Thank his lucky stars he'd got off so lightly. He ran his hand through his hair, from his forehead to the back of his crown, releasing pent-up tension.

Trouble is, I don't feel as if I've had a lucky escape.

An image of Sadie, her marine-blue eyes heavy with concern, her voice soft and appealing, telling him her story on the train. Of Sadie, watching California's rivers and plains rolling before her from the carriage window, her face a quicksilver flickering of delight, excitement, and fear as they drew near to San Francisco and her missing sister.

He couldn't deny the pull deep in his inner self, the draw of this relentless, idealistic woman, an intriguing bundle of contradictions.

She's delivered the message. Nothing doing. You just don't want to accept it.

Thirty-six

With Blackheart as their guide, they'd boarded a city train for a twenty-minute ride out of town, heading south from the teeming streets into green pastures. Literally. Sadie had been nowhere so empty of people. When they alighted in what appeared to be the middle of a rough field, and Blackheart pointed to a waiting coach, she suffered a sudden loss of confidence about the wisdom of the whole idea.

Meeting up with Cobra's sister? In the middle of nowhere? What am I doing?

She and Phoebe stood on a rough country path beside a rustic, uncovered wagon with bench seats down each side, surrounded by untidy pastures dotted with modest farmhouses, the occasional milking cow, and a smattering of native oaks.

Away in the distance, a bulky cliff face rose, like a sleeping mountain keeping watch over the pastoral scene below. She couldn't believe the stinking stews of the Barbary Coast were only thirty minutes away.

"You get on there," Blackheart said, pointing to the waiting wagon.

"You're not coming with us?" she said, her voice thin and faltering.

He gave her a sharp glance.

"More than my life's worth," he said. "When you've done your business, return the same way. Coach to the station, and train link back to town. People commute for work from here every day."

He stepped up to the driver and patted the waiting horse's haunch with one hand, pointing back to them with the other.

"Let them off by the convent school," he said, as they stared after him, not moving. "Second stop near the top of the hill."

He wandered back to Sadie and Phoebe, rooted on the rough path as people strode past them and boarded the coach, intent on getting to their destinations.

"Get on now, or you'll have to walk it," he said. "Second stop. You'll see the convent school walls. Ask for Sister Consuela."

•••••••

Convent school? Blackheart hadn't told her they were going to a school.

I can't let that worry me now.

Sadie let out a lingering, relieved sigh as the full wagon pulled away up the hill. She reached across and took Phoebe's hand, squeezing it for reassurance. Her own or her sister's, she wasn't sure.

Blackheart had boarded the train back to town before their wagon pulled away, and his disappearing back gave her a momentary sense of panic. She was abandoned on a mountain and about to take one of the biggest gambles of her life.

Whenever Blackheart left her, she underwent that feeling of loss, except for that day on the train. He presented a granite-like calm to the world, no matter what turmoil might roil underneath. She found it comforting in this unpredictable city, where she knew no one and controlled nothing except her own demeanor.

They were bumping up a steep hill, breathing in the scent of lavender and a resinous lemony smell from trees she didn't recognize, all because of one fateful conversation at Morrigan's party.

The lure of Consuela. They'd racked their brains about how to get Cobra to commit to the idea of marriage. Phoebe got cold feet about raising it, frightened he would dump her altogether, and Sadie understood her reluctance.

Although Cobra seemed as enamored of his young paramour as ever, he was getting increasingly impatient about the final consummation. Phoebe sensed she wouldn't be able to hold him off much longer.

Consuela was their secret weapon. Their only weapon. That's what they were hoping, and all based on some vague word from Blackheart, who she'd hardly seen in the days since the party.

"It's all going to work out just fine," she whispered in Phoebe's ear. "Patrick wouldn't put us wrong."

She offered a silent prayer that finally, after quite a wait, her faith in him was not misplaced. They went over an especially rough bump and she jostled shoulders with the woman sitting next to her, a dumpy fresh-faced woman nursing a small child on her lap.

"Sorry," Sadie muttered. The woman turned to her with a bright smile.

"Can't be helped, dearie…" She looked her over. "You're new to Bernal Heights?"

A small girl of three or four Sadie presumed was her daughter gazed up at Sadie with liquid brown eyes.

"Bernal Heights? Oh, is that the name of this place?"

Perplexed gray eyes gazed out at her from a round face. The woman's complexion was clear of lines, but the skin on the hands that linked around her child's slim waist was reddened and work weary.

"You don't know? You *are* new here. What brings you out?"

"Visiting a family friend," Sadie said quickly. "And you?"

"Ahhh, Fergus and I are lucky enough to have a place out here. I grow vegetables to sell at market and he gets plenty of work as a builder. Lots of houses going in up here. You'd fit well," she laughed. "Many of them are Micks like us."

"Oh yes, and there's the convent school out here too," said Sadie.

"That's right. Most of the Irish folk send their children there. One of the first in the Bay," she added with pink pride. "Sister Consuela does a great job."

Sister Consuela does a great job?

"Oh? Is she one of the teachers?"

"Sister Consuela? Oh, not just a teacher. She's the principal."

Phoebe elbowed her in the ribs.

The wagon drew to a stop and her fellow passenger slipped the child to the floor.

"You'll have to walk, now darlin'," she said to the child. "Mummy's got parcels to carry."

She stood and picked up a bulky carryall loaded with provisions. She glanced down at Sadie.

"Enjoy the rest of your trip," she said.

In the momentary clatter as the rest of the passengers for this first stop disembarked, Phoebe dug her in the ribs again.

"When we get there, you're doing all the talking," she said. "I was no good with the nuns, if you remember?"

•••••••••

St. Mary's College sat on a rise at the start of what apparently was the village of Bernal Heights, such as it was, surrounded by small farms where dairy cows or pigs grazed, planted too with fruit trees and vegetable plots around the modest dwellings.

The school's cream plastered walls, arched clerestory windows, pitched red tile roofs, and chapel and bell tower echoed its European origins.

They let themselves in through a wrought-iron gate from the street and walked on the balls of their feet up to the arched main doors, trepidation in every step. Sadie had a flashback to their own school days, when she'd led a reluctant Phoebe into the classroom before she attempted fleeing back home, as she'd regularly tried to do when she was small. Phoebe and external authority never mixed well.

But making the tentative request to speak to Sister Consuela was like a magic charm, an Open Sesame.

A young noviate who looked like she'd stepped out of a Renaissance painting, in a white robe rimmed with blue, gazed at them eagerly. "You want to see Sister Consuela?" Her voice sang with the same Irish cadence as the woman on the wagon.

"Of course. Come this way. There may be a small wait. She is busy with something else right now, but if you're patient, she'll be with you soon."

On a hard bench in the corridor outside her office, Sadie had time to compose her opening lines, but as soon as they were shown in and her eyes lit on the commanding presence behind the desk, the words she'd rehearsed flew out the big windows into the garden outside.

Sister Consuela was a coin minted from the same metal as her brother—Sadie could see that at first glance. Even seated behind the desk, it was clear she was tall. Her body loomed over the paper-strewn top, and the hands that were clasped in front of her were big for a woman, the fingers long and strong.

The same roving black eyes as her brother's—capable of instilling fear in one glance—looked out of her handsome olive-tanned face. But where Cobra's fleshly appetites were written plain in his alcohol-flushed cheeks and marauding scrutiny, Consuela's hawk-like gaze carried with it a profound, penetrating peace.

The same consuming energy burned in both of them, but while Cobra looked to satisfy his appetites by force of will, intent to be master of all he surveyed, Consuela's power flowed from surrender to powers that were not of this world.

It was like seeing the angel of light and the angel of darkness brought forth from the same womb, and Sadie took on the instant conviction that these two were not just siblings, but twins, two peas in a pod, grown into very different vines.

Blackheart had given her no counsel about how to handle this audience. Apart from the fact that the nun was Cobra's sister, and he was in awe of her, she knew nothing else.

Did she know what sort of operation her sibling was engaged in? That he unashamedly served the devil while she served her Lord? Did anyone else in this place know of their relationship?

Consuela gestured to two seats set before the imposing desk. Light flooded in from windows that looked out on a courtyard planted with abundant flowering roses set amidst classic marble statues. Sadie assumed they were of various Holy Roman saints. Fragrance from the yellow and pink blooms drifted into the room and an unearthly peace enveloped them all.

Consuela scanned their faces expectantly. Her wide mouth hitched up at one corner in a reflexive gesture which was identical to Cobra's when he was amused or intrigued. But while his smiles were derisive, she merely looked curious.

"Welcome, Sadie and Phoebe is it, and you're sisters, our young Penelope tells me. Has she got that correct?" She flashed them a quick smile, as if to say, 'Well, let's get on with it. I'm a busy woman."

Sadie felt a jolt go through her. The smell of the flowers, the profound peace, the impact of Consuela's personality had her mesmerized. It was almost out of this world. But now, she came down to earth with a thump.

"That's right, Sister. We're here from New York, and new in the area. Our father back in New York has developed a business relationship which brought us here."

She paused briefly, her stomach gripped by a convulsion of anxiety. How she phrased the next bit might be critical.

"I…" She hesitated and flicked a glance at Phoebe. "I am Sadie. And this is my younger sister, Phoebe. We understand you're related to the man our father is in partnership with, and that is why we are here today seeking your advice."

Consuela's thick, finely curved brows rose in surprise. The hands, which had remained linked and poised in front of her, opened wide as she pushed slightly away from the desk and back into her chair.

After a few moments of silence, when Sadie became aware for the first time of a loudly ticking clock, Consuela said, "I see. And this gentleman your father has a partnership with, what is his name?"

Sadie glanced at Phoebe on her right, as if to say, *Your turn. He's your fiancé.* Phoebe tensed beside her, and then cleared her throat and spoke. "We only know him as Cobra, Sister. King Cobra." She swallowed so hard the scrape in her throat was audible to Sadie, and she was confident to Consuela as well.

"I guess he has another name, but I don't know it."

Consuela's mobile mouth went into a wry smirk. "Yes, indeed. He does. It is Cosimo. Cosimo Romano," she added as if in an afterthought. "Cosimo means decency and order, though I'm not sure our Cosimo has lived up to that." She smiled again. "He is my twin brother. Who told you we're related? It's not widely known."

Instant terror grabbed Sadie by the throat. "Please don't tell Cobra we're here," she croaked. "He might be angry."

Consuela's smile broadened into a relaxed grin that sparkled in her black eyes. "Your secret is safe with me."

Reluctance gnawed at her, but Sadie decided she needed to come clean as a gesture of trust.

"One of Cobra's lieutenants told us," she said. "He was just trying to be helpful."

Consuela lifted a skeptical brow.

"And why are you here? What do you want from me?"

Always one to get straight to the heart of things, Sadie thought with warm approval.

This is easier than I thought it would be.

"They brought Phoebe to San Francisco as Cobra's *inamorata.*"

She watched as Consuela's face clouded and then took on the full meaning.

"Not against her wishes, you understand. She fancies Cobra. And my father and Cosimo, they agree on this. But Phoebe—she is a pure girl. She has not yet been with a man, any man.

"And our mother Grace, she was a faith-filled woman. She asked me to swear on the Bible I would protect Phoebe, not let her fall into trouble. On her deathbed, I vowed this."

Consuela's face was grave as the story poured out.

Beside Sadie, Phoebe grew suddenly restless.

"You didn't tell me that. You didn't tell me about the deathbed vow…"

Consuela watched the exchange like a hawk.

"You… Umm… I didn't have a chance. It wouldn't have made any difference, anyway. You say you're in love with Cobra. You left home without telling me. I thought you'd run away. Or been abducted."

She glanced back at Consuela.

"Sorry Sister, family business. The important thing is, we've come to the same conclusion by two different paths. Phoebe wants to be Cobra's woman. Forever. For eternity. Isn't that right, Phoebe?"

Phoebe's cheeks flushed pink, but she gazed imploringly at Consuela and nodded silent assent.

Sadie continued. "And I want to ensure I keep my promise to Maa. So, we've decided. We have to persuade Cobra to marry Phoebe to make it right. And we're asking for your help."

Thirty-seven

Cosimo to marry?

Consuela knelt in the St. Mary's Chapel and did what she did with all the decisions she made in her life—she placed it on the altar before the Lord.

The sisters' arrival earlier that day had been one of the biggest surprises in her life. First, because only a few key people—the bishop, Father Gregory—knew of her twin's existence.

She'd never stopped loving her brother or forgiving his misdeeds, but she'd also never imagined God might bless her family line with another generation from a properly constituted and blessed marriage. Until now.

They were the only two living children of their parents, also Cosimo and Consuela Romano. Cosimo, having chosen his life as a gangster, had naturally taken as he pleased from the many women available to him, but the only wife he'd had died in childbirth and he'd sworn off any other Church-blessed union.

"Better to stick with what I know," he said. "Obviously, God's got it in for me."

To learn he had another opportunity at forty, to marry a twenty-year-old virgin, seemed like a heaven-sent miracle. But she knew she would need to handle the situation with delicacy if she was to help bring about the desired outcome.

Cosimo regarded her as his stairway to the Father, but he was also arrogant and determined to have his own way.

She glanced up at the central image of the altar triptych, of Jesus ascending to Heaven, and whispered.

"If it be Your will, Father, let it be done." And she rose and went to supper.

Thirty-eight

Patrick Blackheart hung his hat on the hook inside the café door and cast his eagle gaze across the room to where Sadie sat in her window seat, steaming coffee cup on the table in front of her.

He crossed the crowded floor in a few big strides, filling the space as he moved with his powerful masculine presence.

"This is becoming a habit," he said with a grin, glancing out the window. "We'd better not let Cobra catch us."

She blushed. She'd deliberately set herself up to catch his eye, but she'd never admit it.

When he'd arrived at "the office," he'd paused on the threshold and glanced back across the street. And there she was, framed in the café window, where he'd seen her last time. Was she ready to acknowledge it wasn't just coincidence that had brought them together again?

She felt like a kid caught out with her hand in the cookie jar. She was thirteen years old again, hot and vulnerable, overwhelmed by a schoolgirl crush for the neighborhood Romeo.

Now, as he stood by her table, he noticed the way she nervously followed his eyes to the street, because he gave a soft laugh and added, "Just kidding."

He glanced to the counter where Belle stood, acknowledging his presence with a rosy-cheeked beam.

"Aren't you going to order?' Sadie asked.

"Belle knows what I want. She'll bring it when she's ready."

He shot her a pleased smile as he pulled out the chair opposite her and sat down.

"How did the visit with Consuela go?"

His closeness overpowered her. The blood boiled in her veins, momentarily leaving her light-headed. She couldn't raise her eyes to meet his.

He's got women at his beck and call. Of course he does.

She reached for the edge of the table, as if clutching something solid would help anchor her wild thoughts.

"Consuela? Have you met her?" She attempted to force confidence into her trembling voice.

"No, I haven't. I daren't let on I know she exists."

"How did you discover she does? Exist, I mean." she asked, interest suddenly piqued.

"I've also got a sister who's a nun," he said. The dark eyes flashed with irony, his eager-beaver confidence replaced by a self-conscious grimace.

"Find it hard to believe, wouldn't you? Two hoods, both with holy sisters."

He gave a self-deprecatory laugh, and then hesitated.

"It's an open secret within the cloisters, but not whispered outside of them. They hold Consuela in too much respect."

Buxom Belle appeared at his shoulder with his coffee, creamy head foaming.

"Two sugars, sir," she said with a quick nod.

So, he has a sweet tooth.

He nodded his appreciation and picked up the teaspoon to stir.

"So how did your visit go, anyway?"

She considered how to answer.

"Sister Consuela's a remarkable woman. The exact opposite of her brother in every respect except appearance. She's an angel of light to his prince of darkness. But if you met her, you'd pick up immediately that they're related."

"And what exactly did you ask of her?"

She pursed her lips, wincing with reluctance.

He'll think I'm a dry brain, with no milk in the cocoa-nut.

"We explained our dilemma. How we'd both arrived at the same conclusion from starts. I told her about Phoebe's hot-headed desire to be with Cobra. How far from being coerced, she was all for it. And of my equally strong conviction I needed to keep faith with my vow to my mother.

"Sister Consuela sympathized and agreed that the best solution was to persuade Cobra to marry." She hesitated and her brow furrowed briefly. "I think she did, anyway."

She raised her eyes to his powerful face, taking in the slash of his cheekbones, the searching hooded eyes.

She flashed him a wry smile. "Funny resolution, isn't it? Dizzy infatuation versus righteous rigor. But Sister Consuela understood."

She relaxed in her chair, look a sip of her lukewarm coffee. Steeled herself to meet his eye again.

"She said Cobra had married very young, and his wife died in childbirth. He's got the idea God has got it in for him, so he hasn't been willing to try again."

Patrick stirred his coffee and contemplated what she'd said.

"Do you think he's right?"

"What? About God having it in for him?"

"Yes."

She laughed out loud. "No. That's just typical male pride. It's the poor wife who died, isn't it? And the baby. It's not their fault what Cobra is or was. Men think the world begins and ends with them."

He watched her for a few moments, considering.

"So. What is Sister Consuela going to do about it? Did she say?" He scooped some of the foam onto his spoon and licked it as his black eyes drilled into her. "Because Cobra's like a man with ants in his pants. He won't hold out for much longer."

She watched him wave the spoon in front of his mouth and then swallow the creamy topping.

"She didn't say. She sent a note saying she'd prayed about it and she considered it a good option. But that's as far as I could go with it. I guess she'll pray about it some more. We can't discount that will make a difference."

"And you? What do you think about it?"

She sighed.

"Of course, I still think it would be best if Phoebe got over the whole Cobra thing. Or he got over her, and nothing came of it. But I accept that's not likely to happen."

"And what about you?"

"What about me?"

"If Phoebe marries him and settles here. What will you do?"

"I hadn't really thought about it. Go back to the Shamrock and look after the kids, I guess."

"You aren't interested in marriage for yourself?"

Dolphie's wry, measured gaze flashed across her mind's eye, and she was startled by a sense of disloyalty, even of betrayal. After all, the man sitting opposite her had risked Cobra's fury by telling them about Consuela.

Here you are, sitting with a man who's probably attracted to you, hankering after someone else. And what's the point of that? You've burned those bridges well and truly.

"I haven't really thought about it," she lied.

"If you stayed here, you'd be able to keep an eye on Phoebe. Make sure she's all right."

She speared him with her eyes, searching for duplicity.

"And what would I do here? I've got plenty to keep me busy at home with the Shamrock and the rest, now that Maa's gone."

He shrugged. "It's up to you. You've got to decide what you want. Something would come up, if you wanted it to."

If you wanted it to.

"Let's wait and see what miracle the Sister and her prayers pull off," she said.

Thirty-nine

Phoebe stretched like a sleepy cat, opened one eye to guess at the time, and closed it again. The sun was blindingly bright behind the shutters on the upstairs windows, so she knew she'd slept late. She rubbed her legs across the fall of the smooth cotton sheets, luxuriating in the warmth and peace of her bed.

It didn't matter that it was late. She had nothing to do when she got up anyway, except sit around waiting for Cobra to show up. A cloud passed across her perfect morning for a few seconds, and then she remembered their meeting yesterday with Sister Consuela, sitting in the nunnery up on the hill.

Consuela was the most amazing religious person she'd ever met, and she'd met a few thanks to her devout Maa. Practically none of them she'd known before had she got along with, but Consuela was different. Consuela was going to solve everything, so she could have her dream life with Cobra.

Consuela would explain the best course of action to Cobra in words he'd understand and respect. If she mentioned the word marriage, she was fearful of his reaction. Would he be furious? Would he lock her up in her room until she complied to his demands? Or, worst of all, would he force himself upon her?

She was aware Cobra was becoming short-tempered and fretful. He'd begun by thinking it was charming to be courting a reluctant virgin. At least she hoped that was what he'd thought.

But in the last week, she'd sensed his temper fraying, and his patience with her was running out. If nothing changed soon, she feared they'd have a most unromantic consummation of the relationship. And that would ruin everything.

Consuela had the answer. She just knew she did.

She shivered with excited anticipation as she imagined the scene. Her in her golden dress and the filmy veil, processing down the aisle on her father's arm to the front of the church. She stopped amid her dream… halfway down the aisle. Her father didn't know they were getting married, so how would he know to be here?

She threw off the sheets and slid off the plumped-up mattress. She had to get word to Brian so he could be here. Halfway across the room, between bed and mirror, she halted. How would she tell her father? She wasn't allowed out, and she had no money. She didn't know how to send a telegram, so she'd have to ask Sadie to do it for her.

She pulled her hair in frustration. Where did she get the idea being Cobra's woman was going to buy her freedom?

●●●●●●●●

By midafternoon Phoebe's mood was souring further. Cobra hadn't come to see her, and neither had Sadie. She suspected someone, Patrick maybe, had warned Sadie off visiting too frequently, but they had so much to discuss! She wondered if Consuela had talked to Cobra yet. And she thought again about Teo.

When she'd had her own personal minder, she'd had a lot more freedom. And that was only right. If she was going to be Cobra's woman, she deserved a personal bodyguard like Teo. Having him around made her feel safe and stopped her from being lonely, like she was now.

But she'd seen nothing of him ever since she'd been in San Francisco, and as a result, she had only seen the inside of the Golden Girl and the unauthorized brief trip out to visit Consuela.

I'll have to ask Cobra where Teo is, and if he's not coming back, request I should get a replacement. It's only right.

A gnawing hole in her abdomen expanded and nudged her lower ribs. She didn't like the feeling, nor did she want to examine it too closely, or to give it a name. Did Teo have a wife and children? Maybe when she was married, Teo's wife and she would have afternoon tea together.

When she was married?

She sighed to herself. Maybe marriage wasn't so important after all. The most important thing was Cobra and her being together.

For the first time in many years, she prayed. To God the Father, or the Virgin Mary? She wasn't sure which would be most receptive to her pleas, but she knew she needed a miracle. Maybe Sister Consuela was going to create one.

She didn't enjoy feeling so lonely, so she prayed that the Sister who seemed so like an angel of peace would draw some miracle down from Heaven soon. Like right now.

Forty

They snuggled together in front of the glowing fireplace, just like they had so many years ago as children, although the mild spring evening made a fire unnecessary for their personal comfort.

Consuela had taken off her veil and was clad in her "off duty" non-religious clothes, a home-woven light wool skirt in a silvery gray color and white cotton shirt. With her hair down and the severe wimple absent, her glowing unlined face looked at least a decade younger than her twin's weary countenance.

"You're getting younger every time I see you, *topolino,* my little mouse," Cosimo said with a sad smile. "Whereas I…" He glanced at her. "…for me, every day is a day closer to death and my accounting with my maker."

"And are you ready for that day, Cosimo?"

Consuela's throat was dry, her voice sounded rusty and rasping, because she knew without him answering what his response should be.

When he didn't respond, she added: "You know my prayers can help you, even there," with a smile.

Cosimo tweaked one of her long black locks. "I'm counting on it. Where would I be without you?"

Cosimo—Consuela refused to countenance calling him by the demonic name of Cobra, with all its connotations of irredeemable sin—draped his brawny arm around her shoulders and she tucked her head, with its crown of long, shining black hair, under his chin.

They had rested like this for fifteen minutes, not speaking, each one lost in a personal revery of childhood moments when they'd been the children of a poor, honest fisherman on the Adriatic Coast.

They'd both rebelled against continuing in the old family ways when they reached their teens, Consuela going into the church instead of marrying and birthing six children like their own mother, and Cosimo into a life of lucrative crime.

After a long time of shared peace, Cobra withdrew his arm and Consuela sat up.

"Why did you call me here tonight?" Cobra asked. "You've got to admit, it's unusual."

"It is, I know," said Consuela. "Fact is, I had a visit from a pair of young women, and it sparked my interest."

"Oh?" he said, his interest drifting off. "What young women? And what have they got to do with me?"

She smiled benignly. "Everything. Everything to do with you, my dear Cosimo. One of them was an extremely beautiful young woman named Phoebe, who I understand you are about to affiance?"

His mouth tilted up in a show of mild annoyance. "However did she find her way to you? She's supposed to be under lock and key for her own protection."

"I have my ways. I've been keeping an eye on you, and I invited her," she lied.

Forgive me, Father.

His eyes widened in surprise.

"I didn't know your sources were that good," he said. "And anyway, it's a rather quaint way to describe a mundane business. I didn't take you for a romantic."

She could see hectic scarlet spots were highlighting his triangular cheekbones even as he spoke.

In their youth, Consuela had many young men offering for her hand, but she'd rejected them all.

"Or are you getting sentimental in your old age?" His words were teasing.

"Neither, *caro mio.* But it's time you stopped playing the gigolo."

Her dark eyes screwed him down, and he saw with surprise that she wasn't joking. She wanted to see him married.

"You know what I think," he said. "And I'm not ready to take the risk."

"Luciana was a long time ago," said Consuela. "You've honored her memory for long enough."

"Is this a word from the Lord?" he said testily. "Because if it's not, drop it."

"I think it's a word for you from your twin sister. Whether it's from the Lord… I wouldn't presume to say. But I do know we'll see no addition to our family line from me. We have left it all to you."

She reached out and tenderly traced his brow with her index finger. When she'd completed that, she moved on to the weary arches around his eyes.

Her sixth sense for such things recognized darkness clothed him, but to her he was still her beautiful, dynamic brother. Always running ahead and not willing to let God catch up.

"You've been out in front long enough, Cosi," Consuela said. "The still small voice says to wait in the cleft of the rock for him to pass over."

His laughter carried a hint of embarrassment. "My dear Consuela. Always ready to talk in riddles."

"Sacred mysteries, perhaps. And this is one. Don't refuse it. She's beautiful, pure, and she believes she loves you. What is there to be afraid of?"

He stared into her dark eyes. "You always know me so well. You already know."

She smiled gently. "I do. You're frightened she'll make you want to be good."

Her finger traced the line of his determined jaw.

"And I challenge you to resist."

Forty-one

"Dolphie, I can't tell you that, because I don't know myself. If I did, I'd happily give you my opinion."

He was asking Sadie about Phoebe, and Sadie fought to keep the irritation out of her voice.

She'd missed out on her Belle coffee this morning, because Count Adolphus Westerhoven had been waiting for her in his coach parked outside the boarding house. As soon as she'd stepped out onto the street, he'd leaped down and accosted her.

Just as well, she thought.

It means I won't have an excuse to see Blackheart today, and that's a good thing.

Sadie screwed up her eyes and ran her hand over her brow, as if trying to smooth out the frown she knew had formed as she wrestled with her answer.

She couldn't pretend she wasn't flattered to see him, although somewhat perplexed as well.

Hadn't she made it clear she didn't need his interference in their affairs? And yet here he was, back to taking an interest.

She cast a sidelong glance at his clear-cut features, the straight, elegant nose and neatly symmetrical brows over a finely wrought jawline made for stroking. Her hand twitched at her side.

Did she just think that?

She shook her head, annoyed at herself as much as him.

This was all getting so confusing.

They rode to the top of the hill and stepped off into Woodward Gardens, two blocks of park superbly suited for gentle strolling amongst birds—the wild ones and captive, like the peacocks—and flowers.

It was a glorious spring day, not too hot yet, and it would have been a delightful outing if not for Dolphie's insistent questions.

Did she feel quite safe?

Had anything more been said about Teo?

"No," she lied. "Not a word." And shuddered at the memory of her most recent exchange with King Cobra, and how she'd sucked up to him.

He's going to be your brother-in-law. You have to get along with him.

"Is Phoebe free to come and go?"

"No, she isn't," Sadie answered. "But is that so different from how any impressionable young woman—your sister, if you had one— would be treated under the circumstances?"

He gave her a searching look and capitulated.

"You're quite right. Some young things need to be protected from themselves."

"You've got it," Sadie acknowledged. "That's Phoebe exactly. I'm glad I know where she is every minute of every day. It would be scary any other way."

"So, what are you hoping will happen next?"

She hesitated, debating inside whether to tell him about visiting Consuela. If she did that, wouldn't she also have to reveal Consuela's identity? She felt guilty about doing that, because the Sister's privacy was important to her.

She shrugged. "We're still working on the hope they may get married…"

She waited for an explosion, but none came.

"Married?" Dolphie sounded uncertain. "You've mentioned that before. You'd be okay with that? Having a mobster overlord for a brother-in-law? Won't that further endanger you?"

"No more than it does already."

She explained about her father's relationship with Cobra and the Bloods. How it was now well-known in New York that they were allied.

"I hate it, but I can't do anything about it. I think the wise thing would have been to stand aloof. Florian got killed in a random street fight. It was an unfortunate event, but Brian can't leave it alone. He wants revenge and he'll end up endangering us all more than before."

But she left out the detail about Phoebe being part of the "war chest." Her cheeks flamed with mortification every time she thought of it.

Talk about bringing dishonor on the family.

And she didn't mention Blackheart's interest in her either. Of course she didn't.

Dolphie gently took her elbow and steered her toward the peacock enclosure and a seat under a flowering shrub with a pleasant lemony scent.

"Life's never dull around you, Sadie. That's for sure. Has it always been that way?"

She laughed. "Honestly, mostly my life has been pretty much dull drudgery. No kidding. Helping with the younger children and my father's business when required. Your life sounds far more exciting."

"My life's been pretty selfish. Yours has been selfless, as far as I can tell. Even this mission out here, motivated by concerns for your sister."

He caught her eye, and his expression grew solemn.

"I respect that about you, Sadie. You are always putting others before yourself."

He held her in his admiring gaze, and a wave of warmth rose from the soles of her feet up through her body. With it, tears threatened.

How long was it since anyone had told her they appreciated her? She couldn't remember.

She swallowed hard and tore her eyes away from his face. She knew her face was flushed pink, so when she glanced back at him, she dove in headlong.

"You're embarrassing me," she laughed, making light of it. "Anyone would do the same in the same circumstances."

Dolphie saw her discomfort. He matched her light laugh, but shook his head. "No they wouldn't. They don't. Not from what I've seen. They're much more likely to wash their hands of it."

She rubbed her face with her hands, trying to erase traces of the last few minutes' conversation.

"They haven't got the deathbed vow," she whispered. "I can't forget it."

He nodded. "I understand. I think. But enough of this serious talk. Coffee is called for…"

He led her to the garden's tea house, and they spent the next hour chatting about everything under the sun except her compromising family. By the time he'd dropped her back at the boarding house, she remembered only too well why she'd been so strongly attracted to him on the train.

And also, as she turned and waved to him from the kerb, why there was absolutely no way for their friendship to go any further than the pleasant exchange they'd shared today.

He'd said it himself.

A mobster for a brother-in-law?

He'd never countenance it. He was just being kind.

Forty-two

Phoebe had the feeling when she woke the next day that Cobra would visit her today. She rose and took a long time shampooing and towel-drying her hair, and in choosing the right dress, trying several on before she decided on the primrose floral silk. That was the one that best set off her creamy skin and darkish hair.

She spent another age in delicately applying skin cream and a hint of kohl to darken her lashes, as subtly as she could manage. Cobra didn't like her wearing makeup, although he didn't seem to object to it on other women. He wanted to believe she was naturally perfect.

Already a walnut-size knot of tension was forming in the pit of her stomach. What would happen when the day came that she needed makeup to cover up the flaws and blemishes that were inevitable with old age? What would happen then?

You can't worry about that now, Phoebe. And that's years away. A lot can happen before then.

She was late slipping down the stairs to the intimate communal area she thought of as her sitting room, but there were no familiar faces amongst the small number of girls who lingered. She was too late for some—they'd already gone to bed after a late night—and too early for others—they were on the late shift.

Such is the life of a bordello party girl, she thought. She gave silent thanks that that wasn't her fate. It would never be, not if Cobra married her. She shivered as the fear she'd suppressed every day that she'd been in San Francisco nudged her again.

What if he doesn't wed you? What then?

She settled on a sofa by the window with an outlook onto Montgomery Street and signaled to Ned at the bar to bring her a coffee. All she had to do now was wait.

Wait, and pray that Consuela's appeals to Heaven on my behalf have worked.

Even with the caffeine kick Ned delivered, she dozed off briefly, and woke with a start. Was this what her married life would be, sitting like a caged canary waiting for the man who fed her to bring her a few crumbs?

She stood to stretch her stiff limbs and shake out her skirt. Luckily, the silk didn't crease too badly. Her back was to the door, and she was looking out the window again, when she sensed he'd come. His electric presence filled the room before he'd taken two steps inside. She turned, her face flushed with delight, and confirmed her instincts. Cobra was here.

She flew across the space separating them, wrapping her arms around his neck, laughing against the bare skin at the base of his throat, his beard tickling her nose.

He responded in equal delight, breathing hard and peeling her arms from him with the sweet endearments she loved to hear. *Tesoro… Principessa…*

He's so romantic.

He scooped her up in his arms and carried her to the sofa she'd just left, sinking down into it with her on his lap. He nuzzled her hairline behind her right ear, sending delicious shivers down to her toes.

"*Caro mio,*" she whispered. "I've been waiting for you."

He sat up more formally and slid her across his knees to settle her more decorously on the sofa beside him.

"*Uccellina,*" he murmured. "How is my *uccellina?*" His baby bird. His chick. Her mind flashed back to the caged canary.

"Happy. Thrilled, now that you are here."

He beamed his wide grin and signaled to the waiter.

"More coffee for the *principessa* and brandy for me."

A little jag of irritation spiked at the back of her neck.

What if I don't want more coffee?

She dipped her head demurely and smiled. "Thank you," she whispered.

He took her right hand in his. "I've got news."

He stroked the top of her head with a proprietorial air.

"I've telegraphed your father to say we're getting married." He sat back, letting go of her hand, transferring one of his two meaty paws to rest on her thigh closest to him in a gesture of ownership. Waiting for her reaction.

"How do you like that?"

She was momentarily distracted by his fat mitt, with its hairy back and sausage-like fingers. She'd never noticed before what clumsy instruments his hands were.

Her attention flashed instantly back to his ruddy face, flushed with anticipation.

"Married," she gasped, the wind knocked out of her. She turned and held his face in her hands. "Truly?" she squeaked. "You want to marry me?"

He released his face from her hands like a rooster fluffing up his feathers to impress.

Ned cleared his throat, the drinks ready for delivery. He glanced at Phoebe as he put the tray down and left them.

"What made you decide to do that?" Phoebe asked as soon as they were alone again.

"Ah well, *principessa,* you are so beautiful. And so young. I don't want any other Romeo getting his hands on you."

"Oh Cobra. You know I'd never…"

"Besides. Your father and I have a deal."

"A deal? What kind of deal?"

"Ahh, *uccellina,* you don't need to worry your lovely little head about business."

He tweaked the curls around her ears, as if rearranging them to his satisfaction.

Again. That trickle of irritation.

"So.. Um… When are you and Father thinking we will be married?" she asked, her heart pounding. She swiped the back of her hand across her forehead, which felt hot and damp. He didn't pick up on her faint edge of sarcasm.

"As soon as he gets here."

She stared at him. "Father's coming?"

"Yes. He's coming immediately."

"Oh. My goodness. Is there anything we need to organize?"

"You don't need to worry your little head about a thing. That sister of yours can look after the God stuff. She seems on close terms with the Almighty. And I'll take care of the rest." His voice had turned sour, and her stomach tightened.

"Sadie? She's harmless. She simply loves her family."

"She's too nosy, if you ask me. But anyway. What else have you been doing?"

What have I been doing? With Teo away, I can't go anywhere. What does he think I've been doing?

She sat up straighter and took in a steadying breath.

"I haven't been doing anything, Cobra. Not without Teo here.

Where is he, by the way? I miss him. When will he be back?"

"Teo?" His face darkened. "What about him? Did he bother you?"

She stared at him, uncomprehending. A long silence drew out between them.

"Of course he didn't bother me. What are you thinking? Far from it. He was always a complete gentleman!"

He was still glaring, and she felt her heart kick up a faster notch.

"Why are you staring like that?" she exclaimed, more emphatically. "I don't know what you're thinking. He was a very good bodyguard. I felt safe with him around. And without him, I can't go anywhere. They won't let me out of here."

She reached out and patted his hand. "That must be your instructions, isn't it? I've seen nothing of San Francisco yet. Just this place. When is Teo going to be back so I can go out? I need to get some things if I'm getting married…"

His face had darkened, and she realized she was gabbling out of fear.

"If you need to go out, you can go with your sister and I'll get Blackheart to go with you. He seems to handle her without difficulty."

He stood abruptly, as if the sweet talk was over.

"Teo is *finito*," he said. "*Finito*." He slammed a menacing hammy fist on the coffee table and she jumped. "Don't mention his name again."

Forty-three

Isla didn't surface at the Golden Girl until late—it must have been close to eleven p.m.—after Phoebe had almost given up on seeing her, even though she kept telling herself she rarely came till late.

As soon as she spotted her Arctic-white hair across the room, she excused herself from a desultory conversation she'd been having with one of the bar girls and made her way to her.

"I thought you'd never come," she said, with no further introduction. "Where have you been the last few days?"

Isla grinned at her. "Here and there. The usual." She put her hands on Phoebe's shoulders and stepped back to observe her.

"Mmm. I thought so. You're obviously getting cabin fever," she said teasingly. She flashed her another sympathetic smile. "Let's get some fruit punch and hear all your news."

All my news.

Phoebe hadn't seen Sadie and apart from Isla, there wasn't another person she wanted to tell "her news" to. She felt a strange sense of premonition, as if telling people she and Cobra were engaged to be married would bring bad luck.

She stopped herself. Were they engaged? He'd never actually asked her to marry him. He hadn't given her the chance to say yes.

Did his announcing his intentions to her father count?

She supposed it did. She wanted to ask Sadie that very question just as soon as she could.

"Have you seen Sadie?" she said as soon as they'd settled in a corner with their non-alcoholic punch. "I want to talk to her and she hasn't been near the place. You hear stuff from Jack and other people. I hear nothing in here. It's dreadful."

Isla hesitated.

"I understand Cobra's warned her off. Maybe not him directly, but one of his men. He's given her the message she's interfering and he doesn't like it."

Phoebe felt an instant charge of annoyance.

"Oh, for goodness' sake. That man is such a pain. I tried to explain earlier when he was here. She's a normal, loving sister. Not a troublemaker."

Then she remembered why she was feeling so sore.

"And what about Teo? Do you know where he's gone? He hasn't been here for days. Ever since we got here, when I think about it."

Isla's face turned nearly as white as her hair.

"Teo?"

"Yes. Teo. The one who acted as my bodyguard. We were together all day, every day. I got used to having him around. And then, Poof. He's gone."

Isla shook her head. "I don't, sorry. The Bloods… they do things their way. I don't know much about them."

Something in the way Isla refused to meet her eyes set off Phoebe's alarm bells. And then there was Cobra's strange reaction when she'd mentioned Teo's name.

"Isla, look at me," she said. Reluctantly, the young woman turned her sapphire eyes on Phoebe. "Good. And now, tell me what you know about Teo. Everything. Leave nothing out."

Isla bit her bottom lip and screwed up her eyes in a worried frown.

"I heard he hasn't been home for several days. His wife, Marisol, is looking for him."

"That doesn't sound like him," Phoebe said. "I hope he hasn't been in a fight and got hurt."

She thought of her brother, his life ebbing away from a stab wound on the street.

She hesitated, licking her lips.

"I asked Cobra where he was and he got furious. He said he was *'finito.' Finito*," she repeated, sounding disbelieving. "Like, finished. What did he mean?"

Isla looked away.

"What's wrong?" asked Phoebe. "Have you heard something you're not telling me?"

Isla began tentatively. "The Bloods, they're ruthless, you know. It's dangerous meddling with them."

Phoebe frowned. "What are you talking about? They look after their own. Cobra always says that. 'We look after our own.'"

"Maybe." Isla wriggled uncomfortably in her chair.

"Why do I feel there is still something you are not telling me?" asked Phoebe. "If you know something, tell me."

"You're sure you want to know?"

"Definitely," she said. "Why wouldn't I?"

"Because once you know, you'll never be able to forget?" Isla's voice was strained and concerned.

Phoebe laughed. "Stop being overdramatic."

Isla scraped her chair along the floor, drawing closer. She looked cautiously around for any eavesdroppers. Then she leaned forward confidingly and said in a low soft voice, "It's *vendicare…* revenge."

"*Vendicare?*" The word had a vaguely familiar ring. A rush of anxiety took her breath away.

"Payback?" she said in English.

Isla nodded. Phoebe shook her head, refusing to let the implications of what she was hearing sink in.

"It can't be. Teo was loyal. He'd never…"

Isla looked around them nervously and held her palm up in a helpless gesture.

"Don't make a scene," she said, her voice low and hoarse. Her eyes were fixed on Phoebe's, communicating a desperate wordless message.

"The walls have ears."

Phoebe starred at her for long seconds, then quietly edged herself off the sofa, still shaking her head.

"I don't believe this. It can't be." She reached out and grasped Isla's arm. "Please. Ask Sadie to come and see me. I need to talk to her. It's urgent."

Forty-four

"Why didn't you tell me before?"

Phoebe's thin wail rang around Dolphie's landau as she and Sadie sat, side by side, facing Dolphie and Isla in the comfort of the four-seater cab, with Elizabeth's driver Bert up front.

"I've explained already. You weren't ready to hear it. And I didn't want to upset you."

"His hand? On the doorstep? I can't believe it."

She bent over her pretty peach dress and quietly sobbed.

There'd been nothing for it but to tell her the facts. No way of breaking the news gently. Sadie and Dolphie had waited down the block from the Golden Girl, ready to pick her up as soon as she'd quietly slipped the leash from the brothel caretakers.

Dolphie had answered an emergency call from Sadie, routed through Isla and Jack, that Phoebe needed to talk to her urgently.

Now they were on their way to Elizabeth's house in Pine Street for dinner. It was the only safe place Sadie could think to meet without being spotted by either Patrick, Cobra, or one of Cobra's men.

Isla reported to Jack that she'd had no choice but to tell Phoebe that Teo was dead. She'd been vague and had spared her the gruesome details, but nevertheless, Phoebe had been distraught.

Isla sensed there was more than the loss of Teo behind her distress, but Phoebe had refused to confide any further. Sadie guessed there was probably some news on the marriage front as well.

By the time they pulled into Elizabeth's driveway, Phoebe's sobs had quieted. She put on a brave smile and stepped out into the rose-scented evening air. They'd barely reached the front step when the door flew open and Elizabeth embraced Sadie warmly.

"It's so good to see you again, Sadie." She turned to Phoebe with a welcoming smile. "And this is the famous Phoebe."

Phoebe gave her a thin smile, and they trooped inside.

Within minutes, they'd completed the round of introductions to Susannah, Cordelia and Jack, and were seated around the dinner table with Mrs. R preparing to serve turtle soup.

Two hours later, comfortably full from a dinner of minestrone soup followed by roast chicken and green beans, the six of them, Jack and Dolphie, Elizabeth, Sadie, Phoebe and Isla, retired to the study for serious talk.

They sat in a half circle around the fireplace, no one quite knowing where to begin. They'd avoided the topic over dinner in deference to Cordelia's presence. Jack had reasoned there was no need for her to be dragged down by the grim realities of gang life, and they agreed.

Sadie cast a sympathetic eye at her sister. "Phoebe, the very first thing I want to hear from you. Has there been any sign that Consuela has spoken with Cobra about you know what?"

Phoebe's cheeks pinkened, and she replied in a self-conscious murmur intended only for Sadie's ears. "I'm sure she has, though he hasn't let on about her. But when he came to see me yesterday, he announced we were getting married."

She rolled her eyes dramatically. "No thought of asking me if I agreed. He just announced it, so I suppose in his world that means it's happening."

There was a shocked silence around the circle. Obviously, although her voice had been soft, everyone was listening with rapt attention.

"And in your world?" Sadie regarded her with an ironically raised eyebrow. "Are you as delighted as you thought you'd be a few days ago?"

Phoebe was very pale, and she swallowed several times. Sadie could see a sheen of sweat on her forehead.

"Honestly? I don't know how I feel about it. I'm just so upset about Teo. I never thought…" She put her hand up to cover her face and straightened in her chair.

They waited, giving her time to recover herself.

"I feel stupid. I feel like one of those people who believed the emperor really had new clothes in that story Maa used to read to us."

She dropped her hand and gazed at Sadie, pain in her eyes.

"I know you tried to tell me, and I didn't want to listen. But today I saw a side of Cobra I'd never seen before. I asked him where Teo was and he got so angry. He told me Teo was '*finito*.'"

She broke down again, and they waited patiently for her to regain her composure.

When she did, she scanned the circle of faces. "I want to meet Teo's wife." Her voice strengthened, and her eyes blazed with determination.

She fixed her gaze on Isla. "You told me Teo had three small children, Isla. Is that right? Well, I want to meet his wife and children. It's something I need to do before I marry Cobra."

Forty-five

"So Consuela worked her magic." The downward intonation in Patrick's voice made it a statement, not a question.

The familiarity of it jolted Sadie from her reverie.

Belle's was especially busy this morning, with every table occupied, and the hum of morning coffee chatter wrapped around her like a consoling blanket.

She blinked and opened her eyes to Blackheart's robust form, holding a steaming coffee in one hand. He glanced pointedly around him, as if making it clear there weren't any spare chairs near them.

"Take a seat," she said, gesturing. "Belle is doing a roaring trade today, that's for sure."

"Because it's market day," Patrick said. "It's always busy when they set up the Farmer's Market in Portsmouth Square."

She dipped her head in acquiescence. "So that's why. I wondered if there was a special reason."

"It's where a lot of that produce you saw growing up on Bernal Heights ends up for sale," he said with a wicked grin. "Speaking of which…"

She laughed out loud. "Cleverly done," she cried. "You want to know how our meeting went with the good Sister?"

"I think I already know part of it. The boss is talking marriage."

A hollow feeling opened up in her chest.

"Really? What did he say?"

Blackheart set his cup down and pulled out the chair opposite her.

"He's already instructed your father he expects him here in a bit over a week. He's made no mention of his sister or of your visit, so I don't know how Consuela pulled it off."

He stirred his cup and watched her across the table.

"I'm relieved to say he didn't seem bothered. He isn't asking questions about how Consuela knew, so I've no idea what she told him, but it seems to have worked."

He grinned. "Looks like Phoebe's here to stay."

His hand holding the spoon stilled, and his gaze on her grew more tenacious.

"And that means you'll have to be making a few decisions of your own. Is that what was making you look so soulful just now?"

She let out a surprised laugh. "You're an astonishing fellow, Patrick Blackheart. You really are…"

"Why?" he asked. "What did you expect?"

She shrugged. "I don't know. Someone less astute, for starters. Less self-aware…"

"So in your book, gangsters can't hold an intelligent conversation?"

Her heart did a peculiar little dance.

This man challenges all of my assumptions. He's dangerous.

"Patrick, in my book, gangsters can't be anything but losers. And you don't strike me as a loser."

He lifted his coffee in a mock salute.

"I've no intention of losing at anything."

And suddenly, the mood between them changed. Her heart was quickening, but the gap between them, the distance of ten coffee cups, was suddenly wider, deeper, darker, and she felt awkward making light of such a serious topic.

Men are killed in Patrick's world, she reminded herself, *and women widowed. Children left fatherless.*

He seemed to sense the change, and he readjusted his dominant frame, stretching his legs out into the surrounding space, edging his body away from her, and slouching nonchalantly with one elbow on the table.

"Is Phoebe over the moon with Cobra's capitulation?"

His tone was still jovial, attempting to make light of whatever cloud had lowered over them.

Without wanting to reveal too much, she caught herself in a quick frown.

He noticed immediately. "I see. Not so much. Women… So why the change of heart?"

She shook her head in partial denial. "She hasn't had a change of heart so much, as reconsidered."

She fingered her cup nervously. She couldn't help it. Her throat suddenly felt parched. She licked her lips.

"I guess she's just realizing marriage is a big step. It's not a game."

He drummed his fingers on the table edge.

"I'm afraid it's too late for second thoughts, Sadie. Cobra's not letting go now he's made the leap. I hope she understands. She's unleashed a tiger."

Sadie nodded in agreement. "Of course. I understand."

She rested her hand on her stomach to quell the inner trembling that assailed her as she spoke the words.

If he knew where she's headed this afternoon…

He drew his stretched legs back under the table and leaned forward with eyes like chunks of coal.

"A little birdie tells me she's planning on visiting Marisol. I want to tell you. That would be a terrible idea."

His coal-black eyes bored into her soul.

She schooled her features to show no response. The quivering in her stomach froze into icy terror.

"Marisol?" The single word came out like a squeaky question.

Pretending not to know who or what Marisol was.

"Yes," he said. "Marisol. You know very well who she is, so don't profess otherwise."

He pushed away from the table and unfolded his rugged frame.

His stern expression was impossible to read.

"I can only go so far in defying Cobra's edicts," he said, warning in every word.

"And you are far too nice a girl to lie convincingly. Stop Phoebe going to Marisol's today, or we may both live to regret it."

Forty-six

Sadie watched Patrick Blackheart's retreating back until he was out the door, and then resisted the urge to wrap her arms around herself to ease the desolation that nearly overwhelmed her.

She'd agreed to the mad idea of pushing Cobra and Phoebe into marriage only because it was the best of the worst options, and she should have known better. She stared at her empty cup, her mind whirling in confusion, when for the second time that morning, a voice she recognized interrupted her musings.

"I saw you in the window," said Dolphie Westerhoven. "Mind if I join you?"

"Of course not," she replied in automatic good manners mode, but her voice held no welcoming ring.

She tried to rally herself. "I mean, please do."

His lean, virile form flowed into the seat Patrick had occupied minutes before, and she snuffed out a quick smile. If Blackheart was a lumbering great black bear, Dolphie was a lithe panther.

"Can I get you a second cup?" he asked, with his best nobleman courtesy.

"That would be marvelous," she said, mustering up enthusiasm. "I need an extra jolt today."

She flashed him a wan smile, and he rose obediently and left to place their order.

By the time he returned, she'd managed to re-gather her energies.

"Thanks so much for your kindness last night," she said. "It can get lonely trying to corral that sister of mine." She attempted a weak smile. "It was very comforting to have you all around us last night, helping disperse the pressure."

He gave a wave of his hand to dismiss her obligation and said, "That's why I came in, actually. I was on my way to catch you and say I'd be happy to take you to see this woman Phoebe wants to visit, when you've got it set up."

A warming on the inside replaced the unsteady feeling that had overwhelmed her at Patrick's warning. It was like the relief of finding a fireside after a frigid walk.

She let out a long, relieved sigh.

"Oh Dolphie, that's so kind of you. You can't imagine how welcome that is right now."

She made a wry grimace and put her hand to her fresh coffee.

"She's got it all set up through Isla for later today. Would that be convenient?"

He nodded. "Totally fine. Happy to be of help."

They sipped their coffees in companionable silence.

Then Dolphie cleared his throat. "Anything else of note been happening?" he asked, his intelligent eyes searching hers.

"Like what?" She had an uncomfortable feeling he had an idea something had changed.

"It's not my place…" His voice trailed off, and he hesitated. Took a quick breath. "Really Sadie, sorry. It's none of my business. Forget I asked."

She laughed. "Forget you asked? I don't think so, Dolphie. What on earth have you heard? I'd like to know."

"I met Patrick Blackheart just now. He was coming out as I was coming in."

Her heart had turned into a lump of stone which pulsed slowly, painfully, in her chest.

"Uh huh? And what did he have to say for himself?"

"He said you were engaged to be married."

"He WHAT?" She stared at him, and the lump of rock shattered into a dozen small pieces, each one ricocheting inside her at high speed.

"He said he had asked you to be his wife, and you'd agreed. He was warning me off."

"Dolphie… He's talking nonsense. He's not telling the truth… He was wrong to…."

She was spluttering, talking gibberish. Starting and stopping in fragments of sentences. Because she felt guilty that she'd allowed things to reach this point.

Dolphie waved his hand. "You're not sounding exactly convincing, Sadie. That day we met on the train. You weren't wholly honest about your encounter then. Were you?"

Her face flushed with guilt. She shook her head and said in a low voice, "No, I wasn't."

"There's no need to feel embarrassed," Dolphie said.

He drained his cup. He'd gulped down his coffee faster than she had. Then he rose to his feet.

"You're entitled to do whatever you wish with your life, Sadie. You don't need me to tell you that. And it doesn't make any difference to my offer of help today. If you want a ride to this woman's place later, I'm happy to oblige."

She quickly stood to meet his gaze.

"I am NOT marrying anyone right now, Dolphie." It was her first coherent sentence of the last few minutes. "And especially not Patrick

Blackheart. And if you are still happy to take us to Marisol's, I'd be incredibly grateful. We'll be ready at the same place as yesterday at three o'clock."

He made a slight courtly bow and left while she sank back to the table in mortified silence.

Forty-seven

Three small children nestled at her side, Marisol sat in a clean, sparsely furnished front room in a cloth-lined waterfront shack at the foot of Telegraph Hill, in the heart of San Francisco's Latin quarter.

She'd once been exceptionally beautiful. Phoebe could see that at a glance. But grief and anxiety had ravaged the smooth skin and crushed her spirit, leaving her a desolate shell of a woman.

A waterfall of black velvet hair still tumbled halfway down her back, and her chiseled features and erect squared shoulders gave her the air of an Aztec ancestor.

But the coal-black eyes looked out of gaunt, sunken sockets, and a hatchet of lines ringed her drooping mouth. A tortured presence, like a mantel of hopelessness, hung over her.

Phoebe's heart pinched as she moved into the room, like a mouse not wanting to disturb a watchful cat.

She paused in front of the hard cane bench Marisol sat on, her arms protectively drawn around the three small children tucked at her sides. Tentatively, Phoebe reached out to take her hand and squeeze it lightly.

The dark-haired girl who had led them into this simple room looked like a bookend to the woman on the bench—almost certainly they were sisters. Her guide spoke into the weighted silence in a clear, firm voice.

First to Marisol, in a Mexican language that bore no resemblance to Spanish and which Phoebe did not understand. Then she completed the introductions in English. "Marisol, this is Phoebe." And then to Phoebe: "Phoebe, Marisol."

She turned to Phoebe. "And I am Pacquita, Marisol's younger sister."

The children stared up with huge brown eyes and snuggled closer to Marisol. A boy, the smallest of them, sucked his thumb. The tallest, a girl of about four years old with a dark fringe that fell over huge worried eyes, clutched a tattered rag doll.

Dolphie's landau had brought them out here from the center of town, because the area dubbed Chiletown in the 1850s hadn't yet been serviced with the cable car or commercial coach lines that were common in many other parts of the city.

Chiletown had evolved into a village of Mexican and Spanish-speaking settlements over the last twenty years, and Phoebe felt as if she'd stepped into a different country.

Sadie and Dolphie hung back in the doorway, uncertain of the etiquette of their visit. The room was small and dim, the small windows shuttered. Apart from the bench the mother and children sat on, there were only two chairs. A cloth pinned to one wall carried a portrait of a dark, heavy-featured man who seemed to watch over proceedings.

Phoebe glanced up at it as she hesitated in front of Marisol. Her eyes filled with tears. It was a very good rendition of Teo, his reproachful eyes in stark rebuke. Like a declaration of his innocence, of reproach, from beyond the grave.

Marisol's sister gestured to the hard-backed chair set next to the bench.

"Sit down and I'll explain to her why you're here." Her English carried a slight Spanish accent but was easy to follow.

She spoke at some length with her sister, Marisol looking up with astonished wide eyes that shafted with fear as it slowly became clear why Phoebe was here.

Before Pacquita's explanation ended, she responded with a cry and turned to Phoebe.

"Cobra? You're going to marry the Cobra?"

It startled Phoebe to realize she spoke English.

She returned to her native tongue to make a sharp, guttural exclamation.

Pacquita interpreted.

"She says don't do it. He is a terrible man. Don't do it."

Nausea hit the pit of Phoebe's stomach.

She turned to Pacquita. "Do you know what happened to Teo? Is it too sensitive to speak of it in front of Marisol?"

Pacquita's strong brows contracted.

"Sensitive? No! We want all the world to know what happened to Theodoro." She glanced at her sister. "Theodoro. That's his full name. It means Gift of God and he was that to Marisol."

Phoebe gulped. "So what do you understand happened? Are you certain he is dead? I just can't believe it."

Pacquita's eyes flashed with pain.

"How do we know? Because that devil Cobra left us his hand to bury. His hand and his ear. That's the only parts of him we had left to put in his coffin."

Her brown eyes filled with tears. Phoebe glanced at Marisol, who, despite speaking in her own language, clearly understood English perfectly well.

She rose to her feet, her face contorted in rage.

"*El asesino,*" she cried.

"El asesino," Pacquita ground out. *The murderer.* Phoebe had heard enough Spanish in Teo's company to recognize the word.

Phoebe's eyes filled with tears.

"And you are certain the Bloods killed him?" she rushed on, not wanting to accept what the women were telling her.

"Maybe it was another gang? Like Satan's Horsemen?" Her voice sounded thin and reedy. She knew she was clutching at straws.

Marisol's eyes were like burning coals as she turned on her with an angry stream of Spanish, her earlier hopelessness replaced by hot anger.

"She says they took his wedding ring, but left the key."

Pacquita made an open-handed gesture.

"She says of course it was the Bloods. It was ordered by that devil King Cobra. She says he is worse than Satan."

"The key? What key?"

"The key he always wore in his ear."

The thundering in her ears told Phoebe she understood. Teo wore a tiny pewter key from a fine chain in his right ear. She'd never known its significance.

"What about the key? Why was that important?"

Pacquita looked at her as if she was an innocent child.

"All the Bloods swear the gang has the key to their hearts. That nothing and no one will come before Cobra and the brotherhood. Not mothers, not wives, not children… Didn't you know that?"

Both the Spanish sisters were staring at her in righteous fury. "Leaving that for us told us they had deemed him guilty. He hadn't kept his promise to make the Bloods first in everything," Pacquita said.

"That's probably why they took his wedding ring, too."

Forty-eight

They drove back to the Golden Girl in ghost-faced silence, Phoebe's white-knuckled fingers locked tight in Sadie's, as if she was heading for her own execution.

"What am I going to do now?" she whispered into the heavy air, not looking for an answer from anyone but herself. "How could I have been so stupid?"

She stared straight ahead. To Sadie, sitting beside her, it seemed as if she was barely aware of either her, or of Dolphie opposite them. She was lost inside herself, in a maze of doubt and recrimination.

As they neared the Golden Girl, the coach slowed to allow for the heavier central city traffic, and she seemed to come back to her usual self. Sadie released her hand and put a consoling arm around her shoulders.

"What are you thinking, Feebs?" She glanced across at Dolphie, who was diplomatically gazing out of the carriage window, trying to make himself as inconspicuous as possible.

He sensed her eyes on him and flicked back to meet them, his gaze full of sorrowful understanding. He remained silent.

Phoebe shook her head, her face screwed up in worry. "I don't know what to think. I need more time," she said.

She turned to Sadie. "Why would they do that? Teo was a good man…"

Sadie's eyes met Dolphie's again, and she raised one brow in a question mark.

'If you really want an answer to that, Dolphie might have an answer."

Phoebe's eyes snapped from her sister to the man opposite.

"What? What do you know that you're not telling me?"

Dolphie let out a long, reluctant sigh.

"Jack's been making inquiries ever since they left the other hand with us," he said. "Of course, we wanted to know as much as you do about who had done this and why. For our sakes. For our own safety."

Phoebe gazed at Dolphie for a long minute, and then said in a quivering voice: "And what did he find out?"

"He's heard strong rumors that Teo was accused of skimming the take from the protection money the Bloods collect, both in San Francisco and New York."

Phoebe was vaguely aware Teo had a share in duties as a moneyman for the security work the gang did, supervising the weekly collection from small businesses and stores in return for protecting them from rival gangs like Satan's mob. The arrangement her father had with Cobra in New York was really a glorified protection racket, with cheap liquor supply thrown in as a sweetener.

She stared at Dolphie, unable to speak. He continued in a gentle voice. "The gossip on the street is that Teo put up the stake without telling Cobra, and kept the difference."

An icy feeling gripped Phoebe's chest so violently, she cried out. She might be an innocent where such matters were concerned, but even she understood being caught out in such a scheme would sign your own death warrant.

She clutched her chest. "I don't believe it. He'd never do that. He loved his children too much to take the risk…"

Dolphie hunched his shoulders forward in a gesture of helplessness. "Maybe he did it because he loved his children and thought money would buy them a better life? Who knows, Phoebe? It appears Cobra believed the story, anyway. Whether or not it is true, who knows?"

Phoebe turned to Sadie, wild-eyed.

"What am I going to do, Sadie? I can't… I never knew…"

She combed her fingers back through her hair and then buried her face in her hands.

"*El asesino,*" she said hoarsely, sobbing into her hands.

"*Me caso con un asesino.*"

"I'm marrying a murderer."

Forty-nine

Phoebe's heart fluttered in her chest like a captive bird's. Cobra loomed over her, his face shiny with sweat, beaming through less-than-white teeth. In his hand he held a velvet bag, its contents tumbled out on his open hand, which he was holding out for her inspection.

A rock-sized diamond ring winked up from his fat palm.

"*Uccellina*" he purred, and licked his kips.

Her mind flashed with a scene from her childhood—not that long ago, truthfully—when she'd found her brother Florian's cat playing with a baby sparrow it had caught in the rough ground behind the bar. The same wasteland where Florian was stabbed to death a few months later.

She'd sprung forward and attempted to rescue the bird, and when she held it in her girlish hands she could feel its tiny heart flickering like candlelight in a draught. And then it had stopped, gone silent.

"It died of fright," Florian said." It's not the cat's fault."

Phoebe gazed into Cobra's face and tried to summon up the ecstasy this ring would have given her even two days ago. Before Marisol.

"Oh Cobra, it's beautiful…"

She detected the tiniest shiver of doubt register in his eyes. Those reptilian eyes, which changed with his moods, granite dark when aroused, a yellow-green when he suspected disobedience or worse, betrayal.

I'm not convincing enough, she thought, and her heart beat even faster. *I've got to do better.*

She slung her arm over his shoulder and kissed his cheek.

"You shouldn't have, but I love it. Thank you." She smooched his face again, then pulled back and offered her engagement finger.

"Come on then. Do the honors." She stared at the sparkling jewel and wished her heart didn't feel as hard as the expensive rock in front of her.

He gave her a searching look, then took up her hand and slipped the treasure on.

She displayed her hand, fingers spread wide, desperately forcing her lips to grin in delight.

"I am so lucky to have you," she said, and kissed near his ear.

He smelled stale and oily. He'd had tuna for lunch, she could tell with one breath. Underneath the fishy smell, a sickly sweet smell of alcohol, probably whiskey, not on his breath so much as seeping out of his body.

She'd never been aware of this aura of odor before. Would this be what her bed smelt like when they were married? She shivered involuntarily.

"Is something wrong?" asked Cobra, a sharp edge to his inquiry.

She snapped to attention.

"Of course not," she crooned. "I'm overwhelmed, that's all."

"In that case, maybe I'd better hold my next news till you've recovered."

Her heart clenched.

"What news?" she asked, plastering her face with the sweetest smile she could summon.

"I've set the date, and I've another surprise. And someone I want you to meet."

She darted her eyes to his face and saw he was watching her closely. Too closely. Again, Florian's cat flashed into her mind. She was a deceptively mild-looking grey and white moggy.

She clasped her hands in front of her body and did a little "so, so delighted" twirl before him.

"You've set the date? When? When is it?"

He visibly relaxed, and his watchful eyes softened.

"In ten days. Your father will be here in seven days, so we're waiting for him."

Oh no. Ten days? Is that all?

"Father will be here? Truly?" She made another mockery of a happy pirouette.

He stepped forward and put his hands on her shoulders, stilling her.

"And I've brought the priest, Father Gregory, to meet you. He wants to be satisfied you're happy with the arrangements. I told him there's no doubt about that! You're even keener on the idea than I was at first."

He gave her a lascivious smile.

"But you need to tell him for yourself."

Fifty

Sadie hovered in the shadows, waiting for Patrick to emerge, frightened to attract unwanted attention, knowing she couldn't risk presenting herself at Blood headquarters and asking to be let in.

She was almost certain the burly guards on the door wouldn't admit her, and she dreaded having to explain herself to Cobra if they did. He had already made his antipathy toward her plain.

I'm a jolly fool, she thought as she huddled in a deeply recessed doorway a few buildings down from the general store, which had closed its doors an hour ago. *I'm gambling on the hope that Patrick is actually there this late. If I'm wrong, I'll be lucky to get back to the boarding house without being molested.*

Whatever happens you're in danger of being molested, you fool.

She wished she hadn't lost her Derringer. She gazed up at the watery sky, and saw the sliver of silver moon was half-obscured by high-level fog.

You don't know that you'll be any safer in Patrick's company than you are on this street.

Look what happened to Phoebe today. She got a horrible shock, and it's quite likely you will too.

She heard a heavy door thumping closed, and a quick exchange of male voices. Her body went rigid with expectation, her ears tuned in for footsteps. Footsteps that came her way.

She waited until a male figure loomed out of the murky evening, wrapped in a stylish woolen overcoat, carrying a briefcase and umbrella. Just like any other respectable businessman.

She was about to step out of the shadows when the figure suddenly stopped. He tapped the umbrella point on the pavement and said, "What are you doing here?"

Sadie stepped out, her hands clammy and her heart racing, and prayed her worst fears were not about to be realized.

•••••••••

They went to a quiet bar on Portsmouth Square. Somewhere, Patrick reassured her, Cobra would never find them. They took up occupation of a very private corner booth with varnished oak walls ideally placed to muffle any confidences they might share.

The place had the warm, slightly tired air of a meeting place that had already seen the crowd come and go and was now just hanging on till closing time. As a bar owner's daughter she recognized the go-slow, almost mechanical arm movements of the staff as they served drinks and cleared battles. Counting the minutes to closing time, when they could quit the closed-up air smelling of beer and cigarettes and be on the way home.

Patrick seemed happy to treat the get-together as a quiet chat between friends, either choosing to ignore or failing to detect her geared-up anxiety. How to introduce the topic which was her sole reason for seeking him out?

Who killed Teo?

And why?

They chatted about what she thought of San Francisco and how it compared with New York.

"I thought New Yorkers were live wires, but they're nothing to here. Everyone's hustling here," she'd observed. "I noticed it from the moment we got off the ferry at the wharf on this side. In New York you'd have to go looking for help from someone to carry your luggage. In San Francisco as soon as you step on dry land you're swamped over by touters, porters and cabmen offering their services."

Patrick had laughed. "So true."

"Belle's a great lady. Have you known her for long?"

"Known her for yonks, as the Sydney Ducks would say."

"Yonks? I don't know the term."

He smiled suggestively, and she was suddenly glad she was wearing one of her buttoned-to-the-neck blouses. She had the distinct impression he was assessing her bosom.

"It means a long time. One of the Aussies' favorite expressions."

From his smile, she wondered if Belle was one of his sexual conquests, and discovered she didn't care if she was.

After what seemed like an eternity, but was only long enough for one drink, Patrick asked, "Want another one?"

She nodded weakly. "I guess so. Tell him to go light on the brandy and heavy on the soda."

He nodded and added gravely: "And then you can tell me why you're really here."

Her hands, which had dried off as they'd sat chatting, instantly felt cold and clammy again. Her stomach churned all the time he was away at the bar, and when he returned, she was tongue-tied.

He placed her drink in front of her and waited.

Glanced across and flashed his wolfish grin. "So what is it, Sadie? Something's bothering you. It's not like you to be at a loss for words."

She leaned across the space between then and said, "Why did you tell Dolphie Westerhoven I'd agreed to marry you?"

Blow me. I never knew I was going to ask him that.

He peered back with surprised, amused eyes.

"Is that really all?"

No, not the half of it, she wanted to say. She stayed silent and smiled in what she hoped was a mysterious way.

He shrugged and took a sip of his refreshed drink.

"I'm hoping it will be true any day now. In the meantime I wanted to deter a competitor. As they say, all's fair in love and war."

"In love and war…" she said. "And what's your definition of war?"

He gazed back, his senses sharpened. Before, he'd been treating this conversation as a joke. Now he sensed a more serious undercurrent. Again, she didn't allow herself to be drawn into further comment.

"War?" His eyes darkened to cocoa brown. Once she'd found that seductive, the way his eyes varied in shade, depending on his mood. Like when his pupils flared when he looked at her. She shivered. Now it seemed threatening rather than appealing.

"I guess war is anything that works against my interests."

"Your interests?" she said. "And what are those interests?"

Again, the cocoa irises flashed, and she sensed he was losing patience with her little game.

"My interests?" He shrugged and glanced away. The piano accordion player was packing up his instrument for the night. Only a couple of other tables were occupied and she sensed the barmaid getting restless.

He stared back, not so warmly this time. The man was mercurial.

"Anything I decide they are."

There was a long, tense silence and then she asked it. The question she'd been planning for all night.

"And would your interests include killing Teo?"

She saw the shock register across his face, the quietly confident sense of humoring her replaced by icy calculation. She saw a man she didn't recognize as Patrick Blackheart.

"Would it bother you if they did?" Prevaricating. Playing for time.

She shook her head. The games were over.

"Just answer the question," she said.

He played his fingers across the plane of the table, as if fingering notes on a keyboard.

"It was him or me," he said, with an odd tone of indifference. "Cobra finally cottoned on to the fact he was being skimmed. Someone had to pay to keep the King happy."

He put a sardonic twist on the words.

"As I say. Either him or me."

Sadie felt the color draining from her face.

Don't ask the question if you're not ready to hear the answer.

"I'm not sure I fully understand. Were you both in on it? The skimming?"

He reached out both his hands toward her, as if to reassure her nothing had changed. She was still going to be Mrs. Blackheart one day.

She shrank away from his touch.

He drew back and regarded her with a mocking glint.

"Of course not. Teo didn't have the brains to double-cross anyone, let alone Cobra."

He must have seen the shock register in her eyes. She drew in a sharp breath and held her mouth tight to stop herself from crying out. She clutched her hands tight to conceal the trembling that had overtaken her whole body.

"You murdered him to cover your tracks." She glanced away from him briefly and then back. The dark eyes glittered and a sardonic smile played on his lips.

He's a fine physical specimen, but rotten at the core.

May as well push in for the final thrust.

"So, have you decided to play it safe from now on?"

He regarded her with appreciative humor.

"Why? Are you going to turn me in?" He laughed at his own joke. And then leaned in to her confidentially. His tone was icy, even threatening.

"Play it safe? Never. I'm going to be a lot more careful. That's all. And keep my eyes out for another fall guy, just in case I need him."

Fifty-one

"The girl is loco. What? Does she think she can lure a man like Cobra into marriage and then change her mind a few days before the wedding? She's loco, I tell you! Who does she think she is?"

Sophia Morrigan ran her hand distractedly over the top of her head, her blazing blue eyes lit with a furious fire. Sadie gaped like a goldfish, still trying to absorb this latest calamitous development.

She'd barely got home after her annihilating meeting with Patrick Blackheart when there'd been a tap on her boarding house door. Isla was there, summoning her to a middle-of-the-night emergency meeting with Sophia.

Apparently earlier in the evening Phoebe had broken down and told Isla she'd kill herself rather than marry Cobra, an admission which was overheard by one of the other "party girls" and passed straight on to Morrigan, who had been livid when she heard about it.

Blackheart's shameless admission that he was the traitor who was stealing from the Bloods had left Sadie in frozen disbelief. Battered by emotional storms like tropical cyclones, she shook with outrage one minute, and grief the next.

His added disclosure that he was the flagrant executioner who had set up a gang brother for the fall and killed him in cold blood? Her mind spun with self-recriminations. How could she have been so naïve as to imagine him—however fleetingly—as some sort of "noble bad boy"?

Yes, she knew the Bloods were a crime syndicate, but she'd allowed his personal charisma, his intelligence, his wiliness, she saw now, to blind her to the full significance of his role.

In that, she was no more discerning than her young sister. When Sadie woke from a nightmarish sleep, she'd been uncertain for a few minutes where she was and if she'd dreamed the whole frightening scenario.

Only Isla's deathly anguished face had brought her back to earth. It was one a.m., and someone was summoning her to a meeting at the Golden Girl to discuss her sister. No excuses accepted.

"Are you listening to me?" She jolted herself back to the confrontation in Sophia's office. Jack had told her Morrigan's ruthless approach had earned her the moniker the Angel of Death and, sitting before her as she ranted, Sadie appreciated why.

The waxy fragrance of the candles burning above the fireplace did not soften the chilling edge of Sophia's words. Sadie was under no illusion. Negotiating any change was not on Sophia's agenda.

"They've declared full-blown gang wars for lesser insults," she roared. "And I am not about to stand by and see everything I've worked for wrecked by some stupid girl.

"If she jilts Cobra, he'll batten down the hatches and strike everywhere he perceives an enemy. He won't be in the mood for expansion, and my deal with him will be ashes in my hand. That will not happen."

Her eyes were cold, and her words struck right at Sadie's heart. She half expected what she said next.

"Phoebe? I don't care about her. She's for the fishes. I'm much more interested in what the humiliation will do to Cobra's reputation. The Bloods will be a laughingstock. Nobodies who considered them invincible will all decide it's time to take a shot at them when they're down and out."

She softened her voice, but rather than being less threatening, it sounded even more deadly.

"She wanted to play in the big league? Well, this is what it costs. There's no room for 'cold feet at the altar.' I can't imagine what's she's thinking."

She pointed a finger at Sadie accusingly. "One more thing. Cobra hears nothing of this. Do you hear me?

"We're all in the line of fire if he does. Now you just go down there and sort your sister's head out. It doesn't matter if she's fallen out of love with him. She wanted him, and she's got him. There's no turning back now."

Fifty-two

Sick to her soul. That's how she felt, and she'd experienced nothing like it ever before. The color, the fragrance, the cheerful pulse of life she'd taken for granted every day, had drained right out of Phoebe's world.

It was as if a thin veil had fallen between her and her surroundings. She squeezed her hands together, just for the sensation of touch, because she felt impervious to everything around her.

The laughter of the other girls, the fragrance of the ripe bananas and peaches in the bowl on the bar, the fluid notes of the birds outside her window, the jingly sound of the little mirrors on her wedding dress…

She corrected herself. She wasn't unaffected by the wedding dress. The robe that had given her such elation, she'd imbued it with her own treasured significance. But now, when she gazed on its shimmering panels, she felt only nauseous dread.

She'd pulled it out of its secure, tissue-lined box to examine her feelings, to stare at it and remember what it used to mean to her, and the experience left her feeling sick to her stomach. Sick stomach, or sick soul. What did it really matter?

My life is over before it even began.

She'd end up like Teo, bobbing through the San Francisco sewers and out to the sharks in the Bay when she failed to please Cobra in their marriage bed. And how could she please him, when the full realization of his wickedness weighed so heavily upon her?

Every time she closed her eyes, the wide brown eyes of three desolate children haunted her, like three little birds lined up on a branch waiting to be fed and ever to be disappointed. She couldn't sleep because of them.

Did she really have to be intimate with the man who ordered their father's death? Pretend to a tenderness and trust she would never feel? She knew she couldn't do it. Not well enough to deceive Cobra. And when he realized it, what dreadful sentence would befall her?

There was a soft tap on her bedroom door, and she rolled over and turned her back to it.

Pretend to sleep and they'll leave you in peace.

She closed her eyes and gaunt, forsaken Marisol's face loomed in her inner sight.

She heard the tap again, and Sadie's voice, no more than a whisper.

"Phoebe. We need to talk."

"Go away," Phoebe bleated.

"I can't. It's important. We've started something and now I don't know how to finish it."

"What's so urgent? Can't it wait till the morning?"

"No. Sorry, it can't. Open up!"

Phoebe grumpily emerged from the rumpled sheets and stalked to the door. She turned the key and yanked it open.

Sadie stepped inside and she closed it behind her.

"Satisfied now?" Phoebe sounded petulant.

"Not really. Seriously, Phoebe. I'm sorry to state the obvious, but we're in deep dung."

"I'm in deep dung. Not you. And tell me something I didn't already know."

Phoebe flounced back into bed and pulled the blankets up around her shoulders. Sadie sat on the edge of the mattress.

"There's lots you don't know, if you think it's just you in the soup. They've hauled me up on the mat before Sophia."

She raised her brows in a wordless challenge and gave a brief smile when she saw surprise register in Phoebe's eyes.

"Yes. It was just like being called up in front of the Mother Superior of the bad old days. Except a lot more scary."

"More scary?" said Phoebe, an edge of disbelief in her voice.

"You'd better belief it."

And she repeated to Phoebe everything Sophia had told her, including how not going through with the wedding would start a gang war.

•••••••••

They talked until the room lightened with the first rays of dawn, and then Sadie snuggled in beside Phoebe and they shared a few hours of restless sleep before they reluctantly opened their eyes to face the luminous day.

They'd gone over every inch of the Cobra-Phoebe affair and agreed the only likely escape route might be if Phoebe appealed to Brian and asked him to intervene.

The problem was, what could Phoebe use as her excuse for her change of heart, without revealing she'd been to see Marisol and bringing Cobra's fury down on her head as well?

Sadie conveniently ignored the fact that she'd kept two critical aspects of the whole affair secret. She hadn't mentioned either Blackheart's betrayal, or their father's "deal" to make Phoebe part of the agreement he and Cobra had made together.

Knowing about either would make everything that much harder for Phoebe, she told herself. Knowing Teo was innocent of any wrongdoing would make her feel even less forgiving of Cobra. And Sadie was secretly terrified that in her upset state she might let slip something about either matter, which could land all of them in an even worse cesspit than they were sinking into already.

She shivered. From what she'd seen of Patrick last night, he wouldn't hesitate to kill again to protect himself. Her life, and Phoebe's, could be at risk, as well as deadly retribution within the gang. She couldn't risk that with Phoebe in the shattered state she was.

"I can't even run away to China. Or Australia. Can I?" Phoebe lay back on her pillow, wide wake now, twirling a brown lock in her fingers as she mused.

"Cobra would still take his revenge on Dad, and you, and the people who helped you. He might even send people after me."

Sadie nodded in agreement. "We can appeal to Daa. But apart from that, there's no getting away from it. Not that I can see."

She tried to be encouraging.

"It mightn't be all that bad. I mean, you were crazy about him. And he will take care of you. Maybe we can help Marisol and the children. Sister Consuela might even play a part with that…"

But she had a bitter taste in her mouth as she spoke the words.

How can you say it, you turncoat? What if it was you forced to marry Blackheart?

The hard reality of their dilemma bit all over again.

"You're not letting me down now, are you Sadie?" Phoebe wailed. "When I'm at rock bottom? I know it's all my own fault, but I need you now more than ever. Please. Don't walk away now."

She turned her face to the wall, held her hands to her abdomen and rocked back and forth, keening, as if the pain was too much to bear.

Sadie fitted her body against her curled back, spooning to calm her.

"I'm sorry, Phoebe. That was a terrible thing to say. Forgive me."

She crumpled her body closer and stroked her sister's arm.

"It's going to be hard, but we'll think of something. You're right. You can't marry him."

Phoebe's keening turned to quiet sobs that gradually faded to an exhausted silence.

Marrying Cobra certainly wasn't the future their mother would have wished for Phoebe. Did that mean she'd been breaking her vow? And what on earth could she do about it now?

Phoebe's breathing was grief-laden but steady. Sadie turned onto her back and stared at the fly specked ceiling.

And gradually, the kernel of an idea formed.

Fifty-three

Sadie pushed herself uphill, her flat leather boots crunching on the gravel path. Her lungs were pumping from the exertion. After two days shut in her boarding house room brooding over her mistakes, asking herself repeatedly how she could have been so stupid to do the things she did, from the vow to her mother on, she emerged, girding herself up to resume the fight.

Whatever that fight looked like. She felt helpless to do anything about Phoebe's situation, and equally unsure about what she should do about her own. Stay in San Francisco and support her sister? Offer hope and comfort in a doomed situation? Or return to New York and her old family duties? Every time she tried to think things out, her brain froze on her, as if the challenge was too overwhelming for her bruised mind.

She'd headed for Woodward Gardens, hailing a hack to the lower gates and then climbing the path to the hilltop lookout on foot. She'd avoided Belle's Café since the confrontation with Patrick, wanting to dodge any reminders of him or the Bloods organization.

And she recalled with a tender nostalgia the walk she'd taken here with Dolphie, although she pushed that to the back of her mind as well. No point in dwelling on botched opportunities. By pushing this idea of marriage to Phoebe, she'd made a mess not only of Phoebe's life, but of her own as well.

If only they hadn't got Consuela involved. If they'd left things to run their course, then Phoebe's fling with Cobra would have taken its carnal run, and then she'd have been assigned to the discard heap. Not a pleasant fate, but better than being chained to a man she despised and was terrified of for the rest of her life, short though it may be.

She strode on, lost in thought, not really seeing anything around her. She was aware of the gentle waft of sea-salt laden air across her face, of the tinkle of birdsong somewhere far away, but of other walkers, or of the flowers and trees she was passing… they were a shadowy mist.

Until she heard a voice close by. On her right shoulder. She stopped mid-stride, transfixed, hardly daring to turn around, her insides frozen.

"Miss McGillicuddy."

An expectant pause. She stood, not turning to confront the speaker. "I didn't expect to see you out so early." Dolphie's voice.

She turned slowly, wishing a hole would open up under her and she could somehow disappear straight into the earth. Be transported, once and for all, far away from the smoldering mess she'd created.

"Count Westerhoven," she said, matching his formal use of names.

One dark brow rose in ironic amusement until he looked into her face. Whatever he saw there wiped the playfulness from his ink-colored eyes.

He stepped forward quickly, one arm reaching out in a spontaneous gesture of comfort. She flinched, bracing herself for his touch. His fluid movement stilled, and with a sharp intake of breath, he drew back.

"Have I interrupted your thoughts?" A flicker of alarm played across his clear features.

He took another step away, as if reassuring her by maintaining his distance.

A movement behind him attracted her attention, and she looked back down the track and saw Jack and Susannah following behind.

The last thing she needed. To have to face this crowd and pretend everything was going just fine. She couldn't do it. The pleasant sense she'd had from the exertion of her exercise, her lungs full of fresh air, turned to panic. The measured beat of her heart as she'd ascended sped up to a tom-tom drumming, telling her to flee.

Her eyes snapped back to Dolphie, and he read her fear. He took one fluid stride to her side and gently grasped her elbow.

"There's nothing to be frightened of, Miss McGillicuddy." He spoke softly, reassuringly, bending into her ear. He let go of her arm and turned to address the rest of his party.

"Sadie and I are taking the side path to the aviary. There's something I want to show her. We'll rejoin you up at the coffeehouse in a little while."

She'd been holding her breath without knowing it. At the touch of his hand, all the tension she'd been holding flowed out of her. With her breath came tears, silent floods flowing down her face. She could not control them. She turned her head to the side, stumbled along the path at Dolphie's side, and had no choice but to let them come.

●●●●●●●●

Thankfully, Dolphie knew the gardens, knew them very well. Long before they reached the popular aviary, he'd guided her onto a side path through a copse of flowering shrubs to a bench seat that looked out to the sea. He'd settled her there and produced a freshly laundered and ironed linen handkerchief.

As she dabbed her face, she smelt the fresh powdery fragrance of laundry soap, felt the pleasant crispness of lightly starched fabric against her skin. She laughed up at him through breathy gasps.

"I must look a sight. Thank you for your kindness."

He scanned her with eagle-eyed brightness and then turned his face away to the view, as if sensitive to her embarrassment. Staring out to sea, he said, "You look beautiful to me in any circumstance, Sadie. Even descending with cobwebs in your hair from a railway carriage ceiling."

He gave a mischievous laugh. "You don't need to worry on that score."

She shook her head, smiling, playing along with his attempt to lighten the mood.

"So much has happened. I confess. It's too much."

"Start at the beginning," he said. "And tell me all."

She glanced around her, suddenly uncomfortable again. "What about the others? I don't want to keep your friends waiting."

He glanced back at her, his face soft with understanding.

"They know the score. They can entertain themselves for a few more minutes."

Sadie blew her nose.

"I've made some terrible mistakes, and I don't know how to fix them." She dabbed at her face.

"We all do that, and nothing's irreparable," he said.

"Oh, but I'm not sure you're right there. This seems pretty hopeless. There's only a couple of faint possibilities left."

Dolphie regarded her steadily. "Last I heard from Isla, Cobra has agreed to marry Phoebe. I thought she'd be radiant at the prospect."

Sadie gave a shuddering sigh. "A few days ago, she would have been. But she insisted on going to meet Marisol, Teo's widow. Teo's three little children were sitting in a bare house, gazing at her with big confused eyes. She said they were like little birds sitting on a wire waiting to be fed. She's gone into meltdown at the tragedy of it all."

She paused. Took a deep breath. "But that's not the worst part."

He turned and gazed out to sea for a few more moments, as if letting the impact of her words sink in, showing no sign of reaction. After a long reflective pause he bent close, eyes smiling, and asked: "Tell me then. What's coming now? What's the worst bit?"

She gave a big swallow to dislodge the lump in her throat.

"She blames Cobra for Teo's death. Jack's information was correct. They accused Teo of skimming off the protection money they collect, an unpardonable sin in Cobra's book.

"So Phoebe's right. Cobra ordered his execution. But what she doesn't know, what I haven't dared tell her, is Teo was double-crossed by one of his Bloods brothers. He was innocent of any wrongdoing. And the guilty party executed him. If she knew that, she'd be even more distraught about the rotten state of the world she's marrying into."

Dolphie had turned to face her as she spoke, his eyes black chips of coal in a somber face.

An extended silence hung between them. Then he opened his mouth.

"And the guilty party was Patrick Blackheart?" he said.

Sadie's hand flew to her throat, where her Adam's apple felt as if it had leaped into her mouth.

"How did you know?"

"Call it male intuition," he said. "When Blackheart came at me the other day claiming you'd agreed to marry him, he had the air of a man who'd stop at nothing to get what he wanted."

Fifty-four

"She doesn't want to do it, Daa. She says it's going to ruin her life."

Brian McGillicuddy glared at Sadie, his face shining red with outrage.

He took a long pull on a two-bit cigar and blew smoke in her face, as if that would express what he thought of Phoebe's change of heart. She dodged the smelly cloud and waved her hand to disperse it.

Her stepfather considered her with narrowed eyes.

She'd invited him out to lunch at Campi's, a popular Italian café on Clay Street which was more wholesome than the usual deadfall dives Brian frequented and was somewhere she could afford and be comfortable doing it.

Seated at long tables covered in coarse gray cloth, surrounded by fellow diners in family groups, women and children as well as the usual men, they'd dined on a seafood salad, followed by vermicelli dressed with beef gravy, Worcestershire sauce and cheese.

Campi's was one of the Bay's most popular family restaurants, and with good reason. The food was tasty, and the mood always welcoming. Brian, however, wasn't sharing in the generous tenor of the place.

When she broached the touchy subject of Phoebe wanting out, he'd got riled up.

"She should have thought of that before she threw herself at him, shouldn't she, darlin'?" His native brogue became more pronounced when he'd been drinking, and today it was strong.

His hand holding the whiskey glass wavered. "And you should have thought of that before you encouraged her to trap him into marrying her. Too big for your britches, you are. Like Davy Crockett said of someone else."

He dissolved into drunken laughter and swayed sideways, knocking the shoulder of the diner next to him, a big-bosomed Italian mama who just laughed and elbowed him back. He was warming up to his topic, and barely registered the exchange.

"Leave you two unsupervised for two seconds and look at what you get yourself into. Persuading one of the most powerful dons in the city—in the state—to marry into the family."

He took a gulp of the fiery liquid and gave her a broad grin. "Well 'n' all, I think it's marvelous. I won't have to worry about security ever again. I should be thanking you."

She snatched away the half-full glass of whiskey that sat in front of him and set it out of his reach. She suspected he was playing up his inebriation to avoid properly addressing the issue.

"Be serious, Father. She will not be able to please him. And when he gets mad at her, we'll all be in his sights. Far from being family, we'll be the traitors, the rotten sheep. She'll be thrown to the wolves in the brothel and we'll be bum fodder."

Brian McGillicuddy's head wobbled in drunken denial. He reached out for the drink she had moved away from him, half rising to his feet as he did. She grabbed at his shoulder to steady him.

"You always look on the dark side, Sadie," he said. "As soon as she gives him a son, she'll be set for life. You know what these Eyetalians are when it comes to family, especially sons."

He took a deep draught from the rescued liquor glass, and gazed around him. "They gave us a good feed here, I'll give that to them."

He burped and turned his attention back to her.

"She's got to go ahead with it. I can't see any other way out of it. It's just silly girl jitters. She'll be fine. We all will be."

He finished the whiskey.

"And that's my last word. I don't want to hear any more about it."

Fifty-five

Sadie…. My beautiful lily is fading away before my eyes.

Long after Sadie had slipped away home, insisting she'd get her own hack back rather than put on a brave face with Jack and Susannah, Dolphie strolled around Pavilion Hill, reflecting on the woman he couldn't get out of his head and her latest bombshell revelation.

She'd carried a careworn sorrow he hadn't ever seen in her before. The marine-blue eyes that usually sparkled with a vital intelligence were drooping with fatigue.

Blackheart, the gangster who fancies himself as Sadie's lover, is the traitor and hit man of the piece. I should have realized….

That day when we met on the train….

I knew I wasn't getting the full story, but I didn't know he was totally without conscience.

A quick recollection of another talk they'd had came to mind… Sadie's distraught face as she talked about her brother Florian's death, and how it had led to the alliance between Brian and the Bloods.

What if Blackheart orchestrated Florian's death to dupe a grieving father into the deal? What if he was already the power behind the throne?

I wonder what else he's had his hand in?

He rested his haunch on an old tree stump and gazed down to the city below. When he'd first come to San Francisco much of the area around the Mission Dolores district that lay before him was pretty much unchanged from the rancho era. It had been the place for racy entertainment—bull and bear baiting, horse racing, fencing and dueling, along with gathering at the famous beer parlor resort, The Willows on Mission Creek.

Now, houses were sprouting up all along the avenues, and Irish immigrants were replacing the earlier Spaniards who'd clustered there.

I want to stay here, make my life here.

And my biggest hope would be to do it with that infuriating Irishwoman by my side.

Seeing her today, he understood she was losing hope of rescuing her sister from trouble. Or of keeping her vow to her dying mother.

She never fussed over her appearance. She always presented an unvarnished, natural self to the world. But today, she'd been pale and dejected, weighed down with worries, her hair straggling down the sides of her face as if she hadn't paid it any attention for days.

She still looked precious to him. The determined set of her jaw, the steel in her sea-green eyes. Her will was enduring as ever. But anxiety was leaving her ragged around the edges. She wasn't about to ask for help, as usual, because she understood the dangers involved and her first thought was always for others.

Whoever held the genuine power in the Bloods, if Phoebe jilted Cobra, it would be a public humiliation he couldn't allow to go unpunished.

How could they avoid that and still get Phoebe off the hook?

He briefly considered doing the job himself. Stepping out of the dark somewhere and giving Cobra the message in a bullet he knew he'd delivered to many others.

He reminded himself he was entering a new season of life. No more renegade acts. He'd only ever shot adversaries in self-defense, and he wasn't prepared to carry out a cold-blooded execution, not even for Sadie.

That kind of thing leaks into your soul, and she already knows that.

No, that wasn't an option. But could he somehow persuade or manipulate Blackheart to declare his hand and assume outright control?

And what would he demand in payment for such a play?

Fifty-six

Sadie glanced down the length of Elizabeth's dining table and felt a flush of pleasure to be sitting here again, as if she belonged here. She catalogued their faces: Dolphie and Elizabeth, of course, and Jack and Susannah.

The welcome she'd received here was the happiest of her life. She'd sensed possibilities, the promise of new beginnings, fresh hopes and dreams…

And how quickly that had all collapsed like a house of cards.

They were meeting because Dolphie had called what he jokingly referred to as a "Council of War" to discuss the next best steps in their drive to rescue Phoebe from a fate worse than death. Sadie had given a little laugh when he'd told her the plan: gather and brainstorm best potential moves until they found something they could work on. But really, she wasn't laughing. She was feeling hopeless.

Phoebe's wedding day was looming fast, and the only "solution" she obsessed over was getting rid of Cobra. Offing him the way he'd dispatched Teo. And she had so many problems with that—moral and practical.

If they killed Cobra, or had him killed, weren't they just as guilty as Patrick was of murdering Teo in cold blood? Was there anything different about the act in God's eyes?

She clasped her hands around her waist and hugged herself, as if to provide comfort from her blackest thoughts. Just because someone was inconvenient to have around, even if he was a desperate sinner, did not give another person the right to kill him.

What was that verse in the back of her mind?

"Vengeance is mine, says the Lord."

She shivered, although it was a scorching afternoon, and glanced up to see if anyone had noticed her discomfort. Her eyes clashed with Dolphie's coal-black orbs. He was watching her with perplexed worry lines across his brow.

What's wrong? he was asking wordlessly.

She shook her head.

Nothing but the obvious. Our dilemma.

They'd finished a comforting meal of baked veal chops and peas. Occasional peals of girlish laughter floated in from the library, where Cordelia was having a tray lunch and playing cards with a couple of new girlfriends.

Elizabeth called the gathering to order.

"We're here to work out how we can release Phoebe from the obligation of marrying Cobra while avoiding the consequences of his wrath. It's a very tricky proposition, I understand that, but one that for the sake of two young women—Phoebe and our Sadie here"—she smiled at Sadie—"we must accomplish. So—some ideas, please..."

She glanced hopefully around the table. Everyone was momentarily tongue-tied, as if the magnitude of the task left them speechless. Dolphie spoke first.

"It's pretty obvious we have to either get Cobra to rescind his marriage proposal, or stop him turning up for the wedding. Either would accomplish our purpose."

Sadie ventured a comment. "From what I've observed in the last week, Phoebe would have to do something terrible to make Cobra want to pull out. And if she did something terrible, it probably would put her in even greater danger, so that's not an option either."

Dolphie leaned forward in eager agreement, hands clasped in front of his body.

"I've been thinking about that. Could we encourage Blackheart to pull off a coup—take control of the Bloods? Do it however he wished. I don't doubt he's already planning for it. We'd simply put up a fee to encourage him to hurry it along. He seems to be motivated by money, so maybe that would work better than anything else."

Sadie scanned their faces and saw Elizabeth's mouth drop open in shock. Even Jack looked slightly askance at the idea. She hadn't told them of Blackheart's duplicity, and it appeared Dolphie hadn't either.

She cleared her throat hesitantly.

"Dolphie is referring to something we've discovered about Patrick Blackheart."

She could feel her cheeks getting hot, and she swallowed hard. Guilt at her own stupidity in ever feeling drawn to the villain welled up inside her.

"He was the one who killed Teo, and it wasn't not simply on Cobra's orders. That would have been awful, but the facts are much worse. Blackheart has been skimming the Bloods' coffers, and Cobra cottoned on something was wrong. I'm not sure how. He confided in Blackheart they had a problem, and Blackheart blamed Teo. He set up an innocent brother and then murdered him to hide his own crimes. And he's continuing with the swindling, blatantly unrepentant."

Elizabeth jolted forward.

"How on earth do you know all this?"

Sadie's cheeks flared an even deeper red. She could feel the heat of it.

"I'm mortified to admit he was angling at making me his companion or wife or something. I'm so ashamed he could even think that would be possible."

She broke off and glanced wildly around, not wanting to meet anyone's eyes.

"I'd rather sink through the floor that admit it, but when I challenged him about Teo's death, he thought it was a joke. I had no idea…"

Bile rose in her throat and cut her off. She twisted away from the table and coughed into her hand.

A painful silence fell, long enough for Sadie to finish her coughing fit, get her breath back to something resembling its normal rhythm, and swing back to face her companions.

"I'm terribly sorry to involve you in something so despicable."

Elizabeth reached her hand out and grasped her wrist gently.

"It's not your fault, Sadie. You have no reason to feel responsible."

"I brought him into your lives," Sadie said, her voice charged with self-recrimination.

"If I'd had any idea…"

"But you didn't," Susannah said.

Sadie's head swiveled in astonishment. Susannah! She was the last person Sadie expected understanding or sympathy from.

"You assume responsibility for the happiness of all around you, Sadie," she said with a tender smile. "You certainly do not need to extend it to some jayhawker."

Sadie felt tears well up, and held herself rigid to suppress them. She could not cry. She gazed at Susannah, her speech stolen from her, and could see from Susannah's answering softness that she understood.

There was another long silence, and then Elizabeth spoke into it.

"Count Adolphus Westerhoven, I would never have believed I'd find myself in agreement with a proposition to hire a hit man."

She set her mouth in a line of grim humor. "That's what you're suggesting, isn't it?"

"That's one way of looking at it," said Dolphie, flashing a cheeky grin. "A slightly less damning view is to say Patrick is angling to grab control of the Bloods eventually and we are making it worth his while to do it now."

"Excellent idea," Susannah said, her voice with the whipping crack of a school principal admonishing a naughty student. "I, for one, am in favor."

Almost as one breath, they broke into uneasy laughter at the absurdity of the idea and then agreed to its necessity.

Fifty-seven

Kate Buchanan's Morton Street parlor house seemed the perfect setting for the urgent meeting with Patrick Blackheart, seeing as it was unthinkable that Elizabeth would ever invite him to her home or converse with him in a public café.

When the Countess was engaged in her charitable work on behalf of abused women and children, Kate had become one of her closest colleagues and friends.

She was a well-mannered, educated woman of middle years, and Elizabeth had never ventured to ask how she came to be running a "boarding house" that was really a front for a high-class brothel. The clientele was discreet. There was never any drunkenness outside or violence inside, and so the neighbors and police turned a blind eye to her activities.

Downstairs in the stately Victorian manor, all appeared seemly, with potted ferns and string quartets and gentlemen relaxing and talking with attractive well-dressed young women. Elizabeth had never ventured upstairs to well-appointed bedrooms fitted out in fine oak furniture, where the revenue-gathering activity took place.

And it was in one of the private downstairs sitting rooms that Dolphie and Elizabeth confronted Patrick Blackheart on the evening following their Council of War.

They agreed, against a background of Sadie's muted protests, that Elizabeth and Dolphie would represent the McGillicuddy interests in a move designed to protect Sadie from her overactive conscience. In truth, Sadie never wanted to lay eyes on Blackheart again, reminded as she was every time she saw him of her foolishness in not seeing what he was from the beginning.

So Dolphie had waited patiently in Belle's Café for Blackheart to make his regular appearance, and arranged this rendezvous for that evening.

Blackheart had sauntered in with his usual confident aplomb, greeting both Kate and her key staff members with familiarity. When Elizabeth had asked Kate if they could make use of her residence, it became clear Kate knew of Blackheart's reputation.

"The classiest hood in the Bay," she said with a sly grin. "Could pass for a well-to-do businessman any day. In fact, I understand he frequently does."

"Don't tell me you've tarried with him, Kate," Elizabeth said, surprise registering in her voice. The way her friend spoke of him carried with it a sense of fond indulgence.

"Oh no, not me," she said with a laugh. "I've got more sense. But there's plenty who have, and I don't mean my own girls. Many a married lady about town finds him irresistible. They happily pay for the room for private dalliance. Whether they pay the gentleman as well…"

She gestured with flat open palms and left the question hanging. "I suspect Blackheart picks up enough business intelligence from their loose tongues to more than make up for his time."

Elizabeth gusted with laughter and put up her hand in a protective gesture.

"Don't say another word, please."

And now the "gentleman" in question sat before them.

"Mr. Blackheart, you'd appreciate, I'm sure, that it's highly irregular for us to be meeting like this. We're only doing it because of mutually unusual circumstances."

Patrick Blackheart inclined his head to her, offering a small courteous smile which belied the dark intensity of his eyes, which she was certain took in every detail in the room. He radiated a watchfulness that went far beyond normal observation. He seemed capable of drinking in mood, private thoughts, the invisible cues that would give him an advantage in any negotiation. Elizabeth suppressed a shiver.

He was cool-headed and handsome, with his roving hawkish eyes and a mobile, expressive mouth, but beneath the facade she thought she could detect the cold devil Sadie had described. But would she have sensed it if Sadie hadn't already warned her? She honestly did not know.

Blackheart barely acknowledged her first words with a slight dip of his leonine head. He remained silent, regarding her with a sardonic insolence that stretched out to the point of embarrassment. Just as she was feeling obliged to continue, he spoke.

"I presume it has something to do with Miss Sadie McGillicuddy? It appears your friend here, the Count"—he spat the title out as if it were a plum stone he was discarding—"has developed an interest in the girl?"

Dolphie stiffened beside her and Elizabeth slipped a restraining hand to his thigh, as if reassuring an unsettled horse.

"Not Sadie so much as her sister, Phoebe," Elizabeth said with a definitive ring.

"Phoebe? What about her?"

She'd surprised him.

"She wants out of the marriage," Dolphie snapped. "And we

thought you might be interested in a deal to arrange that." He regarded Blackheart with icy contempt.

"For a price, of course. A hefty price."

Elizabeth felt hatred emanate from the Irishman as he wolfishly eyed Dolphie, turning over his last statement as he did. Then he responded, slowly, oh so casually.

"Arrangement? What kind of arrangement did you have in mind?"

"It seems clear your intention is to rule the Bloods someday? Supplant the King, so to speak?" Dolphie injected a derisive edge into the words, and Elizabeth saw Blackheart's shoulders rise, as if he were a Sacramento salmon unable to resist a lure.

"Supplant Cobra? Who told you that?"

"No one told us, Blackheart. But an ambitious man like you? You've not going to be satisfied playing second fiddle for much longer."

Dolphie scanned Blackheart from head to toe, as if making himself certain of this last statement, and then cast his eyes to the bookcase in the room's corner before returning them to his quarry.

"Particularly as you are obviously a man of ruthless intelligence. Far greater intelligence than your boss."

Blackheart smirked. "Now I know Miss McGillicuddy has been telling tales. Silly girl. Hasn't she discovered that frivolous gossip is dangerous?"

The coal-black eyes flashed dangerously.

Poor Sadie, for ever being at this man's mercy, Elizabeth thought. Thank goodness she found Dolphie on that train.

"Miss McGillicuddy has nothing to do with it," Dolphie snapped.

Elizabeth patted Dolphie's knee and leaned forward confidentially.

"My friend is right," said Elizabeth. "We are only concerned about Phoebe's plight here. Now if you could bring forward your plans regarding Cobra, there's a handsome incentive in it for you. That's all you need to know."

Blackheart's eyes flashed again. This time, Elizabeth was pretty sure it was with greed.

"You want it done soon? How soon?"

"Soon enough to stop the wedding," Elizabeth said with the sweetest of smiles. "So before Friday."

Blackheart gazed into her face for a long minute. It was like being probed by the devil. She tightened her jaw and called on all the powers of heaven to protect her.

"That's not enough time. No time at all for something this delicate."

Delicate. What a strange word to use in connection with plotting murder, but Elizabeth understood. He had the fastidiousness of a stalking cat for scheming.

"You're a clever man, Blackheart. From what I hear, a brilliant man. I'm sure for one hundred pounds sterling you could advance your plans?"

Blackheart's eyes widened and seemed to get even darker—to a purple-tinged indigo.

"One twenty," he said on reflex.

Elizabeth laughed as if that was the funniest thing she'd heard all week.

"We'll settle on one ten," she said with a certainty that brooked no disagreement, and Blackheart accepted with a curt nod.

"You've got two days," Elizabeth said, rising. "Or else the deal's off."

Fifty-eight

Elizabeth sailed into the breakfast room later than her usual, pleased to catch Sadie still lingering over her coffee. She'd returned to the boarding house to sleep, but they'd arranged she'd return first thing to get a report of how the meeting with Blackheart had gone.

"Did you get any sleep at all, last night?" the Countess asked in a gentle voice, gazing into her face so closely Sadie felt the urge to hide.

Instead, she threw her head back and laughed.

"I know I look like hell. So no, not much. I couldn't sleep for worrying about everything. How did your meeting go? Tell me."

Elizabeth sat down in a gust of high energy, her violet skirts subsiding around her as if they couldn't keep pace with the wearer.

She reached one hand out for the silver coffeepot and paused theatrically.

Sadie laughed again.

"You're enjoying this. Please… Put me out of my misery."

Elizabeth smiled back.

"He's agreed to do it. It's best we know nothing of how he'll arrange it."

Sadie stared at Elizabeth, almost afraid to believe what she'd just heard.

"He will? Phoebe won't have to marry Cobra?"

Elizabeth gave a quick laugh.

"I hate to say it, but she can't marry someone who's dead. At least I've never heard of it happening."

Sadie tried to laugh, but truthfully, all she felt was nauseous. Because of her arrant stupidity, a man was going to lose his life. And that didn't sit well with her, even if it meant freedom for her sister.

Because Patrick was also going to have one more deadly sin against his soul. A temptation she'd presented to him on a platter.

She pinched her lips together and tried to gain control of her rampant emotions. Grief. Fear. Loss. Outrage. Guilt. And relief. She dropped her head into her hands and tried to stop her throat from choking up again.

Elizabeth leaned over and topped up Sadie's morning coffee.

"He's a dangerously charismatic fellow, this Patrick Blackheart, isn't he? I can see why the ladies fall at his feet."

Sadie's head jerked up out of her hands.

"They do? I didn't know that, I confess. In New York, he seemed sensible. It was Cobra who played Lothario."

Elizabeth's smile was full of gentle understanding.

"You liked him, Sadie, didn't you?"

Sadie felt her defenses crumbling again. The tears were hot behind her eyes. She scrunched them shut to stop the flow.

"I don't know what's wrong with me lately," she gasped as she dashed droplets away from under her eyes. "I seem to be falling apart. This isn't how I used to be. I've always been strong for my family."

"Oh, don't blame yourself, Sadie. You've had far too much to handle on your own. And you're not on your own anymore."

The half-eaten croissant with strawberry jam on her plate suddenly felt like too much to swallow, even though the sweet scent was tempting. She took a sip of her coffee and it tasted bitter and cold. The mantelpiece clock ticked loudly in a pregnant silence.

Sadie was suddenly glad it was only Elizabeth present. Jack and Dolphie were off doing some men's business together, and Susannah was taking Cordelia through her lessons.

Elizabeth's kind eyes regarded her in silence, and then she rose gracefully from her seat. "Let's take a round in the garden. There's something I want to show you. Bring your coffee with you to sip as we inspect the roses."

Grateful for any escape, Sadie obeyed. Outside it was a gloriously sunny San Francisco morning. The sun touched their cheeks with a warm glow, but it wasn't burning hot, as it would probably be later in the day.

The air was full of the scent of the surrounding flowers, but Elizabeth quickly bypassed them and led her to a red and orange flowering bush at the back of the garden. She stood on tiptoe and gently pulled aside branches to reveal a miniscule rounded nest about the size of a walnut shell containing two tiny eggs the size of green peas.

"Look," she said, her face alight with the pleasure of discovery. Sadie leaned in and allowed herself to be thrilled with the jewel of nature before her.

"Oh. It's sublime," she whispered. Somehow, Blackheart's dross slipped off her. She felt cleansed by the nest's perfection.

Elizabeth's face glowed. "The female builds the nest alone and also does all the feeding. The male often clears out and finds another mate after the babies hatch."

Sadie felt a choking laughter bubbling up from within her. Bubbling up with such pressure, she couldn't push it down. She stared at Elizabeth, her face streaming with happy tears.

"And there's no doubt a lesson in this for me somewhere?" she gulped through hurried breaths.

"There is indeed, my sweet girl. And it is, don't wind up like the ruby-throated hummingbird. Doing all the work and then getting walked out on."

When Sadie's hysterics had settled, Elizabeth took her hand.

"I understand what it's like to be attracted to a bad boy," she said. She squeezed Sadie's fingers, as if to communicate she understood.

"Thoughts of Jack haunted my early years. I couldn't escape them. Hopeful, infatuated, amorous thoughts of Jack. And Jack had no thoughts at all about settling down with a good girl like me. My mother saw the danger and shipped me off to Hawaii to get me away from him."

Elizabeth gave Sadie a wry, partly sad smile.

"It was completely the right thing to do, but oh, how I missed him."

Sadie licked her lips.

"So. How is it you're good friends now? And he's still not married?"

"Oh, Sadie, that's a long story, and now is not the time. But let's just say he came back into my life after my husband died. And that old tom-tom drum still beat in my heart, even though he was still a rascal.

"We were very close around the time Cordelia was born, but he considered I let him down badly over her care. He wanted something from me I couldn't give.

"He went off and lost himself in the underworld for a few years. When Cordelia vanished, he did too. I'm telling you all this so you'll understand. We're all susceptible to being captivated by the wrong men.

"Of course, Jack's nothing like Blackheart. Nothing at all. He's a basically decent man who rebelled against his family's expectations.

"It's taken him an awful long time to grow up. But you're not the only woman who's got hooked on the wrong messages. Take heart from that. And you've still got a dazzling future ahead. I'm certain of it."

Mrs. Roderiquez came bustling out. "Your next appointment is due in ten minutes, Madame. Do you want me to set up coffee in the library?"

"Oh, my goodness." Elizabeth took a step toward the house and pulled herself up. "Time has flown talking with you, Sadie. There's just one more thing I want to say before I disappear. I want you to come back to Pine Street. Return here as my guest. I insist on it.

"You ran away because you thought you were protecting us, but that danger is now passed, and I want you back. You're the perfect counterbalance to Susannah and Cordelia, and I won't take no for an answer.

"Organize your things and I'll get Dolphie to pick you up. Say about three o'clock? We'll confirm with you later."

Fifty-nine

When Elizabeth sent a messenger boy two hours later confirming Dolphie's arrival at three p.m., Sadie was already packed and ready to go. She still had only one carryall which easily contained the trousers and shirts she'd brought with her and Elizabeth's two dresses, so it hadn't taken her long.

At ten minutes to three she was outside her Kearney Street boarding house waiting, nervously tapping her foot on the pavement, excitement filling her as she watched the swarms of vehicles pass by on the busy thoroughfare. A lumbering truck piled high with hay for the local stables. Wagons laden with bread, vegetables, and beer, being offloaded at every turn to waiting merchants.

Four ladies in landaus out on an afternoon drive, leaning back languidly surveying the scene, white veils floating from flowered hats. Two women in bright satin gowns and lace shawls alighting from a carriage, chattering like tropical parrots, heading arm-in arm for the fashion store or the milliner's, pushing past the apron-clad washerwoman without even seeing her or her chapped hands, permanently reddened by acid soap and hot water.

And everywhere the peddlers with trays of flowers, and hustlers pushing handcarts displaying peanuts and oranges, buttons and penknives. Between the jeweler and the milliner stores, the sellers of fruit, conserves, soaps and shoes invading the sidewalk.

And amidst it all, Chinamen scurrying as if fleeing the scene, their pigtails bouncing down their backs, snow-white stockings showing over boat-shaped slippers. Just another working day on Kearney Street.

She was on the verge of a new life, and she didn't know what she was looking forward to. Would it be here in this dynamic new Pacific Coast city, or back in New York with her family? The one certainty she had was that Phoebe wouldn't be forced into marrying Cobra. Would she?

A tremor of doubt racked through her, a cloud she couldn't dispel with all the sunshine, the dynamism, the energy that fizzed around her. Not that Blackheart wouldn't have the ruthlessness to carry out the deal he'd entered with Elizabeth. She didn't doubt he was capable of executing it. But still she heard a niggling inner voice that said something—everything—could still go wrong.

That she was born to serve others, not follow her own selfish desires. Wasn't that what led her here in the first place? Not wanting to let her mother down? Allowing herself to be pressured into making that vow in the first place? Could others really save someone from making the wrong choices? Could Dolphie and his friends really save her?

She was idling on the sidewalk, lost in daydreams, twirling her parasol in the afternoon sun, when she sensed a familiar presence loom over her. Her legs felt weak, her mind went blank. That familiar scent—of tobacco and leather—enveloped her. Patrick. Her legs felt as if they were going to collapse and she momentarily staggered.

He grabbed her right elbow and leaned close, right down to her cockleshell of her ear. He spoke in a menacing, intimate whisper that sent shock waves through her.

"You're coming with me." She wrestled away from him, staring into his commanding face. The black eyes drilled right through her.

"And why would I do that?" Strength surged up from somewhere deep in her soul. Her voice summoned far more authority than she actually felt.

One side of his mouth curled in a sardonic grin she once might have thought alluring, but which now repelled her.

"That's what makes you so irresistible, Sadie. Your defiant streak. Such a pity you've wasted it on the tribe of the anemic righteous. You've got potential for far greater things than being a slave to your bird-brained sister."

Sadie's face flushed hot and angry.

"I think we've already agreed our ways have parted, Patrick. Never the twain shall meet, and all that?" She sounded snappy. Derisive. And far more confident than her quaking insides should have allowed.

The arrogant smile broadened to both sides of his lips.

"Not quite," he said. "There's an addition, an addendum clause you might say, that I'm adding to the contract. A non-negotiable one. In my mind, it's always been part of the deal, although I wasn't going to haggle over it with the Countess or her blue blood hanger-on."

His face was alight, as if he was producing a winning royal flush before an expectant crowd.

He bent low and murmured. "Unless you to come to me for one night of pleasure, the deal's off." His spittle spattered her cheek. "You might be a virgin, sweet one. Another of the things I find irresistible about you. But I most assuredly am not. And I intend on making it a night you'll never forget."

He abruptly stepped away.

"Who knows?" he called louder, his expression jeering. "You may never want to return to the City of Light. In fact, I'm counting on it.

I mean, what will your pasty-faced Count think when he discovers the Prince of Darkness has deflowered you?"

The intense triumph in his eyes turned her insides to ice.

"Oh, and one other thing. This is between us. No running to the Countess—or the Count—and telling tales, or who knows? Phoebe may not look her pretty self in that gold dress. She'll need to hide under the veil at the altar on Friday. And Cobra will certainly still live to wed her."

His voice mocked her.

Around them, the throng of peddlers, too-hot businessmen in fashionable black overcoats, hostlers scooping up horse dung into handcarts, surged on, no one paying any attention to a man and a woman having what must seem a mild disagreement in the heat of the day. And why should they take any notice?

Sadie felt as if her life were falling apart around her, and there was nothing she could do. If she cried for help, Patrick would fade away. Anyone who came to her rescue would look askance. *What's wrong, lady? Where's the damage? The bruises? Why are you crying wolf?*

And Patrick would have won anyway. If she tried to run? The same outcome.

This was all about power. About proving he was the master of their universe.

He thrust his hand into his coat pocket and pulled out a wad of dollar notes. He pushed them into her numb hand.

"Buy yourself something pretty to wear for tonight. I'm sick of seeing you in those hand-me-downs. And be ready for me. Right here, at eight p.m. Or no deal."

He gave a last triumphant laugh.

"You should be flattered I think you're worth one hundred and ten pounds sterling. There's plenty of desirable flesh available for a lot less."

And in a half minute, he'd gone. All that remained was the leather and tobacco smell still lingering in her nostrils. She gazed around her. The splendid, and the vile. Everywhere.

And if a miracle did not bless her in the next few hours, the vile was her portion. All hers.

••••••••

Dolphie turned onto Kearney Street and peered through the seething crowds with anticipation. A collision a few blocks up at the corner of Clay and Kearney had delayed him by twenty-five, maybe thirty minutes. Nothing he could do about it. A wagonload of timber had spread across the intersection, blocking any passage. He was certain Sadie would still be waiting.

He found a parking spot just two doors down from the boarding house and leaped down to the street. He bounded the few paces to the boarding house entrance, his anticipation rising with every step. He hovered at the entry to her house, casting his sight here and there, adjusting to the throng, expecting Sadie to come bustling forth at any second.

But there was no sign of her. He lingered on the street a few minutes more, thoughts tumbling through his head. Where would she go if she thought he wasn't going to turn up? Would she get a hack under own steam to Elizabeth's? Perhaps her packing had delayed her, though she had little enough to bring with her. Maybe she'd retreated to the quiet of her room?

He ricocheted into the boarding house and found the downstairs office, tucked just off the street. A burly woman with dusty hair pulled back in a bun stood behind the desk, her expression accusing before he'd opened his mouth.

A sign on the desk—one more fitting for a bank director—declared: Mrs. Elsie Morrow. Manager.

"Ah, Mrs. Morrow," Dolphie said, producing his most charming smile. "Miss Sadie McGillicuddy. Is she here, by any chance?"

She glared at him out of a tired face, a prominent wart on the tip of her nose its most outstanding feature.

He found it hard to keep his eyes off it.

She scowled, and the wart slid sideways.

"She's gone. Checked out with her bags—oh—maybe an hour ago. Said she won't be back."

She made every short statement sound like an indictment.

"Did she say where she was going?"

He realized his mistake as soon as the words were out of his mouth.

The scowl turned to scorn.

"Why would she do that? None of my business. Who knows? Maybe she's found herself a fancy man like that codger I saw her talking to on the street. Fine-looking fellow he was."

"Oh? What did he look like?"

The surly Mrs. Morrow peered back, her eyes moving over his form, checking him out, up and down.

Didn't miss much, this one.

"He's the same codger I seen her having coffee with across the road, semi-regular like. At Belle's. Couldn't miss them because they always sat in the window seat. Got the impression she wanted the whole town to see she'd got a handsome chap after her. Maybe he's got what he wanted."

Her eyes went back to the papers before her.

"One thing's for sure," she muttered. "She ain't coming back here."

And Dolphie understood he'd been dismissed.

Sixty

Sadie clutched a handkerchief to her face as the Bernal Heights coach lurched and banged its way over the dusty track to Consuela's convent school. She'd used some of Blackheart's money for the fare here, and she planned to give the rest of it to Consuela as a charitable offering. The handkerchief gave her respite from breathing in the dust and grass seeds that whirled around them.

But it also helped conceal her anguish as she recalled her very recent conversation with Patrick Blackheart.

You may never want to return to the City of Light… I'm counting on it.

She felt sick to her soul. Recalling his words prompted instant nausea, but worse than that. His mockery soiled her. To count the precious things of life so cheaply, and to be included in that assessment. She leaned forward and coughed into her handkerchief. The rawness in her throat combined with the dust made it difficult to breathe.

She'd had just one thought when Blackheart had swaggered away, so confident he'd won. He'd take the money and the girl, all for the cost of a man's life. One he was planning on dispatching, anyway.

And there was one thing she was sure of. She would not be a

bonus chip in Blackheart's perfidy. She had only one choice. Go to Consuela. Tell her everything. She stopped herself. Well, nearly everything. And ask her to warn Cobra about Blackheart's plans.

She'd leave out the part where Phoebe didn't want to marry him. And the part about the deal with the Countess. She did not know where that left Phoebe. But she would not be a sacrificial lamb to her sister's folly, even if it meant breaking her vow.

Did that make her an even bigger traitor than Blackheart himself? She didn't care.

Above the awful creeping sense of being stained through her association with Blackheart, over the grinding nausea in her guts, she heard a roar in her spirit, the thunder of violent indignation. Defiance? Was that it? Was this what Blackheart called defiance?

Well, he'd see what she could do with defiance.

The wagon drew to a stop outside the convent school, and she dismounted and followed a group of young children who ran ahead of her up the path to the main entry. The sense of cool peace that soaked into her as soon as she stepped over the threshold struck her again. Her heart sank at what she would have to confide to Consuela, but she guessed the Mother Superior already had few illusions about her brother's life.

•••••••••

"Sadie!" Consuela rose from behind her desk, both hands extended in greeting, her voice laced with genuine warmth and surprise. "What brings you here? Not bad news, I hope?"

Consuela's kindness, her perspicacity, her galvanized serenity… As their fingers touched, the sadness of the tale she was about to tell boiled over. Before she knew what was happening, she burst into a flood of tears.

Shock. This is what shock feels like.

The same young nun who had greeted them the first time—Penelope, wasn't it?—quickly backed out of the room and closed the door firmly behind her. Sadie sank into the one chair that sat in front of Consuela's desk and mopped her face with the handkerchief she already had in one hand.

Consuela waited patiently, not attempting to console or question, so calm Sadie suspected she had withdrawn into wordless prayer. After the emotional storm had passed, Sadie gazed up at her, and dipped her head in sympathy.

"Bad news it is," Consuela said. "Take your time, dear girl. I'm used to hearing sad stories."

The tale poured out of her. As she talked, Sadie realized it was a relief to share the complete story—well, nearly the complete story—with Consuela. She spoke of Teo, a loyal lieutenant of the Bloods gang, for sure, but also a family man, not given to wanton cruelty, a chap who'd given her sister a sense of safety and companionship when she had little else, and the horrible fate he'd suffered.

She didn't like telling Consuela what her brother's activities involved, but she knew in her heart it would be no surprise. Consuela's face settled into ever graver lines as she continued.

"Does your sister know what happened to him?" Consuela asked in a still voice.

"Yes... Yes she does. I must admit I kept it from her for quite some time, but eventually one of the other girls told her..."

"And what was her reaction?"

This was going places she hadn't intended to divulge.

"She..." Sadie stuttered, hesitated...

"Tell me, Sadie. I want to hear it all..."

"She was very upset. We went to visit Teo's wife Marisol, and their children, and she was even more disturbed."

There was a drawn-out silence. A bell sounded, possibly for the end of class, and Sadie was aware of children's voices, excited but muted, in the corridor outside.

"And?" Consuela's single word was a question.

Sadie shook her head, as if not wanting to tell Consuela the thing she needed to hear.

"She's terrified. She never realized… Cobra seems… She doesn't want to marry him anymore…" She blurted it all out in one big rush of breath.

Consuela arched her fingers and gazed at her over the top of the pyramid.

"But that's not why I'm here."

"It's not?"

Consuela was very good at extracting information with only a few words. Years of practice as Mother Superior, she guessed.

"No. I'm here because I wanted to warn you that your brother is in danger. The same man who murdered Teo is planning to kill Cobra. Kill him soon. I thought you should know so you could warn him."

Consuela regarded her with shrewd eyes.

"And why should you care? In fact…" She spread long elegant fingers before her in a gesture of submission. "If my brother is killed, your sister won't have to marry him. Isn't that a neat solution to your problem?"

Sadie's stomach fell into a bottomless hollow. This woman was wily. Years of the religious life had not dulled her keen nose for the hard realities of the world outside.

"It could be… but it's not right. You helped us. I can't stand by and…"

Her voice trailed off. She really couldn't admit they'd arranged it all, this assassination.

It would have happened anyway, she self-justified. *We just sped things up.*

Consuela sat still and silent for another long period. Sadie had the sudden suspicion she was asking God for answers, but that would be absurd. Wouldn't it?

Then, just as unanticipated as the long silences were, Consuela's serene face blossomed in a smile.

"I suspect there are still things you are not telling me, Sadie, but that is your prerogative. You are quite certain about this fellow Blackheart? That he is the one cheating Cobra? The scorpion at the heart of a nest of vipers?"

Sadie nodded enthusiastically. "I am under no illusions about my brother," Consuela said. "We chose different paths a long time ago, but I still love him. I still pray for him."

"A scorpion in the heart of a nest of vipers," echoed Sadie. "That is so apt."

She suddenly remembered Blackheart's money. She pulled it out and kept just enough for her fare back to town.

"Speaking of scorpions," she said, her heart suddenly feeling a lot lighter, "Here's some of the devil's own money. I'd like to give it to you for your work."

Consuela's eyes widened, and then sparkled with mischief.

"Nothing I like better than taking back from the devil what he stole from the flock."

She kissed Sadie on each cheek and stood to show her out.

"Till we meet again," she said, when they reached the entryway. "I'm certain we will."

Sixty-one

Isla was growing tired of hearing Phoebe bemoan her lot. She'd decided tonight was the night they'd have fun, despite her friend's declared dismal prospects, but the evening didn't start well.

"Sadie hasn't even been near me," Phoebe wailed, as soon as she caught sight of Isla in the salon doorway where they usually met up.

"I don't blame her," said Isla. "First, she helps you score a wedding to the man of your dreams, and then you change your mind on her. You're a hard woman to please."

She rolled her eyes in frustration.

"Good luck, Cobra, is all I can say. Now, what are you having to drown your sorrows? I'm sick of hearing about them."

Phoebe gazed back, her eyes wide with shock, and then her lips quirked into a smile. "Drown my sorrows night, is it? Better than sitting around moping, I suppose."

They were onto their third Pisco Punch when a girl Phoebe hadn't noticed before sashayed in, skirts rippling around her as her hips swayed. She parked herself confidently at the bar on the stool next to Isla.

"What's up?" she said as she plopped herself down in a cloud of heady sandalwood perfume.

Isla's sapphire blue eyes popped open in wild delight.

"Jasmine," she cried, stretching her arms around her neck in a dignified hug so as not to disturb her friend's hair or makeup. "When did they let you out of Sacramento?"

"As of right now, baby. I've graduated to the big time."

She made a sweeping gesture around the space they occupied.

"I've arrived. World, take notice."

Isla giggled and nudged Phoebe, sitting on her other side.

"When you've known Jaz a little longer, you'll understand she makes everything fun. She never lets life get her down."

"That's nice," said Phoebe, aware her face was reddening as she took the sly dig on board.

Isla turned back to her friend. "What are you drinking, Jaz?"

"Same as you," Jasmine said, pointing to the pink and yellow concoction sitting in front of them, straws protruding from their glasses.

"Jasmine was at the same orphanage as I was," Isla explained with a sideways glance to Phoebe. "We were real buddies until they separated us at around age eleven. I became Sophia's personal assistant and Jaz—well, she wasn't as fortunate."

She glanced tentatively at her friend, as if reluctant to tell her story for her. Jaz complied with the silent hint.

"I got shipped off to the Golden Bowl—a sister outfit to this one, one of Morrigan's many. Just like this joint, only with a lot more miners to deal with—and I've been there ever since." She gave Phoebe a hard look and then turned to Isla.

"Who did you say your friend is again?"

"Jasmine, meet Phoebe," said Isla.

"Phoebe…" Jasmine drew out her name with a hint of awe. "I've heard of you. You're the one marrying Cobra. Who would have thought…" She gave Phoebe a quick calculating scan, and then grinned in an open, welcoming way.

"You must have something special, girl. That's all I can say. Something that's not obvious to the naked eye," she added with a cheeky grin.

Phoebe pulled a face before she remembered where she was and corrected herself, but Jasmine hadn't missed the fleeting expression. "What? You're not happy about it?"

She glanced around nervously. "Well, don't let on around here if you want to stay in one piece."

"Change of topic," said Isla, scanning the room for eavesdroppers.

Phoebe put her glass down with a clunk, but remained silent.

Jasmine took up her story. "Actually, I was lucky to be sent to the Bowl, rather than some hick place of Sophia's up in the mountains where the only folks you see are miners and railway workers."

She took a sip of her newly arrived drink and said, "Yum. This is perfect."

Phoebe understood the subject was closed.

There was a long silence as they each applied themselves to their drinks. Phoebe couldn't remember if this was her second or her third, but suddenly, she wanted to remain sober enough to hear what Jasmine had to say. The conviction seized her: Jasmine could teach her a lot.

The place had been empty and quiet when they'd first arrived, but now it was filling up with the usual up-and-coming bankers, clerks and sharebrokers. Merchants and jockeys. Farmers in from the country with a hankering to experience the excitement of the "sinful" city.

Jasmine scanned the room with a knowing eye.

Then she turned back to Isla. "So, I asked already and you haven't said. What's the story? You always seem to have the latest gossip before anyone else, and I'm bored already."

She stretched out the last word *b-o-red* at the same time as she stretched her arms like a languid cat in front of a warming fire. Her dark brown hair fell around her face in exuberant curls, framing sparkling hazel eyes.

Her bubbling "nothing's going to hold me down" manner endeared her, even if you could detect a note of desperation behind it.

Despite Isla's secret dig, Phoebe liked her immediately.

Over the next hour, she deliberately held back on her drinking and took a backseat as she eavesdropped on the conversation. As she did, she had time to reflect on how fortunate she was when compared to the two young women beside her.

She'd lived in a protected family until she'd taken it into her head to chase after Cobra, naïve as she was about the dangers of the world outside the Shamrock's walls.

She listened as her friends talked about this one and that.

"Ellie..? Died in childbirth, poor sod. And no one wanted the baby..."

"Shona? She's down in the Barbary cribs, lost to opium..."

"Tanya? Got sent up to Stockton as a punishment for disobeying Sophia.."

"Ruby? She ran away to marry some hick farmer, but it didn't last. They never do... Normal men don't want a prostitute as a wife..."

Did any of these girls have happy endings?

She appreciated what it must cost Jasmine to always appear her upbeat self.

The crowd circulated. The ones who were seeking further entertainment disappeared upstairs. They once again had the space to themselves, and they moved to sofas and a comfortable armchair in an out-of-sight corner where they enjoyed relative privacy.

That was when Jasmine returned to the topic of Cobra and Phoebe. Something obviously fascinated her with the arrangement, and now Phoebe was much better placed to understand.

"So how did a New York gal catch a big fish like the King Cobra?" she asked, apparently casual about it, but Phoebe detected something else, an urgency to know, in the undertones.

Phoebe shrugged, catching a nostalgic tingle inside once again, the rising excitement of that first infatuation with a powerful older man.

"He was in New York for several months doing business, you know, talking to my Daa, who owns a bar in the Bowery. He was in there practically every night and we just kind of fell for one another."

It sounded so simple. Pity it got so complicated.

Phoebe struggled to explain. "He was so different from all the boys who sniffed around. Mature. Powerful. He wasn't throwing himself at me. Not at all…"

"And how on earth did you get him to *marry* you? That's what impresses me the most."

Jasmine had had her share of cocktails by now, and some of the wear and tear was showing around her shiny edges.

She leaned forward confidentially. "I mean, do you know some special sex tricks or something?"

Phoebe's face flushed scarlet and for a moment she wished she could disappear through the floor. "Oh, no. Nothing like that. Nothing like that at all. I'm a 'good Catholic girl." She flicked her index fingers to hyphenate the phrase.

Do I have to spell it out any clearer?

Jasmine's eyes lit up with a sudden revelation.

"You're a virgin?" she whispered in disbelief.

"Oh my…"

She looked around, her eyes lit with a secret fascination, as if she couldn't leave the topic alone.

"So why aren't you happier about it? I mean, come on. Being Mrs. Cobra? You're never going to stoop to the level of us party girls, are you? Never, ever."

Her words carried such poignant longing, Phoebe felt guilty about not appreciating how lucky she was. How could she explain she could not bear the thought of sleeping with a man who had killed Teo and cut off his hands? Even if he didn't do it himself, he ordered it. She didn't know where to begin. Was it even logical to feel such revulsion?

I should have understood what I was getting myself into. If only Daa hadn't encouraged me.

"No, Jasmine. You are right there. It's very hard to explain."

She took a deep breath.

"It's like I imagined Cobra was one sort of man. And he's turned out to be quite another. Different from what I thought. I guess I was a bit of a schoolgirl with fancy ideas of what I wanted.

"They all came crashing down and now I'm terrified of what's going to happen. It must sound pathetic to you… but I know I won't make him happy. And then I am terrified of what will happen next."

She was trembling all over. "I might even end up as a party girl, after all. You never know."

Jasmine regarded her with soft understanding.

"You are in a state, aren't you? And so many of us would give anything to be in your place." She glanced to Isla. "What a humbug. Phoebe doesn't want it, and I'd grab the opportunity with both hands, just to get off the treadmill I'm on."

She turned back to Phoebe. "I'm nineteen years old. Do you know how long women last in this profession before they crack up or fall down?"

Phoebe gazed at her with large, mournful eyes and shook her head. No, she didn't.

"I've already lasted longer than most because I started so young. I had no choice. I reckon I've got a couple more years and I'll be for the knacker's yard."

Phoebe could feel the tears draining down her cheeks. This girl… She was hardly a woman, even now. She'd had no choice in the cards life had dealt her, and here she was, not giving up, still clinging to hopes of a better life.

"I wish you could take my place," she sobbed. "You'd carry it out so much better than I will ever be able to. And you deserve a chance to break out."

Sixty-two

"Elizabeth. I am so sorry. But I can explain."

Sadie stood just inside Pine Street's front door, her hands clasped tightly together, beads of perspiration spotlighting her forehead.

She'd come straight from Consuela's school to the big house, desperate to make her apologies to Dolphie and explain why she'd failed to turn up. She didn't want him thinking she'd rejected him a second time.

I didn't. Honestly.

"I was caught in a desperate situation," she told Elizabeth. "One I'm almost too embarrassed to admit."

She screwed her face in an abject apology. "Please, hear me out before you decide whether I'm completely unreliable—and ungrateful—or not."

She could sense a hesitation in the way Elizabeth stood. Holding something of herself back, uncertain of how to read the situation.

She waited, feeling suspended between hope and despair. In her mind's eye, she saw herself dangling from a hot-air balloon, hanging on in an empty blue expanse, waiting for an arm to reach out and pull her back to safety.

If they were going to turn away from her now… which they were so understandably likely to do… how would she face the future? Yet she'd let them down so many times, she barely deserved another chance.

Elizabeth stepped aside and gestured for her to come in.

"It rather surprised us when you failed to meet Dolphie at the agreed time," she said, as she turned to lead Sadie down the hall. "But of course, I wouldn't summarily cut you off without giving you a chance to explain."

"I wouldn't." I wonder if Dolphie feels the same?

"Is Dolphie here?" The words tumbled out before she censored herself.

Elizabeth paused and turned to meet her eye.

"As it happens, he is. But I can't speak for him. He was pretty upset about your 'no show' earlier. He waited for quite some time before he gave up on you."

Sadie's stomach did a triple flip. Her throat closed over, so she found it difficult to speak.

Before he gave up on you.

"I… I understand," she said. "It must have looked terrible."

Elizabeth gave her a grim smile. "Not the best, Sadie, you have to concede that. I'm happy to see you're still upright. We wondered if you'd been injured. Taken to hospital… something like that. It would have made it easier to understand."

"Please. Let me tell you what happened and you can judge."

They moved on to the dining room and waited in an uncomfortable silence for Dolphie to come at Mrs. Roderiquez' call. Within a few minutes he pushed open the half-closed door, erect and composed, every inch the cool and formal aristocrat, his lips in a straight thin line, his speech clipped and distant.

"Miss McGillicuddy. Nice that you could find the time to fit us into your obviously busy day."

Sarcasm. He's furious.

"Dolphie.. Please. I deserved that, I know, but hear me out before you make any final decisions."

Elizabeth had led them into the dining room, where they seated themselves around the table like committee members preparing to discuss shared business. Gone was the convivial family relationship Sadie had so cherished.

This is what it's like to be on the outside, looking in. How quickly things change.

Elizabeth and Dolphie gazed at her expectantly. She licked her lips nervously and wondered where to begin. Before she had gained control of herself, Dolphie filled the gap, speaking up in a slow, grave cadence.

"It was more than a little perplexing to be stood up today, Sadie. But it would be churlish of me not to give you an opportunity to explain. So go for it. Explain why it apparently wasn't a priority for you to make our appointment."

He lounged back in his chair, the picture of aristocratic indifference, but his tone was acid.

Wow. The Count reveals his true colors. I've never seen him like this. He's had it with me.

Sadie's face flushed bright pink. She could feel her skin heating as she gazed across the table. Elizabeth's expression was milder, but still reserved. Offering moral support to her nephew, of course.

Sadie cleared her throat. "I've got a lot to confess, and I hope you'll see things my way. I didn't know what else to do..."

She thought of Patrick. She'd practically ordered his execution, and her heart stuttered in her chest. She swallowed hard.

"I was waiting for you on the street. I was early. I was so excited to be returning here, so grateful for your invitation."

Her eyes flickered to Dolphie. He remained unmoved, returning her glance with a non-committal stare.

"Then Patrick Blackheart accosted me. He came out of nowhere. He told me if I didn't add my share to the 'payment' you'd set up, he wouldn't be carrying through with the deal."

She hesitated, licked her lips again. Suddenly her mouth was bone dry. She stuttered.

"I don't need to spell out what my 'payment' was going to be. He said I had to deliver on his demands this evening or the deal he'd made with you was off."

She'd kept her eyes on Elizabeth most of the time she was speaking, occasionally flicking them to the pretty rose bowl that sat on the table between them, filling the air with that glorious fragrance of cinnamon and patchouli.

She risked a quick glance across to Dolphie. He was still regarding her with a neutral detachment. She took a big breath to keep herself sailing on.

"I don't know what was worse. The terror of fearing he might kill me, or the humiliation of the way he put his 'proposition.' He spoke as if I was nothing. Something to be used and tossed aside."

She shifted her hands in front of her, laced them together tightly to stop them from trembling.

"He said unless I complied, he wouldn't go ahead with the deal you made. And he implied he'd rough up Phoebe as well. I suppose he treats everyone that way. I hadn't realized how truly evil he is, though of course I should have. My mistake."

She shook her head and swallowed. Her throat was still as dry as the Sahara. Elizabeth noticed and interrupted.

"Just pause a moment Sadie, and I'll get us some water."

She rose and walked quickly to the door, and in that serendipitous way she and Mrs. R seemed to have, the housekeeper materialized with a tray and water glasses at the moment.

Elizabeth poured them all water, and Sadie sipped a few mouthfuls before continuing.

"After he'd gone, I was a mess, but I couldn't leave it like that. I just couldn't. So I took things into my own hands."

Her heart was pumping so hard her ears thundered.

Will they think me evil, as bad as Patrick, for what I am about to confess next?

"There's one thing I haven't mentioned to you. It was supposed to be extremely confidential. But Cobra has a sister. A high-ranking nun named Consuela, who is principal of the Catholic school in Bernal Heights."

She glanced up and saw surprise, and an easing of the defensive mask, on Dolphie's face. "I know," she said with a slight smile. "Who would have thought it? They're twins, and they're still close."

She took another gulp of water.

"I felt I had no choice. I went to Consuela. I told her Patrick Blackheart was planning to assassinate her brother, and I wanted her to warn him about what was coming."

She eyed them both, feeling her resolve, the iron will that had carried her through so much trouble, flooding back into her.

Her eyes were steady, steely now, and there was no apology in her voice.

"I've pretty well organized for the death of Patrick Blackheart, and I make no apology for it."

She let her hands drop helplessly onto the table in front of her.

"I might have ruined our friendship and for that I am desperately sorry, but I had no choice."

She gave them both a faltering smile.

"And I know. I've messed up the plan to get Phoebe out of the wedding, and I don't know how to fix that."

Sixty-three

Isla stirred. The light was bright behind the blind over the single window. That meant it was later than she usually slept. And although she still felt cozy and dozy, she had someone's feet in her face. She jolted up onto her elbows and gazed about her. She saw Phoebe's golden syrup curls. *That's right!* It all came back to her.

She and Phoebe were top-and-tailing in Phoebe's room. They'd reined in the cocktail consumption halfway through the night, so they weren't exactly drunk. But they'd talked until the early hours, and going out in the raw streets and getting herself home when she'd spent hours among friends just hadn't seemed wise. Plus… something lingered over her, a sense of unfinished business.

Phoebe appeared to be happily sleeping on, the gentle inhale and exhale of her breathing the only other sound in the room, her riotous curls obscuring her face.

"What time is it?" she croaked, watching Phoebe's still form. Her sleeping companion stirred, raised one arm over her head and brushed the hair out of her eyes. She opened her eyes, and drew her legs up in alarm when she saw Isla, pulling the sheets up over herself—and off her friend—as she did.

"Oh. It's you." She completed the movement and swung her legs to the floor, sitting forward with her hands on her thighs, wiping her sleepy eyes.

"Oh, what a night we had. And your friend! What a girl." She yawned and cleared her throat.

"She's amazing."

"She is," said Isla with a quick smile. "Got an iron will. Most girls just can't take that kind of life and bounce back."

"I sure couldn't," said Phoebe. "It makes me feel ashamed I've been moaning on the way I have."

She stretched her arms over her head and yawned again.

"But that doesn't mean that I still wouldn't like to get out of it."

Isla followed her lead and made ready to stand up.

"You know," she said tentatively, staring at Phoebe's turned-away head, willing her to wake up and take notice. "I've been thinking… Or rather, it's like while I was sleeping, something came to me fully formed, and I've woken up to discover it."

Phoebe turned her way, casting her eyes casually over her, still not picking up on the rising excitement in her voice.

"What are you burbling on about, Izzy? Are you still half asleep?" She reached over and gave her a playful light pinch on the arm.

"Wake up, sleepyhead! It's morning!" She glanced around her. "I can't believe we both slept so well in one small bed. Maybe it's even afternoon by now! Who knows?"

Isla walked the few steps to stand plumb in front of her. She grabbed her hands. "You're not listening to me, Phoebe. I've discovered something important while I was sleeping."

Phoebe rose to meet her at eye level, a grin playing across her face, making fun of her announcement.

"And what's that, you silly goose? What have the daimons of the night told you?"

Isla grabbed Phoebe's cheeks in both hands and leaned in close.

"That we could get Jasmine to stand in for you on Friday. She's your height and size. Under a veil, no one would know. And by the time the veil is lifted… Well, it will be too late. And if Cobra makes a fuss… well, I could tell Jack to be ready to take matters in hand. He'd make sure Jasmine didn't come to harm. He's good like that."

She let go of Phoebe's face, stepped back, and jumped up and down in delight.

"I've only just thought of that last bit. If Cobra refuses her, Jasmine can still get her freedom."

Phoebe gazed back, a dazed look in her eyes. "And what about me? Will Jack protect me too?" Isla could see flickers of terror and joy moving in quick succession across Phoebe's face, like feathery clouds chased by a racing wind.

"You could go back to New York. To your Daa. Or you could come and live with me…"

Her excitement sputtered out, like a fire doused with water, as she faced the full reality of what she was suggesting. She hadn't thought of that bit. What would happen to Phoebe? Would Cobra forgive her for backing out? Would she have to go to Australia or somewhere to escape him?

"Darn. I don't know about that last bit."

She drew all her thoughts together. "I guess you have to decide. How important to you is it to get out of this marriage? Are you willing to take the risk?"

••••••••

Phoebe had agreed to Isla's challenge. She had the day to decide what she wanted to do, and depending on that decision, they would then corner Jasmine and ask her if she was interested. It was as simple as that.

Simple…

Phoebe's insides withered.

Isla had tiptoed out in her wrinkled, slept-in clothes to return to Daphne's, promising to return tonight to get her answer.

Phoebe slumped back on her unmade bed, her head already aching from too many cocktails and too much hard thinking.

I thought I was being oh so bold, setting my sights on Cobra, and really, I didn't have a clue, she reflected, combing her hair absentmindedly with her hands.

I mocked Sadie because I thought she was so dutiful, so unadventurous. And I've ended up getting everyone in a heap of trouble, and not being nearly as courageous as I thought I was.

Not nearly as courageous as Jasmine.

She knew that if they made their proposition to Jasmine, she would take it. She had nothing to lose.

But me. What will happen to me?

If I go back to New York, will I have to watch my back at every turn, expecting to be attacked by a Bloods gang member wanting to please the boss?

Will other men be terrified to show any interest in me because Cobra scares them?

Will I be notorious as the woman who jilted Cobra—or whom Cobra jilted, who knows—forever marked as rejected goods?

Is anyone going to believe I'm still a virgin? Will they treat me like used goods, anyway?

What will my life be like if I go through with NOT marrying Cobra?

She put her head in her hands and wept in the quiet of her crumpled bed.

She slept again, and when she woke, the headache was gone.

I've been asking myself the wrong question, she thought, as she opened her eyes.

I should be asking, How many other Marisols are there out there?

And if I marry Cobra, can I look them in the face?

How could I have been so blind? I didn't want to see before, but now I do.

And she had her answer.

Sixty-four

Patrick Blackheart had spent the rest of a pleasant afternoon in the Father's Arms, a tavern in the heart of the Barbary Coast on the corner of Kearney and Pacific Streets, hidden out of sight of any policeman called to a disturbance. Not that he had much to fear from the local cops.

Most of them were in his pay anyway, and people around here understood he was on legitimate business, collecting tributes from the bar and brothel owners from blocks around, hand-delivered by Bloods henchmen.

He recognized the regulars, and they knew him well enough to give him a wide berth. There were the Chilean, Peruvian and Spanish-American cutthroats playing a drunken game of backroom billiards.

Over the other side of the bar, the sharp-nosed villain who'd killed a peddler at New Almaden a few years back sat drinking with his woman. The same one who'd sworn him clear so he escaped jail.

The scar-faced fellow drinking at a nearby table was a *monte* dealer, his companion a one-eyed burglar. And the gal on the bar, Red Lizzie? She was the tavern owner's moll, not averse to sharing her favors if the price was right, and she shared the take with her man.

What better way to spend the late afternoon? Collecting money and contemplating a night of pleasure. Blackheart stretched and sighed contentedly. From today's banking, he'd be able to skim his usual share, and this time, he planned to spend it all on Sadie.

At least thanks to me, she'll be wearing something sexy when I see her tonight.

He'd waited months for this occasion. He'd been planning it ever since he first laid eyes on her in her father's saloon.

Dead Eyes Connelly was the last of his men to bring in the cash. He was a lanky fellow in tight-fitting stovepipe trousers which emphasized his skeletal physique. Sunken, dead fish eyes looked out of a curiously bloodless face, his deathly white skin overhung by a shock of black hair.

Patrick rated him a smart operator, and considered his creepy appearance a bonus, prompting a superstitious deference from those around him. He might promote him to a lieutenant's spot when he took over the Bloods tomorrow.

The last of the money collected and accounted for, he made his way back to the Bloods' Montgomery Street headquarters, tipping his hat amiably at the guys on the door as he headed upstairs for the bullion room, the heart of the Bloods organization.

It was the inner sanctum, the place where Cobra also stowed the extra armaments they stockpiled in case of an out-and-out gang war. These were their biggest assets, the guns, and a work-of-art burglar-proof safe.

It was the latest Herring design, with an outer skin of boiler-plate-wrought iron, and an inner lining of hardened steel, crisscrossed with rods of soft steel that took hours of drilling to penetrate.

Only two people had keys to the bullion room. He and Cobra, and he always meticulously returned the day's takings there before he went home at night. No point in risking being robbed himself, or arousing Cobra's suspicions about his trustworthiness.

He allowed himself a smug smile as he ascended the stairs. Everything was coming together admirably. Cobra had no idea who ran this organization, but he'd be finding out shortly. Tonight, he'd enjoy his payout in advance and then he'd do the deed tomorrow. The slight advancement in the date? He could handle it, no problem. He'd been preparing for this for the last five years, Cobra's destiny with death.

He reached the top of the stairs, unlocked the office and stepped quietly into the secure area, locking it again behind him. Always the same procedure, so they'd never be caught by surprise. One, two. The same routine. Always. And followed only by him and Cobra.

He paused and inhaled deeply. Stale and dusty the air might be, but to his nostrils it had the fragrance of ambrosia. Tomorrow all this would be his, and if he played his cards right, Sadie would be in it with him. Once he'd won her over, he had no intention of letting her go.

He moved softly through to the bullion room's steel doors and repeated the procedure. Unlock, and lock again behind him.

He dropped the brown leather satchel he'd carried from the Father's Arms to the floor and pulled out the money bags. A dozen of them. He deftly opened them and redistributed the coins into two empty bags he carried—peeling off his share.

He'd once again increased the tally on selected merchants without Cobra's knowledge, so as long as there were twelve bags with the expected total, Cobra asked no questions.

Task completed, he stowed his share in his briefcase, opened the safe and stowed the twelve newly collected bags in their usual place— third shelf, right at the front. Right where Cobra could see them the minute he opened up.

He turned for the door, unlocked it, ready to leave, and stepped out into the dim room. Plumb into a waiting Cobra.

His hand froze on the briefcase. "Boss!" he exclaimed. "What are you doing here?"

And how had he not heard him come in? Cobra surveyed his face intently. Patrick's eyes flicked uneasily around the room, and that's when he saw Cobra was not alone.

Standing behind him was gold-toothed Tiny Marino, the six-foot-two security detail Cobra took with him when he had a dangerous job on. The moniker "Tiny" was a joke, a play on his name Antonio, because he weighed 200 pounds and was deadly on the draw. He held his Colt Revolver with deceptive ease.

Patrick's eyes ricocheted back to Cobra.

He slowly brought his hands out in front of him, palms up, so Tiny wouldn't think he was attempting to pull on him.

"I was banking the take from the Coast," he said. "From Grant Street to the water."

Cobra didn't take his eyes off his face.

"Tiny. Search the briefcase," he said in a monotone drawl, his face expressionless.

"Hey! What is this? Don't you trust me?" Patrick cried, working hard to sound jocular as his heart pounded in his chest.

"It's not a matter of trust, Blackheart," said Cobra. "It's a matter of greed. Of thinking you own the place. And keep those hands out in front or he'll shoot you before we even see what's inside the bag. Step away from it."

Patrick did as requested, his head spinning.

Had that bitch pulled a double cross, or was this all a terrible coincidence?

You don't believe in coincidence, a dark voice warned.

"Cobra, you've got it all wrong. I'd never do anything…"

"Shut up." Cobra's response was whip-crack hard. "Tiny, get in there."

Cobra held a gun too, a Remington, and was gesturing with it toward the bag.

In one swift move, Patrick kicked the bag toward Tiny, pulled his Smith and Wesson and fired.

At the same moment he saw Cobra's right shoulder bloom scarlet, his body erupted with a pain so agonizing it robbed him of breath. He slumped to his knees, the revolver clattering to the floor with him. His gun arm was drooping and useless, and blood was spurting from his neck.

"You've got it all wrong," he protested, but his voice was a frog croak.

Tiny tipped open the bag and the two bags of coins fell to the floor with a heavy thud.

"Have I?" said Cobra. He'd risen to his knees, and though he was bleeding, Patrick saw he'd only winged him. His eyes were hard black bullets, his voice granite as he gave the order.

"Finish the dog off."

Sixty-five

"I have to start work in an hour, so I haven't got all day." Jasmine rolled her gold- flecked hazel eyes and pulled a funny face.

"Some of us have to earn their living the hard way, you know," she said with a sly grin. "On our backs. We're not ladies of leisure, like some people."

Isla had sent a note to Jasmine via one of the other girls to meet them here, and she'd readily complied.

Isla dug her in the ribs with a dry laugh, and Jasmine joined in.

"I know," she said. "Poor me."

They were lounging around Phoebe's room again, though in the few hours since Isla had last been here, Phoebe had cleaned up. The bed was tidy, and she had put away all her clothes. Phoebe and Isla sat on the counterpane while Jasmine had taken the only chair.

"We've got a solution for that," Isla said, exchanging a secretive glance with Phoebe.

"For what?" Jasmine said, only half listening. She was contemplating her fingernails, as if her mind was already preparing for tonight's performance.

"For your problem. Earning your living the hard way," said Isla.

"I'm not sure anyone has a solution for that. Not unless some miner throws an entire bag of gold dust my way so I can buy my way out." She rolled her eyes again.

"And I can see that happening. Can't you?" Another droll grin.

"And then what would I do with myself, anyway? It's not as if they gave us much of an *educashun* in the orphanage." She deliberately mangled the word to mock the care they'd received.

"Like they cared what happened to us. No one's taught me to read like you, Isla."

"Listen to her, will you?" said Isla. "You're a smart girl, Jaz. If you wanted to learn to read, you could. But that's not what we're talking about right now."

"It's not? What are we talking about again?"

"I told you. How you can get out of here."

Jasmine's expression sharpened, as if she'd heard Isla for the first time.

"Why didn't you say so? And how would that be?"

"By you taking Phoebe's place and marrying Cobra."

Jasmine's eyes bulged, like they were going to pop out of her head. She gasped, and her creamy skin paled to parchment.

"And what?" she croaked. Even her voice seemed to be affected by the shock.

Isla didn't take her eyes off her. "You said you'd jump at the chance... Theoretically speaking. What if it was more than theoretically?"

"Um... what exactly is the plan?"

"You're the same size as Phoebe, and similar coloring. Phoebe's wedding gown is a slick Indian get-up with a full veil that will only be lifted at the end of the ceremony. What if you stood in for Phoebe? You're a gorgeous woman in your own right, Jasmine. When you lift the veil, we could take a gamble Cobra will like what he sees..."

"And if he doesn't?"

"Mmm… if he doesn't, it will be too late. Phoebe will be long gone… And I've got a good man who'll be there to protect you…"

She hesitated and self-corrected. "Could be there to protect you. I haven't organized that part yet, till I know if we need it."

"Isla," Jasmine said in an exasperated tone.

Isla gave her upper arm a sympathetic tap. "I know. We'll sort it out. And we could try to get Father Gregory onside to exert further pressure…" She pulled her lips into a wry grimace. "Phoebe's already a good mate of his," she said with a grin.

"I guess we're hoping Cobra will decide it's better to have one beautiful woman as his wife rather than none."

Phoebe interjected.

"If you agree, I could see his sister again. She has a lot of influence on Cobra, and I'm pretty certain she's coming to the wedding. Of course we've invited her."

Isla and Jasmine both gaped at her.

"His sister?" queried Jasmin. "Who's she?"

Almost simultaneously Isla said, "You dark horse. You never told me about a sister."

"That's because we were sworn to secrecy."

"We?" said Isla, her cheeks tightening with annoyance. "Who else is in on this when I'm not?"

"Just Sadie," Phoebe said. She cast a sidelong glance at Jasmine and explained, "My sister."

Phoebe shifted her position on the bed, uncomfortable at being caught out.

"You have to promise not to tell anyone," she said. "But Cobra has a sister who is Mother Superior at the Catholic school in Bernal Heights."

"Oh my," said Isla. After a stunned silence, she added, "Who could have guessed?"

"They're twins," said Phoebe. "They look like it too."

Jasmine giggled. "I suppose if Cobra got mad at me, I could always appeal to his sister."

"That's what I thought," said Phoebe. "Especially if she's been forewarned."

They sat in a companionable silence, letting the full impact of what they were proposing sink in, and then Jasmine said with a cheeky grin, "Let me see this wedding dress and then I'll decide."

●●●●●●●●

Jasmine looked glorious in the wedding sari, which fitted her perfectly. Her face glowed above the shimmering gold sheesha fabric.

"I've never worn such a beautiful dress. Never." Her voice was reverent, as if she'd just witnessed Jesus turning water into wine. "I've never dreamed of anything so lovely. And it never occurred to me I might be allowed to wear it."

Isla's eyes had an impish glint.

"So you're sold then. Just show Jaz a beautiful frock and she'll do anything…" she teased.

Jasmine laughed. "Not quite," she said. "But I sure am tempted."

There was a tap at the door, and one of the young girls who helped with cleaning and errands stood shyly in the entry, her blonde hair hanging down her back in a long plait. She stared at Jasmine in the shining frock.

"Your sister is here to see you, miss," she said shyly to Phoebe, twisting her hands in front of her thin little body. "Is it all right if she comes up?"

Phoebe scanned the others and shrugged.

"I guess we may as well let her in on the plan," she said. She turned to the child.

"Yes, Fanny, that's fine. Tell her to come on up."

Sixty-six

They sat in a ring around the Mother Superior's desk. Phoebe, Sadie and Jasmine, and they so reminded Sadie of chicks tucked in a nest waiting for the mother bird to return, she had to suppress a smile.

She'd been astounded to walk into Phoebe's room and see Jasmine in her sister's wedding gown—and she admitted, looking every bit the part of a blushing bride. It was as if the scales fell from her eyes.

But as their story unfolded, something hit Sadie. A truth she'd refused to recognize for months now. Phoebe didn't need her to "rescue" her. She could do that perfectly well for herself, as she was so ably demonstrating.

She stood grinning at the trio of women falling over themselves with excitement in Phoebe's room. They were plotting something daring and loving every minute.

The only drawback was that their scheme to have a "stand-in" bride was like a bucket with holes.

Would the priest play along if a different bride presented from the one he'd been expecting? Would Cobra make an outcry as soon as he cottoned on to what was happening? And how could a marriage be legal if the bride answered to a different name than the one declared in the wedding vows?

(Though Jasmine argued she didn't really care if it was legal in the eyes of the church, as long as Cobra went along with it.)

Sadie decided on the spur of the moment that they needed to consult the woman who knew Cobra better than anyone else—his twin sister, and Phoebe agreed. She'd already thought of it. So here they were.

As Sadie studied Consuela from the other side of her desk, she marveled again at how different she was from the nuns she'd known during her school years. They'd all been pale, cloistered women, rarely venturing out into the world—whether into nature or the community. They seemed to equate holiness with social isolation, and feared mixing in the world, seeing it as leaving them open to the encroachment of evil.

But Consuela's broad, countrywoman's face and tanned skin gave her more of the appearance of a farmer's wife than a Catholic school principal. She guessed Consuela handled much of the care for those perfumed roses outside her window, rather than any gardener.

And her down-to-earth, practical appearance seemed to be matched by a robust understanding of the world and the way it worked.

I suppose you couldn't stay in close touch with a brother like Cosimo without developing spiritual pragmatism, Sadie thought, and had to suppress another grin.

Spiritual pragmatism.

Those were the perfect two words to sum Consuela up, and why she hadn't been afraid to bring Jasmine along with her.

"So let me get this straight," Consuela was saying with a broad smile.

"Phoebe has asked Jasmine to stand in for her at her wedding tomorrow, and Jasmine has agreed. And no one has thought to ask the groom what he thinks of the idea? Have I got it right?" Her eyes sparkled with mischief.

"Err, yes, Mother Superior. We're frightened of what he would say," stammered Phoebe. "He has got a reputation, you know."

Consuela frowned. "I can't imagine what you're referring to, girl," she said in mock reproof. She laced her fingers in front of her as she considered them.

"Father Gregory might want to know something more about what's going on as well. Had you considered that?"

Phoebe's eyes lowered to the desktop, and her lips set in a chastened line. Jasmine stepped in.

"We wondered, Mother Superior, if you might talk to him for us. Apart from Sadie, none of us exactly understands the church lingo, if you know what I mean."

"I think I understand what you're trying to say," said Consuela. "My brother owes me a couple of favors." She glanced at Sadie with an almost imperceptible nod. Her face took on a more serious cast.

"Phoebe, can I ask why you've had this change of mind? You seemed quite set on marrying Cosimo when I last saw you."

Phoebe's brows contracted, and she seemed to shrink into herself.

"Mother, I hadn't really understood what Cobra's work entails. I.. I can't get used to the idea that he .. Well, you know…"

"That he kills people?" Consuela said, her eyes steady on Phoebe's face.

"You can say it without offending me. I'm well aware of my brother's activities."

Phoebe looked up with contrite eyes. "It's so hard to accept, but yes. When he killed Teo, who was so good to me, and I went to meet Teo's wife Marisol and saw their three children… well, it made me feel sick inside. Sick, and frightened."

Consuela turned her hawkish eyes on Jasmine.

"And that doesn't bother you, Jasmine?"

Jasmine flushed red, but she held the nun's gaze without flinching.

"I'm ready to confess my sins, Mother. I've been forced into prostitution since I was twelve years old. I'm as black as sin, and no better than Cobra when it comes to my moral standing. If he'll take me, I'll do my best to please him. I'll do anything to get out of the life I have now. One that I've never chosen for myself."

Consuela regarded her in silence for a long moment, her face soft in the candlelight.

"Our father God sees your heart, my child, and cries for you. He forgives in a moment. You could always say confession with Father Gregory before the ceremony, and ask his blessing on this new life, if you choose."

She looked around the circle of expectant faces.

"Every time I see you, Sadie McGillicuddy, you bring fresh surprises."

She gave a forgiving laugh. "Not that I mind. It keeps life interesting."

"Phoebe, Jasmine, I respect what you've both told me. Now I am going to farewell you, and take all of this to my prayer stool. I never decide anything important without consulting my Lord and Savior, so I don't know what I will do until I've spent time in prayer."

She rose from her seat, pushing up with both hands from the desk.

"I am planning to attend this wedding of yours tomorrow, and I'm glad to be forewarned of the change of plans. That's as far as I can say just now. Good night, ladies. Penelope will see you out."

●●●●●●●●

Sadie had one last task, and that was to visit her father in his hotel and explain it all to him. His daughter would not be marrying Cobra, no matter where that left his "deal" for cheap booze and protection. And she was glad of it.

Sixty-seven

Sadie gazed up at the huge painting of Christ in a voluminous white gown, rising into the heavenlies and bolstered by a cluster of cherubs at his feet as the central part of an ornate triptych that hung above the altar of the Catholic cathedral of St. Mary's on California Street. Excitement surged through her

Cosimo was waiting at the head of the nave, sleekly outfitted in what looked like a new sharply cut suit, virile and alert. His dark hair shone under the candlelight from tall brass tapers set to highlight the matrimonial pair and the altar. The hint of silver in it gave him a debonair edge. If you forgot about the man's morality, he appeared a fine, upstanding fellow.

Father Gregory stood beside him, also robed in white, whispering quietly in the groom's ear. She supposed giving him last-minute instructions. At one point Cosimo gazed back into the nave with a sharp eye, and she wondered what the priest had said.

At Cosimo's right elbow, several unusually well-attired henchmen filled the front pew on the "groom's side" of the church, a mountain of a man with a gold tooth among them. She speculated they were present to provide security and as a show of Bloods solidarity.

Patrick Blackheart was notably not among them, and Sadie's

insides momentarily contracted at his absence. They'd never know the details of his disappearance, but that was the world he'd chosen.

Live by the sword, and you die by the sword.

She shook herself free from the guilt of her part in his absence. Wasted emotion, she told herself.

He gave you no other choice.

And any minute now, Jasmine would appear in her sister's beautiful gold gown, heavily veiled as was the custom. Phoebe had always insisted Cobra would not see her until the formalities had concluded.

And suddenly, hollowness gone, Sadie's heart swelled with anticipation, as if it really was Phoebe who would pace up the aisle. If they pulled this off, Phoebe would be free to make better choices for herself the second time round. And Jasmine would be in a surpassingly more desirable place than she was now.

Less than a dozen of them were here to witness this bringing together of a man and woman in holy matrimony, and apart from Cobra's crew and two altar boys serving the priest, Sadie knew them all.

Beside her in the pew were Elizabeth and Isla, both finely decked out in honor of the occasion. Elizabeth in a royal blue gown highlighted by a headpiece of peacock feathers which would not be out of place at a royal wedding. Isla, in contrast, wore a pale pink gown, elegant in its simplicity, which seemed to gather in and enhance her youthful glow.

Across the aisle from them, Susannah, Cordelia and the Mother Superior sat together, Consuela closest to the aisle. Jack was back at the house, with Brian McGillicuddy, acting as security for Phoebe, who had crept out of the Golden Girl at first light, leaving Jasmine in her room to get dressed in the sparkling sari.

And Dolphie? He'd maintained a neutral distance from her even after her big explanation, but he was about to enter with Jasmine on his arm, standing in as father-of-the-bride. They'd put out a story that Brian had suffered a crippling asthma attack and was too unwell to attend the service.

The organ pealed with the familiar first chords of Jeremiah Clarke's "Prince of Denmark March" and Sadie's eyes shot to Consuela. For nearly 200 years, this music had beckoned Catholic brides down the aisle.

The Mother Superior glanced sideways and caught her eye with the briefest flicker of collusion, and at that moment Sadie's feverish anxiety washed away, replaced by an overwhelming peace. She was certain Consuela had helped choose these opening celebratory blasts of the Trumpet Voluntary, and she had an instant conviction that her capable hand would have woven together the threads for the rest of the service.

Cosimo was her twin, and Consuela would only ever be wedded to Christ. This was the one natural wedding she'd celebrate in her lifetime.

With the exception of Cosimo, his men at the front and Consuela, everyone turned to watch Jasmine and Dolphie progress up the nave to the chancel. Dolphie dazzled in a pale gray suit, his glossy dark hair smoothed and tied at the nape of his neck, his movement as light and fluid as the fencer he was. And on his arm, floated the young woman in gold, a serene, graceful butterfly.

They halted in front of Father Gregory, and Dolphie detached, sliding sideways and moving silently to join her pew at the far end, next to Isla.

The air stirred gently with the fragrance of candle wax, incense, and the faint hint of fresh white lilies from two huge flower-filled urns in the chancel. Paid for by Elizabeth, Sadie guessed, and an urgent gratitude sliced through her. The woman at her side had such grace, to help ensure a girl like Jasmine had a wedding she'd remember her whole life.

And then it was just Cobra and Jasmine, standing in front of Father Gregory, and time slipped away as the priest welcomed the tiny group, making special but tactful mention of Consuela's presence, and moved on smoothly through the service. The opening prayer, the Bible reading, a brief homily about the nature of the commitment, and then on to the vows.

Sadie held her breath. What would happen now?

Cosimo and Jasmine were standing facing one another as Father Gregory began the recitation of the vows.

"Cosimo, will you take Jasmine, here present, to be your lawful wife, according to the rite of holy mother church?" *Jasmine?*

For a few seconds, Cosimo glanced wildly back at Consuela, a question in his eyes. As if in reassurance, she gave a nod which, though barely perceptible, communicated authority.

He turned back to the woman standing veiled in front of him and answered: "I will."

Sadie felt a great release inside her. She'd been standing with her rib cage frozen, waiting for the moment when Cobra would renege on the whole deal.

"And Jasmine, will you take Cosimo, here present, to be your lawful husband, according to the rite of holy mother Church?"

Jasmine's response rang out, strong and vibrant. "I will."

Cosimo put his hand into his pocket and drew out a handful of coins which he placed in a brass dish Father Gregory extended to him.

"O Lord, sanctify these coins," the priest intoned, "offered as a symbol of the settlement which has been agreed."

"Now we will have the exchange of rings," Father Gregory intoned. "Cosimo, you may unveil your bride."

The very air in the still, cool nave seemed to contract into one silent moment, as if at least half the congregation held their next breath in suspense.

Cosimo leaned forward and, with plate-fisted gentle hands, lifted aside Jasmine's long, misty veil and moved it back over her shoulders.

She stood before him, her exquisite features radiating joy in his presence.

His big thumbs traced a delicate line down her cheeks, and his dark brows lifted.

"Jasmine," he breathed, so softly the words only carried to the first two rows of the church, but they didn't need to carry any further. "My wife."

He let his hands drop to his sides and reached into his jacket pocket to bring out two gold rings, which he placed on Father Gregory's brass plate.

The congregation exhaled a mutual gasp of approval and broke into spontaneous applause. Father Gregory smiled a winsome, vague acknowledgment and continued as if there had been no interruption to the sacred occasion.

Within minutes, Jasmine and Cosimo had wedding rings on their fingers. The Lord's Prayer had concluded the proceedings, and they were processing out to a rousing trumpet solo from three musicians who'd miraculously appeared at the back of the church.

Whether that was Elizabeth or Consuela's doing, Sadie didn't know, but it made for a perfect conclusion.

Nor, in the joyous celebrations that followed, could she recall afterwards who had led the spontaneous clapping, but she suspected it was Dolphie.

Sixty-eight

Sadie slipped into the bench seat beside Consuela as everyone else left the cathedral, momentarily bowing her head in grateful prayer as she did.

When she raised it, the nun's tanned broad face was suffused with quiet delight.

"I never thought I'd see the day Cosimo wed," she said quietly in Sadie's ear. "And thanks to you and your sister, that day has come."

Sadie smiled in gratitude.

"I consider it's largely thanks to you we saw this go so smoothly," she said. "Tell me, how did you do it?"

Consuela shot her a cheeky grin.

"I confess, I forewarned him of what was coming. I prepared him for it. And I convinced Father Gregory we could use an ancient French ceremony accepted in the canons of the church for slightly irregular circumstances, shall we say? Irregular, but not invalid."

She gave Sadie one of the soft, grace-infused smiles she was coming to recognize as Consuela's signature.

"I believe Jasmine is just the wife Cosimo needs. She's had a hard start in life. It's given her an understanding which someone marrying Cosimo will need."

Consuela took Sadie's hand gently in her own.

"I am going to slip off back to my duties now, Sadie. It's not possible for me to sup with my brother and his cohorts in the public domain. But thank you from the bottom of my heart for making contact and bringing all this together.

"In due course, I look forward to being Auntie Consuela to Cosimo and Jasmine's children. And that will bring all of us new blessings, I'm sure."

••••••••

Sadie trailed out of the church to see a small knot of people still gathered on California Street. Cosimo and Jasmine had climbed into an open carriage, and Isla was gaily throwing rose petals at her friend as she pulled away from the kerb.

She turned as she saw Sadie approaching.

"That went extraordinarily well," she said with a delighted grin. "Now they're off to get to know each other over a sumptuous dinner in a private suite at Lick House. And us…"

She turned and surveyed the emptying grounds with a question in her voice.

"I guess we see how Phoebe's doing after all this, shall we?"

They joined Elizabeth and Dolphie in a silent ride up the hill to Pine Street, Susannah and Cordelia having gone on ahead. Everything had gone off without a hitch, and now they were all feeling a deflating sense of anti-climax.

Until they reached Pine Street and Phoebe came flying out to meet them, their father trailing in her wake.

She flung her arms wide to greet Sadie.

"You are such a star," she said, throwing her head back and laughing. "I don't know what I'd do without you."

And suddenly, Sadie felt fabulous. She didn't care that Dolphie wasn't talking to her. Or that Patrick Blackheart had got what was coming to him. Or that it seemed highly likely she'd be getting on a train back to New York with Brian to resume her family duties at the Shamrock.

Phoebe was safe and happy. Out of trouble. And she'd fulfilled her vow to her mother.

Sadie wrapped her arms around her sister's neck and was surprised to see it was wet with her tears.

"Silly goose," she gasped through her laughing sobs. "You were the clever one to think of recruiting Jasmine—and it turned out so well!"

Her father had rumbled up and was standing back sheepishly.

Sadie turned to him and wrapped her arms around his shoulders, kissing him on the cheek.

"Hello there, Daa… Phoebe and Jack have been keeping you in order, I hope?" She grinned impishly.

"Come inside and let's all recover from all the excitement."

They were met by Susannah and Cordelia, wearing waitress's aprons and directing them to the dining room. "What's this?" Sadie asked with a giggle. "Have you found a new vocation?"

Susannah smiled teasingly.

"Elizabeth's got a surprise for us all," she said. "Make your way to the dining room and all will be revealed."

They did as they were told, and entered a room with the table set for a festive meal, with silverware, glasses, candlesticks, and bowls of fragrant white lilies and jasmine all out waiting.

"Oh my gosh?" said Sadie. She was feeling slightly light-headed. "It looks like a wedding breakfast."

"That's exactly what it is," Elizabeth said with delight. "It's the wedding breakfast you have when you haven't had a wedding."

She smiled at Phoebe. "You gave away your magnificent wedding dress, but I didn't want to see you go without some good memories. I thought it would be fun to mark this occasion, anyway. It is a special day in more ways than one.

"Phoebe successfully escaped a fate worse than death, Jasmine and Cobra both met their match, methinks, and I've discovered the memorable Mother Superior. Now seat yourselves and we'll eat."

Sadie glanced down the table for Dolphie and saw he was already seated, with Jack on one side and Isla on the other.

So that's how it's going to be, is it…? Silly girl, you're still kidding yourself.

She grabbed the chair back in front of her and hurriedly sat down, with her father on one side and Phoebe on the other.

Sixty-nine

Two hours later, after many courses of food and much free-flowing wine, Sadie quietly withdrew and found her way to the beautiful rose garden at the back of the house. The party had been wonderful, and just what Phoebe needed to fill a sense of anti-climax that her much anticipated wedding day had come and gone and here she was, still a spinster.

"Don't worry," Sadie had whispered at one point when she sensed Phoebe's enthusiasm was flagging. "I'm older than you and I'm still a spinster too." They exchanged a shiny-eyed look.

"You understand perfectly," Phoebe whispered back. "I didn't want Cobra, but I would like someone."

Make that two of us, Sadie vowed fervently, eyes darting down the table. Dolphie was engaged in a voluble exchange with Jack that she couldn't quite hear the ins and outs of. Her eyes dropped to her plate, and she kept quiet.

Now, out in the night's still coolness, she let all the fake bonhomie leak away. She listened to a night bird warbling in the nearby bush and let the sadness which had been brewing inside her wash over her like a healing shower.

She could be honest with herself, even if she wasn't willing to admit it to anyone else.

The prospect of returning to her old life in New York, and of relinquishing her hopes of something more with Dolphie, loomed over her like a storm cloud.

He'd obviously decided she was… What? Unsuitable? Didn't fit in his world? She couldn't argue with that. The final straw seemed to have been her disclosures about Blackheart. She stood and strolled idly along in the gloaming, leaning in to smell the roses, filling her soul with the glory of the anonymity of the night and the sweetness of the fragrance.

I don't have to be anyone other than who I am, she told herself.

I don't have to meet any standards but my own.

I've learned a lot here, like not having to be responsible for everything and everyone in my family. That I can let my vow to Mother quietly fade, because it's not fair to expect anyone to direct other people's lives. Phoebe can stand happily on her own two feet.

She spotted a bench seat in a far corner, partly obscured by a bush bearing cinnamon-scented flowers.

Just what I need. Somewhere to hide and think.

She stalked across the lawn to the seat just as she heard the French doors into the garden squeak open. She increased her pace, attempting to waft like a night moth into oblivion.

She slipped to the end of the bench, partly obscured by an overhanging branch, and peered back to the house. Dolphie scrutinized the garden, scanning directly toward her. And then he stepped down and began a slow, intentional lope across the lawn in her direction. She cringed back in the shadows and hoped against hope she was invisible.

"Mind if I join you?" She noticed his voice carried the slightest hint of his European origins—the "f" on the *if* was ever so slightly more heavily pronounced than a native English speaker would say it. Funny, she hadn't noticed that it charmed.

"Do I have a choice?" *Graceless, wasn't it?* But she was past pretending.

He stopped, and a slow smile spread over his face.

"Well, if it's like that… I can make it quick."

She felt her resistance melt away. He had an incorrigible quality she enjoyed. Pity it didn't extend to admiring the same quality in others. Blackheart's handsome, ruthless face flashed into her mind for a second, then vanished again.

She pressed herself further along the bench, increasing the likely distance between them as he sat down.

"Lovely night," he said. She stared into the inky evening, listening to the little bird, which still trilled.

He let his words lie unanswered for a long minute or two.

"Not talking?"

"I was just seeking a little peace," she said, sounding huffy.

"And I'm disturbing it. Sorry."

He didn't sound in the least sorry. He sounded unrepentant.

She couldn't help herself. She laughed at the idiocy of it.

"You sound it," she said.

Another long silence dropped like a blanket between them.

Finally, she turned full on to face him and said testily, "You said you'd make it quick."

He gave her a mocking grin. "I said I *can* make it quick. I haven't decided yet if I will or not."

He let the silence envelop them once more, and she was close to deciding she didn't mind sitting in the dark here with him saying nothing, when he interrupted her thoughts again.

"So what's a dragon-slaying woman like you going to do next?"

She looked at him in blank surprise.

"I don't know what you mean."

"I mean, what's your next trick? Surely you've got one? You've hidden in railway carriage ceilings. Decked the bad man. Saved your sister from a fate worse than death. I'm wondering what the encore is?"

Is he making fun of me?

Suddenly, it all felt like too much to take. She stood up abruptly, wanting to escape, to run away, before he saw her eyes were filling with tears.

Her head hit the branches of the low shrub, filling her nostrils with the heady scent. She swiped her arm across the greenery, blindly trying to make an escape, but he'd leaped to his feet to block her path.

"Sadie, I…" He held her gently by her shoulders. Gazed intently into her face, and registered her distress.

"I'm making such a mess of this, but I'm not letting you go. Not till I've told you how I feel."

"How you feel?" she demanded, finding her voice at last.

"After you've given me the chill treatment, made me feel like a discard because Blackheart tried to use me as a pawn in his power game, and now I'm supposed to care how *you* feel?"

She gave him her most withering stare.

"How about how *I* feel?"

His face had registered shock when she first started raising her voice at him, but now the irritating man appeared to be enjoying it.

"All right," he said. "Fair enough." He let go of her shoulders, stepped back out of her space.

The greenery he'd been holding back slapped back against her and she went with the motion, sinking back onto the seat.

"Tell me how you feel. Apart from discarded," he said with an apologetic wince. "I'm truly sorry if I made you feel like that."

"I feel like a fool," she said, before she changed her mind. She'd decided she was done with pretending. And what did she have to lose? He didn't rate her, anyway.

"Firstly, that I felt a smidgin of attraction for Patrick, I admit it. Right at the beginning. He seemed to understand. To sympathize. But it wasn't my fault he turned into a toxic monster."

"I understand," he said. "And I completely agree. It wasn't your fault he turned out to be Dr. Death." He sat down with a bump. "What else?"

"I feel like a fool second, because at the beginning, I thought maybe there could be something special between us. But pretty well from Day One, everything's been going wrong. First, I ran away in a misguided attempt to protect you. I've discovered I spend far too much time trying to save other people."

She stopped and considered. "Except I was bringing trouble into your house, and I wanted to avoid that."

"And then?" Dolphie prompted. "Let's get it all out."

"And then. Well, Patrick happened and Consuela happened and you weren't talking to me anymore…"

She let her head fall to her hand and raked her hair fretfully.

"Nothing worked out. So I've decided I'll have to go back to New York with Daa."

He gazed at her for what seemed like minutes on end and said, "I thought you said you were over saving other people?"

"Well, I am, but… Daa needs me more than anyone else does." She knew it sounded lame. She hadn't really thought this through to the end.

Dolphie let the silence grow, extended and pregnant with unsaid things, and then in a low voice he spoke.

"He doesn't need you as much as I do."

Her heart stopped. "I beg your pardon," she said. "Say that again."

He pitched forward on the bench, so he turned his body to face hers. His eyes were intent with meaning.

"I said, 'He doesn't need you as much as I do.'"

"Oh. So I heard you right the first time."

She felt weak at the knees.

What's happening? Does he mean it?

"But I don't understand. What are you trying to say?"

He scooted along the bench so he was right next to her. She could sense the warmth radiating from him and shivered, suddenly realizing she felt cold in the night air. He peeled off the jacket he was wearing and draped it around her shoulders.

"Sadie, what I am trying to say is, I need you in my life. Like the morning needs dawn. Like dry earth needs rain. I need you by me. By my side." He leaned back so he wasn't crowding her.

"I want you to stay in California. Give yourself a chance to see if you can forgive me for being so insensitive. For not understanding you better."

He stood and faced out into the darkness.

"I wasn't chilling you out. I was furious you handled Blackheart all by yourself. That you didn't trust me enough to confide what had happened. To handle it together."

He gave a bleak laugh. "The big man wanted to be wanted. And then, to make it worse, you did brilliantly without me. You beat Blackheart at his own game with no help from me."

He glanced sideways, his long lashes briefly shadowing his cheek.

"Do you know what that does to a man who wants to love and protect his woman? To have her go off and slay dragons without a backward glance?"

To love and protect his woman?

Only one phrase resonated in the slew of words that were pouring forth.

To love and protect his woman?

She looked up at him, with what must have seemed like disbelief on her face, because he took her hand in his and kissed it.

"You don't believe me? I love strong women, but a man can only take so much. You've got to let me share the load."

She squeezed his fingers and started laughing.

"I thought you didn't like strong women."

He laughed at her laughter. "I don't like strong women who can do without me."

She stood abruptly and melted into his arms.

He stroked her hair fondly and whispered.

"Please stay a while longer and see if you can find it in your heart to forgive me."

"I already have," she said. And for another long minute or two they stood like that, enfolded into one another's arms.

Before Phoebe came out and called them inside for the toast.

Epilogue

One year later

Sadie sat in the afternoon sun that filtered through the leaves of the native oak at their front door step, her arms gathering her light peach skirts around her ankles. She watched with a joyous grin as her husband strode toward her up the steps of their Dolores Street home, his jacket casually slung over one shoulder, his lithe fencer's body swinging from side to side, carefree and purposeful.

"Everything went well?" she inquired in greeting, eager to engage before he reached her.

He teasingly put a finger to his lips and then sprinted the last steps two at a time to reach her, leaning down to muzzle her neck as soon as he got there.

She giggled and pulled away. "Dolphie! The neighbors will see!"

He swung his backside down to the masonry step and nestled closely beside her.

"Let them," he said. "I want them to see I have the most delectable, eatable, desirable…" He laughed. "Do you want me to continue?"

She gazed into his sparking eyes and affectionately ruffled her hand across the top of his hair, pulled back as usual in the neat ponytail anchored at the back of his neck, a signature of his pared-down, aristocratic style.

"I think I get the idea." She smiled, her cheeks blushing prettily.

He tweaked at her light cotton skirts. "I love you in dresses. I do. But you're going to have to get into those horrendous khaki trousers again someday soon. Just so I don't forget the oddball I married."

She tapped his thigh playfully and in one accord they rose and turned to go into the house.

When they were into the cool of their sitting room, they sank onto a sofa, arms still entwined.

"You didn't answer my question," she said. "Is the business set up?"

"Swimmingly," he said. "Jasmine was a sight. Their baby is due in what—two months? But you'd think it was next week."

Sadie grinned. "And Cobra came through with the money?"

"Without a peep."

"That's so good," Sadie said with a contented sigh. "To think we helped set it all in motion the day I jumped on that Overlander to come here and rescue Phoebe."

She ran her index finger over his dark brows.

"And thank goodness I discovered my Prince Charming on that train."

He gave her a light peck on her lips.

"Jasmine's 'rescue mission' for girls being sold into indentured service wouldn't exist without you," Dolphie said, affectionately nuzzling her neck.

"Or you," she said staunchly.

Jasmine and Cosimo's "arranged marriage" had sprouted wings that carried them into lives neither had ever imagined for themselves… and as an offshoot of the changes, Cobra was willing to support Jasmine's desire to help young girls in danger of being sold into prostitution.

Youngsters with no one to defend or protect them. Jack and Dolphie had agreed to be part of the support committee to provide business backup, and today they'd been signing up the legal papers to get it all formally established.

Dolphie absentmindedly stroked Sadie's face as he went over details.

"I don't know how much time Jasmine will be able to give to it once the baby comes, but I' sure she'll manage somehow," he opined.

"She's a capable woman, no doubt. The way she manages Cobra…! She's got him eating out of her hand."

Sadie smiled. "She'll be able to show me how to do it," Sadie said with a sly grin, watching Dolphie's face as she delivered her news.

"She'll what?" said Dolphie, his brow momentarily furrowing as he followed the gist of her words. As their import hit, his mouth dropped open and his eyes widened in delight.

"You're not…? We're not…?" He was watching her face, which had broken into a broad beam. Her head was nodding.

"We are…!" He stood and wrapped his arms around her waist, pulling her against him and whirling around in a circle.

He was laughing and panting and as he set her gently down he said, "I won't be able to do that so comfortably in another six months."

They stood, gasping and gazing into one another's eyes. When they'd regained their breath, Sadie slipped her hand up from Dolphie's waist and stroked his cheek tenderly.

"Does it matter to you whether it's a boy or a girl?" she asked.

He gazed down at her, his eyes luminous with love. "As long as he or she carries the same incorrigible spirit as their glorious mother, it doesn't matter one bit."

Eight months and twenty-one days later, Alexandra Sarah Elizabeth Westerhoven was born. And from her very first days, they called her Sadie Two.

THE END

WHAT'S NEXT?

The second book in the Home At Last trilogy, Susannah's Secret, will be published later this year. Here's what is coming,

Drawn by New World promise, three California musketeers stake all on realizing their dreams in a Pacific El Dorado.

Adolphus Westerhoven, newly minted European count without land or riches, chooses the New World over the Old.

Jack Cabot, world-weary New York blue-blood intent on creating a new life after losing himself in the Barbary Coast.

Alexandro de Vile, adopted Senator's son, grappling with his unrecognized natural father's Spanish heritage.

Together they'll face adversity, right wrongs, and encounter, and despite themselves love, feisty women who will change their lives forever.

There, they'll find their way, home at last.

ACKNOWLEDGMENTS

As ever I had tremendous fun searching out justification for some of my character's more colorful exploits, and none more so than for Sadie's non -conformist taste for pants. A wonderful online post, *Wearing The Pants: A Brief Western History of Pants* by Kathleen Cooper did the work for me, lending some colorful detail. I know some of the anecdotes mentioned in the article referred to the earlier Gold Rush years, but I choose to believe some lingering rebellion remained in female hearts.

Herbert Asbury's two volumes on the vice-filled side of life in both New York and San Francisco –in his two lively accounts, *Gangs of New York, An Informal History of the Underworld*, and *The Barbary Coast, An Informal History of the San Francisco Underworld,* - helped flesh out the mobster side of the story.

Other online sources proved a treasure trove for the part railways filled in life at this time –like a Scribner article on an Overland journey from New York to San Francisco in 1873, and other material about the Overlander and Railroads at: http://cprr.org/Museum/index.html#Travel helped make travel at the time come alive.

I am indebted once again to copy editor Stephanie Parent (in the U.S.) and proofing editor Robyn Welsh (in Auckland) for making the manuscript as 'right' as we possibly could, but of course any errors –hopefully very few, are entirely my responsibility.

Formatting once again handled with skill, good humor and

alacrity by Marina and Jason Anderson at Polgarus Studios in Tasmania.

The second book in the Home At Last series, Susannah's Secret, will be published in late 2022.

If you'd like to get updates by becoming a friend of Jenny's books and getting the latest news of releases and free book offers join us at: https://www.jennywheeler.biz/free-poisoned-legacy-tangled-destiny-ebook/

Enjoy this book? You Can Make a Difference

Reviews are the most powerful tools in my kit for getting my books noticed. Much as I'd love it, I don't have the budget of a big publisher to buy bill board ads and other national advertising. But I have the promise of something more powerful–something publishers envy. And that's a committed and loyal bunch of readers. Honest reviews of my books help them gain the attention of others who might appreciate them, too.

Post Your Sadie's Vow Reviews Here:

For Amazon: https://www.amazon.com/dp/B0B1DMM5ZS

For Goodreads:

https://www.goodreads.com/book/show/61125922-sadie-s-vow

Bookbub: https://www.bookbub.com/books/sadie-s-vow-home-at-last-book-1-by-jenny-wheeler

ABOUT THE AUTHOR

Jenny Wheeler is the author the new Home At Last Trilogy and of the Of Gold & Blood Old California mystery series:

Poisoned Legacy #1.
Brother Betrayed #2.
Double Jeopardy #3.
Tangled Destiny (Christmas novella and Prequel.) #4.
Unbridled Vengeance #5.
Hope Redeemed, A Spanish Novella, #6.
Boxed Set/Book Bundle Of Gold & Blood, Books 1–3.
Boxed Set Book Bundle #2 Poisoned Legacy and Tangled Destiny
Tainted Fortune #7.
Book Bundle /Boxed Set #3 Book #5 Unbridled Vengeance and #6
Hope Redeemed.
Book Bundle/Boxed Set #4 Book #7 Tainted Fortune and #8
Captive Heart.
Captive Heart #8.
Three Holiday Novellas–Book Bundle/ Boxed set Books #3, #6, and #8.
Ancient Deception #9.
Dangerous Desires #10.

WHERE TO FIND JENNY

Jenny's online home is at jennywheeler.biz or email
Jenny@jennywheeler.biz

You can connect with Jenny on:
Facebook: @JennyWheeler.Biz
Twitter: @Jenny_Biz
Instagram: @jennysbingereading
Pinterest www.pinterest.nz/Jennywheelerbooks
Goodreads: goodreads.com/author/show/11371547.Jenny_Wheeler
Bookbub: www.bookbub.com/profile/jenny-wheeler